When Horses Had Wings

Also by Diana Estill

Stilettos No More

Deedee Divine's Totally Skewed Guide to Life

Driving on the Wrong Side of the Road

When Horses Had Wings

Diana Estill

When Horses Had Wings

For information about special discounts for bulk purchases, contact:

Corncob Press, an imprint of
Totally Skewed Productions
120 E. FM 544, Suite 72, PMB 135
Murphy, TX 75094

ISBN-13: 978-0-9799708-8-7

ISBN-10: 0-9799708-8-1

Library of Congress Control Number: 2011942445

1 2 3 4 5 6 7 8 9 10

First Print Edition

www.TotallySkewed.com

Cover design by Laura Estill

Cover image © Roman Podvysotskiy/Dreamstime.com

For children who've suffered

ONE

I'd like to offer some kind of deliberate purpose for this ruinous decision, the one that cheated me of childhood and stripped away the last of my self-confidence. But if there was one, I've yet to identify it. Whether by design or choice, my memory isn't what it used to be. Some things are better forgotten anyhow.

You might think I'd have relished the details of that fateful day well enough to recall them forever. To be honest, my initial offense has, over time, become far less memorable than its penalty.

All I can tell you is that it happened in a stand of live oaks, somewhere off of a deserted county road in North Texas, one sweltering afternoon in August of 1971. There, in the blistering backseat of a Plymouth Fury, I succumbed to a young boy's attempt to set my body and both our futures ablaze. Like a prairie grassfire, my reasoning followed no particular path. I simply yielded to his pent-up needs and our secluded setting—took advantage of a rural opportunity, if you will. This single stroke of bad luck, or poor judgment, depending on how you choose to look at it, led Kenny Ray Murphy and me straight to the front door of the Second Baptist Church in White Rock, where Daddy was a deacon.

We didn't exactly live in White Rock proper, the largest town in Limestone County, population 5,090. But how else can I describe that physical location, a flat, treeless twenty acres simply called "unincorporated land?" The parcel that Momma and Daddy owned looked like a child-sized sliver cut from a whole buttermilk pie. For the most part, our neighbors, the Caldwells, with their five-hundred-acre spread, owned the rest of that pastry. Every summer when whirlwinds transformed honey-colored strands into millions of miniature pompoms, the Caldwells graciously, and no doubt jokingly, baled Daddy's six acres of oats.

Anyone who saw our barbed-wire-enclosed, three-acre black-eyed pea patch would have known that Daddy was only a weekend farmer, not a serious sodbuster; heck, he didn't even own a horse, much less a tractor. So he improvised by using me and my younger brother Ricky as livestock. It looked something like this: Imagine a horse-drawn plow, the kind used before the Industrial Age, and then substitute two kids where you'd expect to find a work beast. We walked abreast, pushing against a leather strap that crossed our ribs, pulling a giant spade behind us, and praying that nobody we knew or might ever see again would recognize us. Daddy proclaimed the contraption ingenious. We called it humiliating.

The harness was nothing more than a series of interconnected men's belts. This makeshift device didn't hurt my midriff half as much as it distorted my thinking. Often when hitched to that plow, to distract myself from the drudgery, I pretended to be a unicorn. I'd envision soaring off to a place where there were no crop dusters swooping low over human life forms, threatening immediate asphyxiation and the deformation of future progeny. Several times a year, we heard the ominous plane engine sounds and rushed to close the house windows. The few times we didn't move fast enough left the family gasping from pesticide sprays that seeped through the window screens and invaded our lungs. The noxious mist stole our breaths, interrupting normal respiration and thoughts of anything beyond survival for several minutes.

I'll be the first to admit that Daddy wasn't fully dedicated to agriculture, but he appeared resolute about his religion and doing what was right—which was why he took Ricky and me out of the big city schools and moved us to a place so remote that even Marijuana couldn't find us.

Or so he thought.

At least twice, sometimes three times, a week, Daddy drove the eight miles to White Rock so we could witness Brother Sontag's preaching. However, I seldom listened to the minister because he was always shouting about planning to meet Jesus when I was more interested in learning how to approach boys that I could see and touch.

But on the day Brother Sontag asked, "Do you, Renee Anne Goodchild, take this man, Kenneth Raymond Murphy, to be your lawfully wedded husband?"

the reverend had my strict attention. For about a millisecond, I thought I might actually have had a choice, but then I remembered my daddy was standing there with us.

At that instant, I must have been contemplating the outcome of my next response, because I recall holding my breath so tightly and my chest so high that you'd have thought someone had just yelled "AT-TE-EN-TION!" By the time I finally said, "I do," it came out sounding more like a sigh of exhaustion than an oath of commitment. But I was simply relieved to have said it without splitting a seam.

Momma had made my gown, which was no secret to all ten of my guests, from a Simplicity pattern that she remembered I'd liked. She'd run out of white thread near the end, so she'd made do with beige on one sleeve. She said no one would notice, or recall that she'd used the same pattern to sew my band recital dress the previous year. The fact that Momma was even less of a seamstress than she was a cook never seemed to stop her from trying at either. On her second attempt to master a basic shift, albeit satin, her sewing skills hadn't improved much, unless you consider the facing, which she'd taken care to tack. This time.

Though I'm sure that dress fit me poorly, other than my memory, there's no proof of it today. Our wedding photos, shot on Grandma's Polaroid, failed to develop, so I can truthfully say that our ceremony didn't contain any Kodak moments. Grandma said the film might have been underexposed—unlike me. I was three months pregnant.

It wasn't the best of times for a marriage. I'm sure Momma and Daddy would have done more for us, given us some money or something, if Daddy hadn't lost his job five months earlier during the 1971 recession. Daddy had worked in electronics for the better part of his life, but new technology, something he called "solid state," had suddenly surpassed his understanding. Kind of like his daughter.

Daddy was the type of guy my schoolmates would have called a "nerd," a man who read *Engineering Today*, listened to Hank Snow records, and voted for Nixon—both times. His hairline, which receded all the way back to his crown, and his oval face made his nearly square black-framed glasses an ill-suited choice, sort of like the navy socks he sported with his royal-blue suede athletic shoes. He was the type who could tell you how your radio operated and yet remain dumbfounded when it played the lyrics to *Light My Fire*. So it came as no surprise that Daddy didn't wonder how Kenny and I were going to make it after we married.

"Me'un your momma seen plenty o' lean times," he said. "You'll be okay, long as you cling to the Lord." His own momma had conceived him during the Great Depression, so Daddy might have thought I was merely carrying on a family tradition.

He didn't know that by the time I'd turned seventeen, I'd already been accepted into the PWT club. At least, that was what I heard others whisper when I cashed in the cola bottles Kenny had found at his job to buy groceries.

"Poor white trash," women whispered when I passed.

"Look at her belly."

"Already hatching out another one! You know, that's how they do."

"Ignorant little Jezebel."

They could stare and think whatever they wanted. I didn't care because I was planning to eat a sumptuous steak, possibly my first taste of meat in a week. Mmm. I imagined the smell of pork fat simmering in red-eye gravy. Yesiree, I could cook those thick pork slices, ones better grocers wouldn't carry, until they resembled the finest beef cutlets Bonanza Steakhouse ever served. My garage-sale skillet could scald as well as any. I'd dust those strips with flour, salt, and pepper, and then I'd brown the heavily marbled meat in bacon grease that I kept stored in an old mayonnaise jar. We never threw away anything that could be reused.

I reckon bacon grease was about the only thing we had that was plentiful, unless you count the stray dogs sniffing out back for scraps. Pork, our primary source of protein, was cheap, cheaper than cold cuts or yellow-fatted chickens. So every morning, about five-thirty, I'd fry up six pieces of slab bacon, the leanest I could find, for Kenny's lunch. Two bacon and mayonnaise sandwiches, one to eat, one to exchange with his fellow sanitation workers.

Kenny always said, "You can't believe what some of them boys'll trade for a damn B-minus-LT." That was what he called our version of the traditional sandwich because ours never included any produce. Too expensive. However, lettuce or not, Kenny knew he'd stand a better chance of having some variety in his meals if he could trade up. "Ain't exactly their favorite," he'd say of his fellow crewmen, "but a bacon sandwich's about as close as I intend to get to pigs' feet." Sometimes he'd brag that he'd made off with a family-size bag of potato chips or a thermos mug full of hamburger stew, foods he'd have been hard-pressed to find at home.

I couldn't imagine how Kenny could feel like eating *anything*, sitting near one of those garbage trucks with trash heaped on their beds and moving parts compressing decayed animal carcasses and unnaturally colored foods, yellow lettuce and blue-green bread, unidentified dark liquids dripping from all sides, flies circling. There could have been a hacked-up human in there somewhere, and I bet no one would have noticed.

The stench from those two-ton rigs leapt onto Kenny's sludge-colored uniform and followed him all the way home. I could smell him even before he sauntered past the front door, a pungent aroma of rotting fruit mixed with methane gas.

"Where's dinner?" he'd ask right off.

Cupping one hand over my nose and mouth, stifling a dry heave, I would set a couple of mismatched Melmac plates on top of our gray Formica dining table, the one Kenny had brought home from work one day. He found all sorts of worthwhile items on bulk-trash days. If Kenny had a specialty, this was it: claiming what others didn't want and putting it to good use.

The whole while I set out macaroni and cheese or beans and cornbread, our standard fare, my stomach groaned with confusion. Many times, I didn't know which I wanted more—to eat or puke.

On better days, Kenny would wash his hands before he sat in one of the two metal folding chairs we used for dining. I'd fill a plastic tumbler with Lipton Tea, his favorite liquid refreshment other than beer, and set it next to the TV schedule he insisted remain on the table at all times. I'd moved it once, and he'd hollered, "Leave it be. How you 'spect me to plan my evening?"

My nights didn't require much preparation. Given the options—cleaning house or watching cop shows—the choice was easy. I'd pretend I was Kenny's personal servant, which didn't take much imagination, and gather uniforms he'd shed throughout the house: pants that could practically stand alone and shirts that reeked of rancid waste. I was spared the challenge of washing them because once a week Kenny lugged his work clothes to the City where they were laundered, starched, folded, and returned looking like they'd arrived brand new from some big-name department store.

For the most part, I performed my domestic chores responsibly, including washing Kenny's hair in our kitchen's old farm sink whenever he insisted. That wasn't an inconvenience, really—more like self-defense. He only asked me to do it about once every other week, and by then I was ready to perform a full baptism if it might improve his appearance or smell. Dutifully, I'd run his bath water in a tub that still had legs and sponge him all over. I guess I thought that proved me a good wife, unlike the ones in those soap operas Momma watched. Those starlets were nothing but a bunch of self-centered, loose-legged, motor-mouths—gals who were pretty to look at, but tragically useless, as far as I was concerned. I'd studied them, wishing to look the way they did in their fancy, store-bought clothes. But I suffered no delusions. Being a small-breasted, blotchy-faced, uneducated girl, I felt sure my only options were to become a decent wife and mother, even if I confused the order. And I feared what might become of me if I succeeded at neither.

I'd quit school in the eleventh grade because the thought of my classmates teasing about my condition was more than I could bear. They'd already humored themselves enough at my expense. Until my neighbor showed me a newspaper article about my high school band, I hadn't given much thought to becoming a dropout. I couldn't believe the headlines: *White Rock's Marching Band to Perform at Mayan Pyramids.*

Pyramids! I'd always dreamed of standing on top of one and gazing like some kind of princess warrior into the vast distance. Nevertheless, it looked as though the closest thing to a pyramid I would see was sitting on top of our Admiral TV: a pair of rabbit ears linked by a single strand of aluminum foil. And the only picture coming into clear view was the chance I'd missed.

I remembered David Lassiter, first-chair drummer, and wondered what he might be doing now. Was he somewhere gently holding another girl's chin the way he used to cup mine whenever I'd look away while he was speaking to me? Would he be heading to college after high school next year? Or would he, like so many others, settle for pumping gas at the local Fina station? Maybe work down at the roof truss plant ten hours a day, the way Kenny had after he failed algebra the second time?

Technically, I'd been David's girl first, before I became blind to everything but Kenny's senior high school status. Kenny had practically guaranteed my acceptance with the cheerleader crowd, being two years older and all. And David's ability to play a perfect *In-A-Gadda-Da-Vida* drum solo hadn't been enough to compensate for his freshman ranking or lack of a driver's permit. I didn't want my classmates to question my social maturity since most of the boys were already making fun of me. They'd bark when I passed them in the school hallways. "Arf, arf," the sports jocks would shout. Benny, one of my school's star track members, would yell, "Hey! You know you're a real *bow-wow*?"

Yeah, I knew.

My unruly brown hair was thick with waves that went every-which-way except together, nothing at all like Cher's. My eyebrows, a mocha color three shades darker than my frizzy bangs, refused to arch but agreed to meet at the bridge of my nose. The surface of my face changed daily, depending on the number of colas and candy bars I'd consumed and, with both my knees pressed together, you could still pass a basketball between my thighs. I wasn't about to give those unmerciful ambushers any more excuses to launch one of their embarrassing attacks. As it was, I already had to avoid the north wing, the one leading to the school gymnasium. If anyone had thought I was dating a freshman, I might have had to remove ceiling tiles and crawl through rafters to escape torment between classes.

Other than David, no boy would have dared risk asking me for a date. I imagine it was more acceptable to join the canine patrol. If romance was to become a part of my high school experience, I knew I'd have to search for it outside of White Rock High.

Kenny lived in Lolaville, a town named after a popular hot spot that had stood in its midst for a

11

half-century: Lola's Fruits & Vegetables. This small settlement of farmers, quarrymen, misfits, and social renegades was twelve miles southeast of White Rock and, thankfully, in a different county and school district. Kenny wouldn't have known of my reputation as White Rock High's sophomore class joke. In fact, if it hadn't been for a band party at the County Line Skateland situated halfway between our two rural communities, I'm sure we never would have met.

I'll always believe Kenny's lack of insider knowledge accounted for his willingness to notice my pathetic existence. As for David, I don't know how to explain his attraction to me other than to say he might have had a thing for Cocker Spaniels. Long after I'd kicked sand into the flames of his first romance, he'd refused to forget about me. "If anything ever happens to him," he'd say about Kenny, "I want to be the first to know." He'd made me promise, and I'd agreed, though neither of us imagined the significance.

TWO

Every morning after Kenny left for work, I wondered what I'd do with myself for the next nine hours. I kept my ears trained for noises of any kind, hints of welcomed punctuations in my otherwise silent existence. If the germs Kenny brought home from the trash trucks didn't kill me first, I feared I'd die of boredom.

The familiar sound of tires crunching gravel told me someone, probably Momma since nobody else ever visited, had parked a car in our driveway. Occasionally, she'd drop by to tell me something noteworthy—like Ricky took third-place on his science fair project or Daddy found a lucky double-yolk egg that morning—some important incident or gossip that couldn't wait to be shared.

Momma let herself inside before I could open the screen door. "Hey," she said stepping out of an early autumn mist, "know what Sunday is?"

"Of course I know." I rolled my eyes. "It's Daddy's birthday."

"Ya'll be there 'bout noon?" she asked, marching straight through to my kitchen like she paid my rent. The idea of me being the lady of the house hadn't had time enough to fully sink in.

Kenny and I would have sooner suffered a beating than to have eaten Momma's cooking, but I nodded to spite myself.

"Brought this for you." Momma pointed to a small football-shaped object she'd set on my dinette table. I studied Momma's deposit, though I couldn't say I was bowled over by curiosity. Whatever it was, if she'd made it, it was sure to be a disappointment.

Momma followed me back to the bedroom where I'd been cleaning and sat on one corner of my bed. "How's your neighbors? You seen 'em yet?"

"You mean the Hendersons?" I jabbed a thumb to my right, motioning toward the bedroom's east partition, the dividing wall of the duplex Kenny and I shared with the elderly couple. "Can't help seeing 'em and hearing 'em. Two old codgers fight like a couple of game roosters. Cussin' each other out all the time." I made a fake smile. "Reg'lar love birds. But what can you expect for sixty-dollars a month? Lolaville ain't exactly filled with perfect housing or perfect people."

Momma cocked her head. "Don't hear nothing but a dump truck going by right now."

"That's 'cause Ol' Man Henderson done disappeared this morning, like he does most mornings." I opened the Venetian blinds and peered between the dusty slats, calculating the time. "Hard to have a cock fight when you only got one rooster."

I turned and mimicked Granny Henderson. "I'm gonna outlive him! He kil't his first wife, but I'm damned sure gonna outlive him. You just wait and see." Granny's eyes had shimmered like tourmaline when she'd said this. And for weeks afterward I'd listened, one ear to the wall, checking for any hint of strangling or suffocating noises, before I'd learned that Granny had a broad definition of murder.

Momma gasped. "He killed his first wife?"

"Died during childbirth." I chuckled. "But Granny says, 'Same thing.'"

Momma took in her surroundings as if seeing them for the first time. "Your daddy says this..." She swirled her hand in a semi-circle. "...is a shotgun house."

I kicked a pair of Kenny's dirty briefs underneath the bed before Momma could see them. "Mm hmm. He told me that, too. Said you can fire a shotgun at the front door and pellets will fly right out the back." I squinted and thought about that. The doors between our living room, bedroom, and kitchen aligned squarely with the front and back entryways. I could see Daddy's point, though I hoped no one ever tested his theory. I remembered the day I'd asked Granny Henderson what she knew about shotgun houses. She'd studied the porch ceiling and said, "I knowed they's built simple on 'count o' they's built to house slaves." And I'd thought, *Figures*.

Momma shifted and leaned forward, placing her hands on her knees. "I wish you hadn't moved so far, Renee Ann. Out here, pregnant, and no telephone."

We lived ten miles from my folks so Kenny could be close to his mother, Neta Sue. He hated the thought of her being alone now that he'd married, given that his daddy had run off when Kenny was a toddler. Before Momma could work up a case of nerves, I said, "Oh, don't worry. It'll be all right. The Hendersons have a phone...said we can use it anytime. Granny's always home because she's crippled and can't drive. The old man takes the car off somewhere every morning and leaves her here."

Momma stood up as though something had bitten her behind. "I better get going." She scurried toward the front room. "Daddy'll be real happy to see you Sunday." I followed her as she eased open the torn screen door and made her way onto the porch.

"Wait. Before you go," I said, "could you please buy Daddy a couple of bookmarks from the bookstore?" I handed Momma the three dollars I'd found earlier that morning when I emptied Kenny's uniform pockets. "I don't have a way to get there."

Daddy loved bookmarks, especially ones with scripture on them. It wasn't much of a birthday gift, but it was all I could afford. Actually, it was more than I could afford.

"Sure." Momma stuffed the bills in her purse. "Hey, don't forget to try some of that cake I put on your table." She scooted into her station wagon and cranked the engine. "I didn't have any baking chocolate, so I used instant cocoa." She dismissed the substitution with a wave. "Aww, it's all the same, anyway."

From the veranda I watched until Momma's car faded out of sight before I wandered back inside. There sat the plastic-wrapped brick loaf, looking deceptively promising, like those Halloween candies wrapped in shiny papers printed with names that no one has ever heard of, the kind that taste like cow manure. Not to say that I'd ever officially conducted a taste test.

I poked a forefinger at the chocolate icing that had solidified into a coal-colored enamel. Yep. She'd used that same recipe again, the one that called for equal parts of water, granulated sugar, and baking chocolate, the one she never got quite right. With a sigh, I tossed the cake into the wastebasket before Kenny had the chance to take a nibble and make fun.

That night, right after I'd cleared the supper dishes, I told Kenny about Momma's invitation. "What do you mean we're going to your momma and daddy's for dinner Sunday?" he groused. "I'm gonna watch the Cowboys play. Right here." He smacked one hand against the beige vinyl sectional he'd found behind Weir's Funeral Home. "From my own sofa."

I stared at his knuckles, traced the worn out cushion seams, and wondered if the couch pillows had ever held a corpse. Kenny hated it when I tried to guess the original upholstery color, which might have been ivory, tan, or even taupe. No way to be sure, the grime had been there too long. Still, Kenny had said I should appreciate the sofa because it, like most of the furnishings in our house, was one of his employee benefits.

"Come on, Kenny," I whined. "We can be home in time to see the game. It's Daddy's *birthday*. What do you want me to tell Momma? That you won't let me come?"

"Oh, yeah, you'd like to tell your mommy and daddy what a rotten guy I am, wouldn't you?" He said that as though it might be a lie. But I'd never admit it, even if it were the gospel truth, because if I did I'd have to acknowledge the fuzzy image growing sharper every day—a vision of me living in squalor with a man who worshipped his television and hated his life. No. I knew my place, when to speak, when to shut up, and when to pretend I was the happiest girl since Shirley Temple sang that song about a ship named after a sucker.

Perhaps if I were more lovable, a decent wife, or at least a better-looking one, Kenny would kiss me on the cheek and say, "Anything you want, Sugar Pie. What time they want us to be there?" He'd ask me what he should wear and if I needed money to buy a gift. Maybe he'd even offer to sign Daddy's birthday card.

"Change the channel," Kenny said, as though I'd failed my duty to read his mind, notice he was bored with Dolly Parton talking about towels and laundry detergent, and switch the set to *The Untouchables*.

"Ken-ny?"

"Put it on channel eleven," he commanded.

I spun the dial fast, overshot my goal, and wound up at Channel 13.

"Whoa! You passed it, damn it." His look warned I'd better hurry and get it right.

The channel safely adjusted, I relaxed and began again. "Kenny, I swear we'll be home before the game even starts. Can't we please go to Momma and Daddy's Sunday?"

He grunted something almost inaudible.

"Huh?"

"I *guess*," he bellowed. "Now will you leave me the hell alone so I can hear my show?"

~

On Sunday, Momma outdid herself. She'd set out her white lace tablecloth and wedding china and cooked an almost adequate-sized pot roast and three-vegetable assortment for Daddy's birthday dinner. She'd even wrapped my gift using leftover paper that I recognized. I had to give her credit where it was due. Momma was one resourceful woman.

Daddy didn't wait to finish his dinner before opening his gifts. "Why, thank you, sweetie," he said, tearing the pink rose-petal gift wrap from his bookmarks. "You know I always like this kind." He stared at the uppermost marker and read aloud, "*The Lord is my light and my salvation; whom shall I fear? The Lord is the strength of my life; of whom shall I be afraid?* Psalm 27:1."

19

Gazing into my lap, I said, "You're welcome, Daddy." And then I gave my brother Ricky the evil eye, daring him to smart off. He giggled and choked on an ice sliver.

"Sa-a-ay," said Kenny, turning to Momma. "Can I have some of that...that there...uh, meat?"

"You mean this pot roast?" Momma smiled like Edith Bunker. She passed Kenny a Blue Willow china bowl full of charred chunks of beef.

"Yeah, pot roast." Kenny tapped a fist against one of my knees.

I shoved away his hand.

"Wasn't Caroline Sontag's solo right pretty today?" Daddy asked.

Momma nodded as she circulated a dish of fried okra. "Lovely voice."

I knew Momma would agree. If you wanted to know her views about anything, all you had to do was ask Daddy. No point in forming her own opinions when his were just as good, if not better.

"Real sweet girl, that Caroline," Daddy said. "And a downright *natural* beauty, at that."

Caroline was Brother Sontag's fifteen-year-old daughter. Because of her, I'd come to suspect that virtuous men produced ravishing children. However, if this were true then I was living proof my daddy had been either a hypocrite or tragically overlooked. God had blessed Caroline with her father's olive complexion, her mother's crimson lips, and the kind of blue-black hair typical among Native Americans. She'd once told me that her grandmother had been a full-blooded Cherokee Indian. If I'd ever been sure of anything, it was that Caroline Sontag would never need Cover Girl cosmetics the way I'd come to rely on them.

Every time Daddy mentioned Caroline's name, I felt a pain that penetrated flesh, tore through tendons and ligaments, and burrowed deep into my bones. I was neither pretty nor musically gifted, so I didn't measure up. That was what I heard him saying. And I thought if he'd wanted a naturally beautiful daughter like Caroline, maybe he should have married Caroline's mother instead of a third-generation Irish immigrant. In my face, underneath my skin, I could feel a burn seeping.

Momma glanced at me, her head still bobbing as if attached to a coil, then zeroed in further. "Did you do something different to yourself?" She gave me a suspicious look. Two weeks earlier, I'd plucked my eyebrows out of pure boredom. She'd just now noticed.

"Change your makeup or something?" she asked, critically scanning my face for clues.

Kenny bent his head to take a better look at me. "I don't see nothing different."

"Oh!" Momma gasped. "That's it! Ohmigosh, you shaved your eyebrows off."

Momma wouldn't have known the difference between shaving and tweezing. She'd never plucked anything other than a few corn-silk hairs now and again, and she'd probably last shaved her legs during Eisenhower's administration. Her hair hung wild, like mine, only gray, and her weatherworn complexion revealed her skin care regimen, which included no facial creams or lotions of any variety. "That stuff doesn't really make wrinkles go away," she liked to say. Maybe so, but her choice of cleansers didn't help matters. When she was out of Ivory, she washed her face with Daddy's Lava.

"I didn't *shave* them, Momma. I *tweezed* away the extras," I said.

"Extras?" She knitted her own unibrow. "What extras?"

"The part that made me look like Groucho Marx."

Ricky asked, "Which one was Groucho?" but Momma paid him no attention.

"Well, honey, there's a new teen model out named Brooke...Brooke something." She searched for help. "Wha— What's her name, Jess?"

Daddy shrugged and continued sawing at his blackened beef.

"Anyway, she has eyebrows just like yours. Or like yours used to be. And she's not worried about hers."

"Fine. She can keep them, then." Before anyone had the chance to say any more about my facial features, I announced, "We've got to leave at two-thirty 'cause Kenny wants to watch the ball game from home."

Daddy set down his stainless steel fork, giving Momma the cue. She grabbed her plate and raked it into Ricky's, gathering scraps for the chickens.

"Well, I'm right proud to have ya'll here anytime you can make it," Daddy said with a tone I'd seldom heard. Any other time, Daddy would've spouted off his usual remarks, said sports were nothing but senseless wastes of human energy, suggested only brainless people knock their heads together intentionally.

I helped Momma clear the dishes and then said my goodbyes. Later, on my way to the car, I noticed Kenny standing behind the vehicle with the trunk open. Ricky flanked him, his eyes wide and hands clutching a brown paper bag. I thought how grown up Ricky looked, unlike his old portrait Momma kept on her dresser. His blond hair was beginning to darken, and he'd soon be as tall as I. Those Sunday trousers of his had climbed up and over his ankles, which caused me to grin. In some ways, I felt sorry for him. That Surfer Cross, which Daddy insisted was a swastika sign, hidden underneath his button-down shirt might have escaped Momma and Daddy's attention but it hadn't sneaked past mine. Poor kid. I knew what it was like to live with those two and try to stay in step with popular trends. I remembered how, when I was in eighth grade, Momma and Daddy had refused to let me play basketball on account of religious reasons. I'd been heartbroken the day Daddy said, "God never intended for girls to wear shorts in public."

Kenny shut the trunk lid, and I wondered why he'd opened it. "Wha'choo two looking at in there?" I asked.

"Nothing," Ricky blurted.

Kenny shook his head as though I'd said something ridiculous. "Just some junk I found at work the other day." He smirked.

Nothing worth investigating, I decided. Probably an antique soda bottle or some seventy-eight records. I recalled Ricky's paper sack. Maybe illegal fireworks.

A vague nausea, one I'd later identify as morning sickness but right then attributed to Momma's pot roast, suddenly made me swoon. I held on to the Fury's side panel and leaned through the lowered passenger-side window to release the door. Someday, I vowed, I'd own an automobile with handles that worked from the outside, one with dual-controlled electric windows, too. And I'd raise and lower mine whenever I wanted.

Frozen in thought, I rode home like a statue. Mentally, I dwelled on family, both the one I'd come from and the one I'd soon have. My hair whipped against my face, stinging my cheeks and slicing at my eyes. But I never complained. I simply sat there with my gaze fixed firmly on the American flag waving from the Plymouth's antenna.

THREE

Some rural folks think of neighbors as security. However, Kenny and I never suffered that delusion. From the beginning, the Hendersons proved that living next door to them only increased our risks.

Over the sounds of a blaring televised football game, something blasted like a sonic boom. I heard Granny Henderson yell, "Fhar! Fhar!" She hobbled out onto the front porch, her arms waving above her like helicopter blades. Her right leg, which normally dragged behind her left, moved with newfound strength. Partially crippled since birth, she lurched about in ways I wouldn't have thought possible as she announced that the other half of our duplex—her side—had ignited.

Mr. Henderson emerged with a grunt, the tips of his snowy hair broiled brown as toast, beard singed, his dungarees dusted with what looked like chalk dust. "Damned old woman. You just got to go runnin' off before you know what's what."

"I s-s-saw fhar!" she insisted. "I heard it explode!"

"What happened? Are you okay?" I asked.

"Well, is there or ain't there a fire?" Kenny asked, no doubt irritated his football game had been interrupted.

"No. No. I done put it out with some flour," Mr. Henderson huffed. He waved us off, then tottered back inside. Granny and I followed him.

"Crazy old fool. I told you don't light the pilot that way," Granny scolded.

"Oh, shut up. Nobody wants to hear you talk." The old man mumbled as he made his way to the back of his house to inspect the damage.

From the looks of the place, Mr. Henderson had turned on the propane and let it build before he'd struck a potentially lethal match. He'd leaned inside his oven, which had once been white but now appeared charcoal, and been thrown backward by the blast, flames licking at his face. That sonic boom I'd thought I heard had been the Henderson's kitchen window exploding into shards. It now lay scattered along the easternmost side of their house.

"Lookee here what he's done," Granny said, her head gyrating from palsy. "If he can't kill me, looks like he aims to kill our stove."

~

Some days I could have sworn our duplex was haunted, both sides of it. The spirits of others who'd stared head on into the eyes of misery seemed to want to share their despair. Those ghosts whispered to us and made us angry; at hard living, I supposed, but we took it out on each other.

One March afternoon after we'd returned from having Sunday dinner with Neta Sue, who I generally tried to sidestep the way I do spooks, Kenny's woes must have outstripped his patience. He parked his near-dead car in our front yard, and then we both sat there, too full and unenthused to get out. Overhead, a blanket of cucumber-colored clouds threatened to break our monotony—though the storm was still a good half-hour away by my calculations. Being seven months pregnant, I had no inclination to rush anywhere until my water broke.

For the past several minutes, Kenny had been recounting his good fortune at having recently run into an old girlfriend from high school. "She invited me to go to church with her tonight," he said, as though he might be contemplating the offer.

"Really? That's great." I finally found enough initiative to hoist myself from the vehicle. Grunting, I tumbled out into the thick afternoon air. "I'll go with you." If anyone needed to ask for penance, it was Kenny. I surely didn't want to let a petty thing like spending an evening with an old flame get in the way of his salvation.

"No you won't," he said, lumbering behind me. "I'm going by myself."

"Why would you do that?"

"'Cause it's gonna storm." He pretended to study the sky. "Besides, you got no business out runnin' round at night. You're pregnant."

"I'm not dumb, you know. I can tell you're up to no good. Maybe you want to be with someone you didn't get pregnant—yet." I turned my back and strutted ahead of him in my unlaced bowling shoes, the only footwear that would fit my swollen feet.

"Don't you accuse me of cheating, you stupid bitch!"

Before I could respond, something knocked me off my feet. One minute I was looking at our front porch, and the next I was examining pea-gravel at microscopic range. The ground had risen to meet my nose before I'd even sensed I was falling.

That was how it began, with what otherwise might have been a simple shove had I not been so top-heavy that I'd ended in a prostrate sprawl.

Kenny glared as I righted myself. "How was I supposed to know you'd fall?" he asked, seemingly offended by my accusing look.

I considered his remark. Perhaps I was even clumsier than I was unattractive. How could I have been so foolish? Why wouldn't Kenny be tired of spending every evening with me? I was grotesque. Wasn't I simply fortunate to have someone as cute as Kenny Murphy speak to me, let alone take me as his bride?

This teen-idol look-alike had chosen me, the mongrel, out of all the other girls at County Line Skateland, to slow dance with him. We'd swayed to the Bee Gees' *To Love Somebody* and suffered an ache that you might say short-circuited both our brains, a primal yearning so strong that, afterward, we hid shamefully in the dark recesses of the rink, breathing deeply.

Ever since I'd been fifteen, Kenny had teased and flirted with me. He had swallowed me with kisses that promised passion but had led instead to bitter resentment. If I was sure of anything in that moment in the gravel, it was that Kenny Murphy didn't know what it was like to love *anybody*.

I brushed the finer bits of rock cinders from my maternity smock, the one that Momma had recently sewn for my seventeenth birthday. Checking my stomach for abnormalities, I found none. My baby and I were okay. For now.

Though I could readily dismiss my immediate hurt, I couldn't shake several stubborn questions: How could anyone shove a pregnant woman to the ground? What did that forecast for my or my baby's future? If Kenny would risk harming his own child, what else might he be capable of doing?

I opened the screen door leading to our living room.

Kenny had already made himself comfortable in front of the television, his butt squished down into the fake-leather sofa cushions like a potato trying to take root. "You aw-right?" he asked.

I eased my way between Kenny and the most important thing he owned. "It ain't me I'm concerned about."

"Aw, now, don't be stupid, Renee. You know you're aw-right." He paused, then yelled after me, "Gimme some tea, will ya?"

Later that night, Kenny put one arm around my shoulders and said, "Just to prove I didn't mean to hurt you, I'll cancel my plans. I can always go to church some other time." He kissed my forehead and gave out a horselaugh. "They ain't missed me being there yet!"

I was delighted to have won back his devotion. He'd stayed home with me when I knew he'd fancied being with someone else, someone much more physically attractive.

I didn't tell anyone what Kenny had done, not even Granny Henderson, who, at the time of my fall, had likely been cooking on what was left of her stove. I didn't share the news with Momma, who probably would have simply felt bad about it, or Neta Sue, who'd have denied that *her* son would ever purposefully do such a thing. The whole episode was too atrocious to admit, too shaming. If I didn't talk about it, maybe it would go away, pass right out of my memory like my childhood had, and then maybe I'd stop dreaming about deformed babies dying of malnutrition.

~

For several days, Kenny called me "Woman" but acted like he'd said "Sugar-Pie" instead. He only laughed one morning when I overslept and forgot to pack his lunch. And later that afternoon when he returned from collecting garbage, he even brought me a gift.

"Here, I found this today. Thought you might like it." He dangled a heart-shaped golden locket like a pendulum in front of my face.

I stood over our stove, stirring a pot of pinto beans and wondering whether he was trying to impress or hypnotize me. Possibly a little of both, I decided. "What is it?" I stopped the locket in mid-swing.

"I dunno. You put pictures in it, I guess."

"Pictures?" I laughed. We didn't own a camera.

"Oh, you *know* what it is." Kenny let go of the chain and unbuttoned his uniform shirt with the KEN insignia on it to help everyone, including me, remember who he was. He took a few steps, then stumbled and grabbed at the kitchen doorjamb.

"You okay?" I asked, setting down the necklace.

Kenny staggered to our bed and then caved onto it. He lay crosswise on his back, his legs hanging limply off one side of the mattress, an arm thrown over his forehead, eyes closed. "I'm fine," he said. "Got a little dizzy all o' sudden."

I turned down the flame under the beans and joined him in the bedroom. "You want me to get a cold rag?" I reached to touch his mottled cheek.

He caught my hand and caressed it. "Would ya?"

Lifting his legs, I righted him and positioned a pillow under his head. "I'll be right back with a wet towel and some ice water."

Kenny patted my arm and smiled. For the first time in many months, I thought he actually saw me.

When I returned, I dabbed at his face and neck with a damp cloth, wondering at his almond-

31

shaped eyes and dark lashes. Those were the orbs that had lured me in and invited me to dance, kiss him, and eventually have sex. And there I was, about to have his child. Gently, I pulled him from his shirt, loosening one sleeve at a time.

Within a few months we'd be parents, however unprepared either of us might be to fulfill our roles. I vowed to make the most of it. After all, as Momma had said, this was "my bed to lie in." With that thought, I wrapped the spread around me, encasing the two of us inside a chenille cocoon. Maybe we could emerge transformed into the perfect family I'd fantasized.

The smell of burning beans soon awakened me, the pungent odor a roiling reminder of dinner and my limitations. I slipped out from underneath the covers and scurried on tiptoes into the kitchen, grateful, for once, that it was only five steps away. Dousing the pan with tap water, I managed to save our supper.

The locket was where I'd left it on the stovetop. I lifted the piece for inspection. My fingers traced the tarnished necklace as I imagined the accessory made of 14-karat gold, a gift purchased from one of those fancy mall jewelry stores—the kind where couples with hopeful eyes hover around dazzling display windows. What would it be like to *plan* a future instead of succumbing to fate? I longed to know. Maybe I could start setting goals instead of idly waiting to see what each day might deliver. Maybe I could salvage my situation the same way I'd saved our supper. Maybe that was what Kenny had been trying to do when he'd brought me the necklace.

It was a good gift, a thoughtful one. Later, I'd have our family portrait made. And inside it, I'd keep a photo of the three of us: me, Kenny, and our baby. Smiling at that image, I split the pendant open and noticed the clasp was broken.

FOUR

The smell of baby oil permeated the bedroom even with both windows open. I'd been greasing my belly because Granny Henderson had sworn that if I kept my stomach and breasts anointed, my stretch marks would vanish along with my pregnancy. And I'd believed her on the grounds that anyone who'd had seven babies ought to know. However, most of what Granny Henderson told me was suspect. Like when she said that if I stared at that stray dog, the one that had been run over in front of our house, I would mark my baby. "Your child's gonna have a birthmark shaped like that flattened mutt." But I'd looked anyway, out of pure identification with the victim.

"Wanna see Mr. Wiggly?" Kenny said, stroking himself. I didn't know why he felt the need to name his privates.

"No. Really. I'd rather not. I don't feel well." I rubbed at my belly, hoping he'd notice, then climbed into bed, socks and all.

"You never want to *do* it with me anymore," he fumed. "Ever since you got *pregnant.*" He said it as if pregnancy was something I might have purchased through mail order or found packaged inside a cereal box. Rolling onto his side, Kenny walled himself against my assorted ailments, sneering under his breath, "You ought to be glad I still find you worth screwing."

He was right, I figured. Nobody but Kenny would take a second look at me. On a regular basis, he reminded me of that. "You think anybody besides me would want your fat ass?" Then he'd add, "But I'll keep you, I guess. You're still young enough to train. Like they say, old enough for bleedin's old enough for breedin'." But he saved that kind of talk for intimate times like these.

"I'm sorry." I traced his lower back with my fingertips. The apology turned him around. Substituting my hands for his, I took up his rhythm, hoping that he might settle for something less than expected. But he didn't.

Two hours later, I felt a tightening in my abdomen and pressure mounting along my spine. A steady squeeze gripped me like a python. The torturing pains tapered off, only to return again within twenty minutes. My middle grew rigid; my toes curled under. I held my breath, but that only made things worse. If this was labor, I wanted none of it.

"Kenny?" His back was turned to me, in typical fashion. I nudged him with one elbow. "Kenny, wake up."

"Nnn. Huh? Wha'da you want?"

"I think I'm in labor. We've got to go to the hospital. Now!"

He turned his face away and pulled a pillow over one ear. "Go back to sleep. It's nothing."

Right then, more than ever, I wanted Momma. If only she were there to protect me, take my hand and guide me through this mysterious passage, I'd be okay. I needed to grasp the palms of someone experienced, someone comforting and compassionate. While that might not have fully described Momma, it didn't remotely identify Kenny Ray.

The contractions rolled over me in waves. I tried telling myself that each one would be the last. Midnight. Any minute, the pain would stop and I'd go to sleep. But no amount of denial could make the spasms cease.

I checked the clock: two a.m. Had I dozed off? I couldn't be sure. My insides rose and fell like the seas. At any second, I feared it would be high tide. If only I could hang on a little longer maybe the moon would free me from its gravitational spell.

I drifted into a twilight sleep and dreamed I'd fallen overboard from a ship. Above, passengers milled around, sipping cocktails, and nibbling hors d'oeuvres. "Hey!" I called. "Down here! Help!" Didn't anyone notice the woman bobbing in the waters below? Why didn't somebody hear or see me?

Caught up in the vessel's wake, helpless, I watched the crew sailing farther away. Darkness rendered me invisible as the ship drifted beyond any chance of reach.

A sudden sting in my right side startled me from the nightmare. Five a.m.

Soon Momma would be awake. She'd rise to make Daddy's, and later Ricky's, breakfast, though it was Saturday, and she could sleep in if she wanted. If only I could get to her, everything would be better.

Momma was a creature of habits, mostly good ones, a woman to whom routine brought security and a sense of purpose. She was predictable to a fault. And in my immediate need, I recognized that predictable meant reliable, too.

"Kenny!" I pushed him hard. "I need to go to Momma's."

"Hmm? What?" He peered at me through narrow slits. "You wanna go to your momma's? Now? What time is it?" He propped himself on one elbow and then collapsed back onto the mattress.

"It's five o'clock. I've been awake all night." A pain stole my next breath, spiraling through my chest and ribs. "Please." My voice weakened and climbed to a new range. "I need to see Momma. Please, get up and take me there, then you can come home and go back to sleep."

Kenny rose, becoming a bit more coherent. "Aw-right, aw-right," he growled. "Just let me get dressed first. If that ain't asking too much." He scratched his buttocks and then shimmied into yesterday's crumpled uniform. "Might as well wear this, bein' as how you're making me work on a Saturday."

By the time we arrived at Momma's, another hour had passed. She took one look at me and asked, "When did you have your first pains?"

"Around ten o'clock."

37

"Ten o'clock?" She looked confused. "Last night?" Her normally stoic expression evaporated. "And you're just *now* thinking of going to the hospital?"

How could I tell her that I'd married a deadbeat, a good-for-nothing, irritable oaf who bullied and ignored me? How could I let anyone know that I'd pulled this guy out of the gene pool and chosen him, of all the men in Limestone County—not that there was a large selection to choose from—to father my child? What kind of statement would that make about me? I'd only end up looking more foolish and wretched than Kenny, if such a thing were possible.

"I didn't believe, right away, that it was labor." Something warm and moist escaped from underneath my housecoat before I could finish explaining. I stared with disbelief at what had broken free and pooled beneath me. It didn't look like pee with all that white stringy stuff laced through it. Nothing had strained the liquid. I hadn't bothered to put on any underwear because I'd feared I might go full-circle and wind up giving birth right where I'd conceived: in the back seat of Kenny's car.

Momma grabbed a dishtowel from her kitchen counter and threw it at me.

I paused, not knowing whether to clean up the mess I'd made or wedge the cloth between my thighs. Before I could decide, another spurt gushed out.

"You take off," Momma ordered Kenny. She snared her purse from the kitchen table. "I'm right behind you."

~

At the hospital, Momma sat with me in a holding room where I remained until my baby's head crowned. "This'll soon be over and you'll have a beautiful baby to hold," she cooed. But I didn't care if I delivered a possum or if I croaked right then and there. Whatever it took to stop this backbreaking punishment, I'd have gladly welcomed. I considered my limited options. I couldn't afford anesthesia. And to my dismay, no one would administer a lethal injection.

My parents were the only ones fortunate or unfortunate enough, depending on which one you asked, to share my son's birth experience. Kenny's momma didn't come to the hospital right away because nobody thought to call her. I guessed Kenny didn't contact her because he was too busy pacing the halls and eating that king-size candy bar he'd purchased first thing after I'd been admitted. I heard him say to Daddy, "Comfort food," followed by the sound of wrapping paper crunching, and then, "I need it to get through this ordeal." I believed if a contraction hadn't hit me right then, I'd have screamed a string of obscenities at Kenny that would have given my daddy yet another reason to feel sorely ashamed of me.

FIVE

Birthing a baby was a bit like celebrating Christmas; afterward, it was difficult for me to wind down from the mental overload. Alone, pain-free, and exhausted, I couldn't sleep. Possibly I was too hyped-up on hormones. However, I suspected it was something more like maternal love. Lying in the dark, I marveled at the miracle that had taken place, the awesome, unyielding power of creation—of motherhood. I had gained a knowledge that couldn't be taught and experienced emotions I hadn't known existed. My life had changed in ways I couldn't yet fathom. Had my mother and every other mother on the planet undergone this kind of transformation? All I knew was that if Momma had felt like this on the day I was born, from what I could tell, the spell hadn't stayed with her very long. Or maybe Ricky's arrival had broken it.

A lighted bank sign pivoted outside my hospital window, inviting trade at an absurd hour. I focused on the red neon glow and thought about the coming day. When the sun rose, people would enter that bank. None of them would know that I had been there all night, steadily watching and eagerly waiting for them to arrive. I needed to see that sign to prove that I was still in Limestone County and to confirm that, despite my current state, the outer world and what kept it divided hadn't changed.

Inside the hospital muffled cries originating from the nursery filled my room. *That's my baby*, I thought, hearing his distinct vocals. That one was *mine*. On the farm, I'd learned how an animal's brain was imprinted by the first sight of its mother. In much the same way I'd been imprinted by my baby's initial sounds. I needed no one to tell me which cries were his.

What color were his eyes? I squinted and tried to remember. Blue? His hair? Did he have hair? His grapefruit-size head had felt dewy and warm against my chest. His miniscule fingers had clung to my gown. Instinctively, that small oval mouth had searched for me before the nurses had whisked him away. Why hadn't they let me hold him a bit longer? Was something wrong? He'd been born three weeks early, and he'd weighed a scant five pounds. "A lightweight," the doctor had said before giving one of the nurses a suggestive nod. What code had been hidden within that gesture? Like some kind of inside joke, the RNs had both seemed to understand. Whatever it was, they hadn't let me in on it. Why was I, the mother, left out?

My baby would be all right. He had to be. I'd accept nothing less. For him, I'd endured unspeakable punishments and put up with all manner of stupidity. If a reward was to be had, he was it. Thinking of him heated me through, filled me with rapturous feelings,

41

and renewed my hopes. No longer did it matter that I was homely or uneducated or neglected, because I was that child's mother. And that, alone, made me someone significant.

~

Maybe folks without insurance recovered faster than those who had hospitalization coverage. That was all I could figure. Twelve hours after giving birth, I was released from Limestone County Memorial Hospital—without my baby.

I'd named our son Sean in honor of his Irish heritage and a James Bond actor that I found particularly handsome. Sean looked as perfect as morning sunshine on a field of winter wheat. Though I'd suffered fears to the contrary, I'd produced an exquisite baby. If only he would eat. My nurse said it was a common condition in "preemies." But I thought maybe Sean had enough of Kenny in him to make him want to go back to sleep and be left alone.

Nothing about my pregnancy had gone the way it should have. Now our son had arrived too early, before we even had a crib for him to sleep in. However, as it turned out, it would be a while before I needed to worry over that.

Neta Sue turned downright hostile after being left out of her first grandchild's birth. But what had she expected me to do? Get up off of the delivery table, ask the doctor for a dime, and waddle to a pay phone?

Instead of being angry with Kenny, she'd blasted me. "You'd think the *least* you could have done was *call* me when you checked in." She didn't say, "Hello. How are you feeling? What a beautiful boy!" or anything the least bit courteous. To boot, she'd entered my hospital room carrying a sawed-off milk carton stuffed with chicken wire and filled with artificial flowers. Her floral arrangement appeared even more bizarre than her behavior. How, I wondered, could she be so insensitive to a woman who had just given birth? And where in nature might anyone actually find *blue* roses?

Neta Sue never liked much about anyone. Sometimes I wondered if Kenny's father might not have run off at all. Possibly one day his femur bone would surface in Neta Sue's flowerbed. As conniving as she was, I put nothing past her. To hear her tell it, she was superior to everybody, from pediatricians to the President. No one but her could do anything right. Nobody except maybe Kenny. So knowing Neta Sue, I expected she'd find some way to blame me for Sean's extended hospital stay, a setback that guaranteed he'd be a bottle baby and we'd be indebted for years.

Initially I'd planned to nurse Sean, not so much because Neta Sue had told me how much better this was for babies but because Kenny had stubbornly insisted upon it. He wasn't about to get stuck buying baby formula. "That stuff's more

43

expensive than gold," he'd declared. "I could buy a set of mags and a CB radio for what six months' supply of formula costs!"

Kenny knew I hadn't been keen on nursing. My breasts had always been tender and sore, even when I wasn't pregnant. The thought of having my delicate glands gobbled at by a hungry infant, someone who didn't understand the word *ouch,* terrified me. Besides, I'd seen what all that pulling did for a cow's udder, and I hadn't found it too becoming. Now it looked as though my nipples had been saved, but those auto accessories Kenny had been eyeing had moved farther beyond his reach. And Kenny didn't deal well with being told he couldn't have something when he wanted it.

"Wha'da ya mean?" he yelled the day Momma brought me home without Sean. She'd dropped me off at my front door and then hurriedly left so she could be home when Daddy came in from work. "How long is he going to be in that damn hospital?" Kenny asked.

"I don't know. They said maybe as long as two weeks." I lacked the strength to offer any more of an explanation than what should have been apparent. His interrogation threatened to choke the life out of me. I'd grown numb. My insides felt empty and hollow. How would I survive being separated from my baby for so long?

All of my hopes for a better life lay packaged inside a shoebox-sized bundle stored beyond my reach. I'd been separated from the one person who was supposed to love me no matter how grave my flaws. As I stood there arguing with Kenny, it seemed as if Sean might have been a hallucination. I pressed my hands to my swollen breasts and felt the wetness between my faded T-shirt and fingers. The faint smell of lactose and talcum powder reassured me it hadn't been a dream.

"Two weeks!" The whites of Kenny's eyes grew crimson. "And how much goddamn money is that going to cost us?" His gaze shifted from me to the floor and then to the dish strainer where I'd set a case of baby formula. For no reason that I could see, the hospital staff had sent me home with a free supply of Similac and a grocery bag filled with four-ounce glass bottles. He'd spotted both.

"I *tode* you— Tell'em you're gonna nurse."

When Kenny was mad, some of his "L"s disappeared, leaving me, often at very inappropriate times, to think about an amphibious creature.

"I did tell them. What do you expect me to do?" I cupped my hands to my breasts. "You want me to nurse a baby from twenty miles away?"

"You did this deliberately. Whore."

Like some sort of psychomaniac, he darted from room to room in search of his car keys. Finding them, he raced out the door, shouting, "You damn sure better hope I calm down before I get back."

I heard Kenny rev the Fury's engine several times before its tires gave a spin. Rock cinders flew and popped against the car's metal chassis. That caused me to remember that Kenny still owed his momma fifty bucks for the retreads he'd just put on the vehicle. Now that we had to pay for Sean's extra hospital bills, we'd probably never have the money to repay her. But she wouldn't care. She'd interpret our delinquent debt as proof that Kenny, unlike his father, still needed her.

As the sounds of rage dwindled in the late afternoon air, I faced my emptiness, no more alone perhaps than I'd ever been. Abandoned. Confused. In need of a womb where I myself might crawl back inside and await better times—if ever there would be any.

From my bed, I stared into our box window fan and watched the blades turn. Round and round the propeller spun, churning air, yet making no real advance.

Mesmerized by the flickering fan motion, I let my thoughts wander. I envisioned Sean's tiny head. Like some kind of perfect pearl, it seemed impossible that it could have ever formed inside of me. Sean was a beautiful baby, despite my being half-responsible for his looks. He had the complexion of a new peach, flawless and covered with soft blond fuzz. His eyebrows, two faint ivory lines, didn't even resemble mine. Somehow, he'd been spared. He didn't look like a puppy after all.

Every time I thought of my baby, I felt as if I had a chicken egg lodged in my throat. I wanted him there with me, to hold, to caress, to rock in my arms, and to make him the kind of promises a mother diligently wishes to fulfill.

I had to concentrate on something else to keep from choking to death, so I turned my thoughts opposite. What would Kenny do when he returned? Would he strike me with his fists, as he had threatened so many times before? Would he drag me by my hair, curse me, and tell me how hideous I was? Or would he insist on having sex while I was still sore and bleeding?

Frightened, I telephoned Momma from the Hendersons' residence. Granny eavesdropped the whole time, but she never said a word. She didn't even come outside and sit with me on the front porch while I waited for Momma's arrival.

"What on Earth has gotten into him?" Momma asked right off. "He's never been this way before." That was what Momma thought, anyway. I hadn't told her about the time Kenny had shoved me down, or the day he had mashed my mouth until my teeth had split both my lips, or about the assortment of degrading remarks he regularly spewed at me. Right then, I was too emotionally upset to mention the past. The present was disturbing enough.

"I don't know," I croaked between sobs.

We stepped toward Momma's station wagon, and Ricky relinquished the front seat so I could have it. Hysteria had a way of unleashing Ricky's charity.

Momma drove in silence for most of the way to her house. But when she pulled her car into the

47

driveway, she said, "Oh, I see your father's home already."

"Uh, oh," chimed Ricky from the back seat, where I'd all but forgotten he was sitting. "He's gonna be mad."

But Ricky was wrong. Daddy didn't say a word about his missing supper. In fact, I thought he took things pretty well as he listened to me rehash Kenny's tantrum. That was, until he pushed his chair away from the table, stood, and left the room. I heard him walk down the hall and into his bedroom. It sounded like he opened something, maybe his chest of drawers, and then I heard the back door slam shut.

"Where's *he* going?" Momma asked in a way that suggested I should know. I had only the vaguest hunch that it had something to do with finding Kenny. I'd have never suspected that, along with him, he'd carried a loaded 22-caliber pistol.

SIX

No one ever knew what might set Daddy off. So it was easy to see why Momma spent the better part of her time steering clear of it. Ricky and I, though, weren't as shrewd. One day while mowing the yard, we'd managed to cut a swath directly through the full range of Daddy's wrath.

It must have been a hundred degrees on that Saturday afternoon in early July, the summer before Kenny and I had married. I shooed away a hen from the utility stand inside our garage. When the menacing bird stood, I caught the moist bone-colored egg that wobbled out from underneath her. Chickens would do anything to avoid the sweltering heat, right down to laying their eggs on metal shelving. I lifted an already-opened oil can from the ledge that only minutes before had been occupied by poultry.

I handed Ricky the container. "I've got to go get ready for a party, so you have to mow. Daddy said to be sure and add this before you crank the lawnmower."

"Daddy says you can't go to the party if there's going to be dancing," Ricky warned.

"*I'll* decide where I'm going."

"He's just trying to *steer* you in the right direction."

I glared at him. "I'm not a horse."

"Long as he's driving that plow, you are." He wiped his forehead with a greasy mechanic's rag and gave me the stink eye. "It ain't my turn to mow."

"Yes, it is. I did it last time. Remember?"

"No, you didn't." He snatched away the oil can. "You don't know. You weren't even here when I did it." Squatting next to the motorized contraption we both hated more than Momma's burnt chocolate pudding, he let the greenish-black liquid flow. "You were off on one of your soldier drills."

That was Ricky's way of making fun of my band practices. I hadn't had one since early May, so I knew he was lying.

Momma opened the door leading from the house to the garage where we were quarreling. Holding a tumbler filled with ice water, she stared at Ricky. "What's that all over your face?"

Ricky gave her a dumb look. "Sweat." "Here. I poured this up for you. It's too hot to mow without water."

Momma wiped his forehead with the hem of her apron, then offered him the glass.

Ricky took a swig and pushed the tumbler back at her. "I can't hold it while I'm working. Set it down over there." He pointed to a case of antifreeze Daddy had found on sale four years earlier. We'd never had a reason to open it.

Momma set the cloudy water on the cardboard box and returned to less hostile surroundings.

"You do the front and side nearest the peas," I said, helping myself to the remains of Momma's hospitality. "And I'll do the back and around the garage. How's that?"

Ricky positioned himself behind the mower. "If I can go first," he said, like that made some major difference.

"However you want to do it." I cut my eyes at him and left.

About the only time Ricky wasn't first was when he'd been born. I'd beaten him to that one. And he'd spent his limited years searching for a way to overcome that. However, I had a secret phrase, one I used on him anytime he got too full of himself, one that quickly put him in his correct place—a distant second position that might just as well have been dead last.

The high noon rays would soon cook Ricky's fair skin to extra-crispy, and I knew that. But I didn't have time to feel sorry for him. An important television program was about to begin. While I sat in what felt like a walk-in freezer by comparison, the sun, straight overhead, baked Ricky's shoulders to the color of raw salmon.

Soon Ricky returned indoors and fell into Daddy's recliner, one leg draped over its harvest gold armrest. "I can't do this no more!" He looked up at the ceiling. "It's too..." He peeked to see where Momma might be, "*Damn* hot."

"Damn?" I laughed at his daring vocabulary. "How much did you get done, anyway?" I asked, still watching Dick Clark and mentally perfecting my dance moves.

"Half."

Glimpsing sideways, I observed Ricky fanning his face with his hands.

"Maybe less," he admitted.

Ricky chugged about a gallon of ice water before he lit up as though he'd suffered a brain freeze or a brainstorm. I wasn't sure which. "What happens if you don't add oil?" he asked. "What'd you say 'bout that?"

"Burns up the engine." I shot him an irritated look. "How many times have I got to repeat it?"

Ricky grinned. "If I dumped it all out, would you tell?"

I thought about that for a second. If I didn't see it happen, then I couldn't be blamed. And if Ricky was successful, I'd be relieved of mowing duty. "Nope. I watched you put oil in it. That's all I saw, and that's all I wanna know about." I returned to studying something of higher importance than Ricky's burnt up face: an Herbal Essence shampoo commercial.

What happened after that, I wasn't clear on. I presumed it had something to do with Ricky and an upside-down piece of landscape equipment.

Daddy spent the next few nights in the garage working on that mower. He cleaned the carburetor and refilled the oil tank, talking first kindly and then hostilely to that resistant engine. It repaid him with an occasional start that sounded like a can full of marbles rattling. Then it blew white smoke in his face. Beyond the overwhelming smell of boiling petroleum, I detected Daddy's smoldering temper.

Angry and defeated, Daddy finally took the contraption in for repairs. It irked him to admit he wasn't smart enough to fix that lawnmower himself, which made it all the more enjoyable when Ricky pulled the same prank again three weeks later.

After the Johnson grass in our front yard sprang to knee-high proportion, Daddy brought the newly reconditioned lawn eater home. "Got ya'll a present. Somethin'll keep you occupied this weekend."

I prayed some half-wit farmhand had jack-rigged that mower, but it purred like a tiger on a full belly. You'd have thought it was brand new. Ricky wasn't threatened, though. After he took his turn with the monster, I saw him zip past the living room window. A few moments later, the lawnmower sputtered and coughed. Out of gas, I hoped. Otherwise, even Daddy might get suspicious. It seemed inconceivable that Ricky would have been brave enough to empty the mower oil *twice*.

But I underestimated Ricky's hatred for lawn care.

The choking carburetor sounds I'd heard had come from the back yard, so I moved from the TV room to the kitchen window to get a better look at Ricky. Sure enough, there he stood, one hand on his hip and the other animated, as he spoke to Daddy, who'd been standing outside inspecting cantaloupes.

Momma joined me at the sink. "What's goin' on?"

"I don't know. Heard the mower stop, so I came to see."

Daddy made a couple of attempts to revive what Ricky had obviously killed.

Ricky sauntered back to the house and opened the kitchen door. Looking down at his feet, he passed behind Momma. Then he halted and stood next to me.

"What happened?" I asked.

Ricky shrugged. "I dunno. Bad repairman, I guess."

"I can't *be*lieve after all he's *spent*, that thing won't run," Momma said, still watching Daddy yanking out his guts as he tried to restart that machine.

I turned back toward the window for further entertainment. Daddy had ceased his futile resuscitation efforts and looked as though he'd been beaten by the class wimp; though in reality, it had been his thirteen-year-old son.

Behind Momma's back, I gave Ricky the thumbs-up signal. At that moment, I was proud to be his sister. Maybe, I considered, I ought to quit telling him that he'd been adopted.

Whack! Wham! Wham! With a sledgehammer, Daddy beat the lawnmower. Over and over he swung at it. I watched until he'd flattened the innocent machinery into something unrecognizable.

"Jesse? Jesse! What are you doing?" Momma screamed through the single-paned glass.

Ricky and I pressed in close to enjoy the view.

Exhausted and near a heat stroke, Daddy had finished the job. He'd put the beast down. Ambling into the garage, he put away his weapon. With no further fanfare, he opened the kitchen door and stared into three anxious faces. As if a sledgehammer might be the standard tool used to regulate lawnmower engines, he passed behind us offering a two-word explanation. "Needed calibrating."

Ricky's eyes widened, Momma shook her head, and I made a mental note: when Daddy was provoked, nobody, not even Momma, could guess his limits.

SEVEN

After that lawnmower incident, perhaps Daddy's sudden shift toward destruction shouldn't have come as a major surprise. But it took Momma a good half-hour before she thought to inspect the bureau drawer where Daddy kept his gun. I heard her shriek. "Dear Lord, he's taken the pistol with him! We've got to do something!" She wrung her hands and paced. "Ricky, you stay here in case he comes back and wonders where we've gone." Next, she turned to me. "Renee, get up from here, right now. *You* got him into this. The least you can do is help me get him out."

I got him into this? Like *I'd* told him to leave or had hired him to shoot my husband. All I'd wanted was for someone to protect *me*. And that wasn't supposed to have required firearms.

"What do you want me to tell him if he comes back?" Ricky asked. His voice quivered, mouth hung slack. "I want to go with you. Don't make me stay here. Let me go, too."

"No. Somebody has to be here if he comes home," Momma insisted. "I need Renee to help me find Kenny's momma's place."

"Neta Sue's?" I couldn't imagine why we'd look for Daddy there.

Momma gave me a curious look. "Why sure. Where else?"

56

How about over at Kenny's worthless friends' houses? Or down by the gravel pits, where Kenny went to shoot snakes and drink beer? I thought those questions, but didn't offer up the suggestions because Momma seemed hell-bent on heading to Neta Sue's. I half-hoped Kenny was sitting someplace out of harm's way. I didn't want him to get hurt. But I surely didn't want him to injure me or my daddy either. Right then, I thought of Sean. Thankfully, he was still in the hospital, snuggled in blue flannel, and sleeping in his see-through bed. Despite the drama unfolding, his world remained safe. If only I could have been equally as fortunate.

Momma skittered about, searching for something, before she found her car keys hanging on a hook.

I sank deeper into my chair.

"Get up," she commanded. "We've got to go."

Ricky sulked and opened a bag of potato chips.

I rose from my seat at half-speed, none too anxious to follow Momma. "Save yourself, now," I cautioned Ricky. "Get out a dictionary and look up the word 'condom.'"

~

By the time Momma had driven cross-county, the sun had set. It was going to be a clear night, a cloudless one. Already a full moon had risen. A jackrabbit crossed the road in front of us. Momma

57

swerved to miss it, shouting, "Move! Dern you." She never ceased to amuse me with her substitute words for 'damn.' It seemed as if she thought the heavens might part and brimstone rain down if she ever uttered a curse word.

"Let's go by the duplex, first," I said, trying every way I could think of to delay the inevitable catfight between my momma and Kenny's. Momma was no match for Neta Sue, who'd picked her teeth with women bigger than Momma. She could cuss out the postman, argue with the power company, and threaten her paper boy, all in one day. Before breakfast. Nothing civilized was going to come out of that old sow's mouth. And I could just hear Momma saying something back to her, like, "Dang it. You can't talk to me that way."

"You think Kenny might have come home?" Momma asked. She hooked a left and started down a country road, one that would take us in the right direction—farther away from Neta Sue's house.

I shrugged. "He might have."

If he was there, maybe I'd tell Momma to drop me off and I'd take whatever consequences I needed to suffer to protect Daddy from pulling twenty years in Huntsville State Prison. Suddenly, I was no longer my primary concern. One person's beating seemed but a small price to pay for sparing a whole family from ruin.

I didn't want to fight. I only wanted to go home, crawl into bed, and pull the covers over my head. Why had I called my parents into the middle of all this? What had I expected them to do? Rescue me from my own stupidity? At that point, I thought if we could all survive the night, that would suit me fine. And if we could manage to avoid Neta Sue's polecat personality, so much the better.

~

The dirt driveway in front of our duplex sat empty. All the lights in the house remained out. Granny Henderson sat in her porch swing, blissfully waving and no doubt silently wondering why in tarnation we'd driven by without stopping. Momma or I might have asked her if she'd seen Kenny. Certainly she would have told us if she had. That was the whole reason she sat out there in the first place—to see what was going on in other people's lives, whether or not she knew them. But the way I had it figured, Granny wouldn't understand why I'd called Momma to escape Kenny, and then asked her to drive me around trying to find him.

Momma made a U-turn in the Rambler. "He's at his momma's. I'm sure that's where he went." Now we were heading straight for disaster.

"What makes you think he'd run to his momma's house?" I asked.

"Because he's a momma's boy." She looked like an elementary school teacher conducting class. "He wants to act like a *child.* So he'll go there. For sympathy."

"Sympathy? Why would *he* need sympathy? *I'm* the one who's just had a baby. I'm the one who's being treated like dirt here."

Momma hesitated before she answered. "He's scared, Renee Ann. And he doesn't know how to show it. He's frightened by all the responsibilities he's taken on. He's not sure he's man enough to handle 'em."

"Hmph. He isn't." I stared out the window and into the darkness.

"Then you got to be strong enough for both of you. 'Cause ready or not, you two have a child now. That means you can't be children yourselves, anymore." Momma turned into Neta Sue's driveway and switched off the headlights.

Neta Sue's garage door was closed. Normally, she left it open. The lights were on inside her living room, and the blue tint of the television flickered against the windows. She was up all right. More like, lying in wait.

Momma pushed open her door. "You comin'?"

"Where?"

"Up to the door. Where do you think?"

"But he's not *here,* Momma. Look." I pointed to the empty driveway. "His car isn't here."

Momma wasn't listening. She climbed out of the station wagon. A hand on one hip, Momma seemed determined to enter the lion's den. "I got something to say to her, either way. You comin' or not?"

I couldn't say I was exactly roaring to join Momma on that stoop. But then I realized I couldn't let her go alone. The whole episode had been my fault. Though it would have been smart to dodge Neta Sue at any time of day or night, I needed to run interference for my naive parent.

Momma rang Neta Sue's doorbell while I struggled to catch up to her. The entry door opened, rattling the "This Home Protected by Smith & Wesson" sign Neta Sue had posted beneath the peephole.

"Why, what are you two doing here?" Neta Sue asked.

Wondering the same thing, I looked at Momma and awaited her response.

"I'm here about your son," Momma began. "It seems he's caused quite a ruckus tonight."

Neta Sue stood between her entry and outer storm door and listened, refusing to invite us inside. Not that we would have accepted if she'd offered. "I don't know what you're talking about," she said. "I haven't seen or talked to Kenny today. *I* been up at the hospital holding my *grandbaby*." She gave a smug smile. "Noticed none of your people were there. Poor little thing." She made a sad face. "Nobody but those ol' nurses to love on 'im."

"Well, I don't know when *you* were there," Momma said, taking the detour, her tone now defensive. She clutched her handbag tight. "But *we* were there until noon, when we checked Renee out and brought her home. Seems that's when all the trouble started."

Neta Sue poked at her up-do, one that appeared permanent. She claimed her beauty parlor reset it each week, but I felt sure it was a hairpiece. No one, not even Kenny, had seen her with her hair down. With all her makeup removed and that teased-up hairstyle of hers, until she opened her mouth she could pass for a Pentecostal. "I've been lookin' at my show..." She gestured to something behind her. "So like I said, I don't know what you're talking about."

"I'm not here to pick a fight with you," Momma said. "I came to tell you that, if you care about your son the way I care about Renee, you'll tell him to settle down before somebody gets hurt."

"*I beg your pardon!* You don't threaten *me*...or my son, for that matter! Who do you think you are, coming here, bothering me with your girl's problems?" Neta Sue's face turned two shades darker. She blurted her words so fast that a spray of spittle flung onto the glass in front of her. "If she—" She pointed her index finger like a weapon at me. "—can't keep her husband happy, it ain't none of my fault."

Momma gasped. For a second, I thought she might burst into tears. Eventually, she fired back. "This isn't about keeping Kenny *happy*. It's about keeping Kenny *alive* and my husband out of jail." Momma adjusted her eyeglasses and attempted to look mean, but she was no Dirty Harry.

"Jesse's out there, right now, looking for Kenny. And he's got a gun," Momma warned. "All I'm asking is for you to tell Kenny to stop threatening Renee so her daddy won't lose his temper and do something terrible."

Neta Sue grinned. "Oh, I assure you there's nothing to worry about. Kenny can take care of hisself, and Jesse, too, if need be. He's a Murphy. And us Murphys don't take shit off *nobody*." She took a step back. "You two need to get along now and worry about yourselves. Me and Kenny'll be fine." She gave out a cackle and shut the door in our faces. From inside the house, I heard what could have been a TV sitcom laugh track, but it sounded more like Kenny's guffaws.

Steering toward home, Momma cried the kind of tears a hurt toddler might shed. "I can't *believe* you just stood there and let her talk to me that way." She said it as though it had been my role to shield her. But I'd been too busy sizing up the odds, wondering whether Kenny's car was inside Neta Sue's garage, questioning if Daddy had maybe sought to gun down the wrong person.

"What did you expect me to say?"

"I don't know. But you could've said *something*."

Up ahead, maybe twenty yards, about where that jackrabbit had crossed our path earlier, I could see the Rambler's headlamps reflecting off a parked car. "Hey, isn't that Daddy's Volkswagen?"

Momma braked to a stop. "It sure is. Why would he be here? There's nothing out here."

Momma eased her car in front of the other vehicle, and then we both exited to search for clues: no keys in the ignition, windows up, doors locked. Daddy's ball cap rested on the passenger seat, next to his Bible. It looked as if he'd abandoned the Bug.

"Sweet Jesus, I hope he's okay," Momma said.

"Maybe we should check home before we worry. He could have broken down." I wanted to believe that, wanted desperately to have the night end peacefully because I'd lost my last nerve on Neta Sue's doorstep.

First, Kenny had expected me to be a magician. Then Daddy had tried to turn me into a widow. And Momma had wanted me to act as her therapist while running a reconnaissance mission with her. All I wanted was to feel okay for ten seconds. Hard to imagine that, a mere twenty-four hours earlier, I'd been staring at a revolving bank sign, wondering what tomorrow would bring, and expecting something wonderful.

~

We found Daddy in front of an empty fireplace sitting in a chair he'd pulled from the dining room table. A jolt shot through me when I saw him there with a pistol in his lap.

Momma rushed to his side. "Jesse? Jesse? Jesse, please tell me you didn't fire that gun." She looked up at the ceiling. "Dear God, I can't bear this. Jesse?"

Daddy raised his head. "I fired it. Hit a car."

Momma fanned her face with her hands.

"Engine needed calibrating." And then, for no apparent reason, he burst into laughter. "By golly, if that old Bug didn't give me up. I couldn't get her started to save nothin'. Couldn't see out there on that dark road, neither. Flashlight batteries had burnt out."

"So you shot the Bug?" Momma asked, already aware of the answer.

"I didn't even know you had a pistol—" Ricky chimed.

"And you can forget you ever saw it," Daddy said.

"You'd have shot him, Daddy?" I was more concerned about his intentions than his temper fit with a Volkswagen. "He's my husband. I mean..." I snared my purse from the kitchen table. "I'm sorry. I never meant...I shouldn't have called you."

Daddy carried the pistol to the kitchen countertop and set it down. He let out a sigh. "You should have told me sooner so I could've put a stop to it."

Momma studied the weapon. "With a gun? Jesse Goodchild, do you mean you'd let that man damn your soul to Hell?"

"He's my *husband*. This...I need to go." I eased toward the back door hoping Momma would rise to the opportunity and return me to my original doom.

Daddy stepped toward me. "I'll take you home."

I waved him off. "I can't be responsible for you getting into a fight. I'm sick of fighting."

Daddy put his arm around my shoulders. "Not going to be no fighting. I'll take you home. I need to check on the Bug, anyway."

~

"I'm coming in with you," Daddy said, when he witnessed Kenny's car parked in the dirt drive.

I shook my head, but Daddy ignored me.

"Just want to be sure everything's okay before I leave. No trouble. I promise."

When Kenny saw me and Daddy, he raised his Naugahyde throne upright. "Where you been?" he asked, as though I'd failed to obtain a pass for temporary leave.

"Went for a visit." My eyes dared him to say more in front of Daddy.

"Ever hear of leavin' a note?"

Daddy removed his feed store cap and approached Kenny. "Look here, son. I know y'all been having marital problems. But there's a right way and a wrong way to settle differences." With his calloused fingers, he squeezed the rim of his hat.

Kenny kept his seat, refusing Daddy any respect. "Yeah? What's the right way? Call your daddy?"

His jaw pulsing, Daddy stared down at him. "Any man who'd strike a woman is a lowlife."

"I ain't never hit her. She's a liar."

I tugged on Daddy's free arm. "Kenny's never hit me. I never said he'd hit me."

Daddy scrutinized me. "Shoving don't count?"

I tried to think if it did. Were there different degrees of violence? Did I need to suffer a black eye or broken bone before I could call Kenny a horrible husband?

"Well, what do you call a man who cheats?" Kenny asked. "One that slips off to the motel with a girlfriend who drives a better car than he does?"

In a roundabout way, Kenny appeared to be asking questions similar to the ones in my head. I understood him to be suggesting how much worse some guys behave. Someone more astute and less concerned for her safety might have connected the dots differently. But I didn't.

"It's late," Daddy said. "I'm going to leave you two alone to patch things up."

For the moment, Kenny had escaped Daddy's ire. However, it hadn't felt like the hand of God in action. More like His little pinky, maybe.

EIGHT

Granny Henderson had a way of prying into family matters as innocently as if she'd asked for the time. "It ain't none of my business, but if you wanna talk about it, you can." She pushed her good foot hard against the cement, setting her porch swing in motion. The bench seat's faded wood peeked through the final remains of cracked, cheap paint. Granny searched the pockets of her floral-print apron for a tissue. Finding one, she set it in her lap as if to suggest one of us might soon need it.

Granny Henderson and I spent the better parts of our fair-weather days sitting under the roof overhang and watching the traffic on Hawk Creek Road, a narrow county byway that bordered our drives with its two lanes of occasional use. Hawk Creek Road was Granny's second best source of entertainment. No doubt, I was her first.

Fumbling with her tissue, Granny anxiously awaited the day's top story.

"Not much I can say about it." I settled into an Adirondack chair that, together with Granny's porch swing, could have been the only property improvements any tenant had ever made to that duplex. The metal lawn chair didn't exactly rock, but it had just enough spring in it to loosen my thoughts.

A gravel truck passed by heading toward the quarry, going too fast, as usual. Its driver craned his neck and waved like he was thrilled to discover people actually lived out in these parts.

I adjusted my denim cutoffs, ones I was proud to fit into again.

Granny's right hand went up and around and shook in such a way that I wasn't sure that trucker ever was clear she'd properly acknowledged him. I stared at the vacant asphalt he'd left behind.

"Well, I know your baby's still in the hospital and doin' okay," she started again. "'Cause your daddy said so."

I sat forward and gave her a suspicious look. "When did you speak to my daddy?"

"Other night." She straightened her apron for maximum effect. "When he came a lookin' to shoot yore husband. Least, that's what he told me he planned to do when he found 'im." She looked up and to her left. "Said he was gonna blast Kenny's nuts to where they couldn't cause any more harm."

I gave out a snort. *My* daddy talked like that? I could hardly believe it. "Well, you can relax," I said, after I quit laughing. "All Kenny's parts were there when he left for work this morning."

Granny wanted the rest of the story, in detail. To me, none of it seemed worthy of repeating. So I just sat there quietly, staring at the road, waiting for a chance to change the topic. Granny, however, didn't let much time pass before she started up again.

"You know, I'd never wanna be accused o' meddlin', but if you ask me, I think maybe you oughta let your momma and daddy work out their own problems—and you and Kenny take care o' yours." She was in the mood to lecture again. However, that day I wasn't in a frame of mind to listen. "You got a child of your own, now."

Before I could reply, Granny's screen door opened and out stepped Mr. Henderson, his thick hickory walking cane in one hand, black felt derby in the other. He shuffled past without speaking, navigated the porch steps, and staggered over to a vintage-model Chevy sedan. From the first time I'd seen that car, I'd been curious as to how an automobile that ancient could still operate.

"Would you look at that?" Granny said loud enough for him to hear. "Past Easter and he's still wearing that winter hat. I tell you, that man ain't got no sense at all."

"Can he see well enough to drive?" I was more concerned with his safety than his sense of style.

"See?" Granny gave out a laugh. "Not past that front bumper. Even drives with his cane."

"With his *cane?*"

"Yeah, with his *cane*—instead of his foot. Says his legs get too stiff."

Amazed and happy to have found something else to talk about, I stretched this subject as far as I could. "Where does he go?"

"Who knows? Who cares?" Granny shrugged. "When a man leaves, you gotta make better use of your time than t' spend it asking pointless questions." She studied the Chevy as it rolled backward fifteen feet, stalled, and then headed west on Hawk Creek Road. "Maybe a gravel truck will get 'im." She sounded as if that would make her day.

Whatever had made Granny so mad at her husband had to have been hugely memorable. If there was ever an affectionate word exchanged between the two of them, I never heard it. Mostly they just tried to stay out of each other's way, except late at night, whenever their fights must have grown as exhausted as their decrepit bodies. Somehow they slept together in the same bed—without either of them finding a better use for their pillow.

"You drive?" Granny asked matter-of-factly.

"Sure." I swatted at a gnat that threatened to violate my nose. "Got a driver's license, anyway."

"I ain't never seen you drive y'all's Plymouth." Granny sniffed and scanned the roadway for any signs of traffic.

"No. I guess you wouldn't have...and likely never will. Kenny won't let me."

"Anybody that don't drive gets driven." Granny let those words hang in the air like they held some secret meaning. "Let somebody else drive you, you never know where you'll end up."

I lifted a jelly jar at my feet and took a long swig of cold tea. I'd made the beverage for Kenny's

71

supper that evening, but I'd snuck a glass for myself. "Kenny says there ain't no place I need to go that he or Momma can't take me."

Granny's eyes narrowed and she stewed on that for a bit. "If it was me, and it ain't, and if I had me two good arms and two strong legs like yours, I just b'lieve I'd *find* me some place else to go then."

NINE

I didn't think much about driving during those first few weeks after Sean came home from the hospital, in part because Momma found about a billion reasons to visit. She'd found a crib for five dollars at a garage sale. I needed to go with her to buy some "bumper pads." She wanted to take me to get Sean's picture made. My baby needed more diaper shirts. And Momma needed to know that she spent more time than Neta Sue did with her grandbaby. But eventually Momma settled into grandparenthood with the same enthusiasm she'd brought to parenting, and she returned to her normal routines. That was when I caught a touch of cabin fever.

Somehow, I had to concoct a scheme to get outside the house by myself, go away someplace where I could hear my own thoughts again. I was beginning to lose them the way I'd lost most of my ambitions. Gradually. Diminishing a little more each day, until over time I couldn't recall that I'd ever had any.

There'd have to be something in the deal for Kenny if he was ever going to let me drive. That much I could guess. So I decided to begin by asking to motor myself to the place he hated most: the Laundromat—on a Saturday. "You know, you don't *have* to drive me this morning," I said. "If you'd let me drive myself, you could keep Sean inside where

73

it's cooler. I'd be back in two hours." I nodded toward Sean's crib. "He's just gone to sleep. He'll be down for the first hour, at least. What would you think about me going alone?"

Kenny peered through the doorway between the living room and the bedroom where Sean slept. The crib took up one side of the room, and our double bed occupied the other. "I was thinking about a nap, myself."

"Go ahead and take one, then." I tried to sound nonchalant. "Give me the keys, and I'll hurry back."

"You better," he said, handing me the permission I needed. "And you better not go anywhere else. I can't deal with a crying baby." He paused, then added, "And I ain't about to change no dookie diapers, neither."

I couldn't have been any happier if I'd opened my front door and greeted someone from Publisher's Clearinghouse. Not only did I regain the privilege to drive again for the first time in more than a year, but I got to listen to radio music, the kind *I* liked, and to lose myself in two hours of uninterrupted thinking. It didn't matter that the Laundromat was filled with dozens of tired women and energetic children, or that the heat inside had pushed past the temperatures outdoors. For once, I'd driven myself where I wanted to go. Granted, it wasn't somewhere exciting. Until I opened a dryer door.

Right on top of a pair of Kenny's freshly laundered jeans was a crisp, hot, twenty-dollar bill. The Laundry Fairy had visited me! The money couldn't have been Kenny's because he never carried around bills that large. We rarely had twenty bucks to our names unless it was payday. Regardless of its origin, that bill was now mine. All mine. No way did I plan to tell Kenny about it, which was why I later hid that cash inside my sugar canister. Everything would have been hunky-dory if Neta Sue hadn't decided to bring us a gallon of strawberries.

~

"These here strawberries don't taste sweet," Kenny said.

I wanted to say, "How could they? Your momma touched them," but instead, I replied, "It's getting late in the season. Those probably aren't from the Rio Grande. Maybe that's California produce." I set the lid on a pot filled with canning jars and turned on a burner before scuttling to retrieve a glass Kenny had left on the living room floor. Sean sat happily in his playpen, so I saw an opening to do some chores.

When I returned to the kitchen to put away the glass minutes later, I met Kenny standing large in the middle of the room. He'd apparently been looking for a way to sweeten those berries. Now he faced me, pinching the corners of my prized twenty-dollar bill between his thumbs and forefingers. "You wanna explain *this?*" he asked in a way that was more of a dictate than a question.

"Where'd you find *that?*" I asked, having all but forgotten about the hidden money.

"Well, the sugar bowl was empty. So I thought I'd just get some out of *here.*" Kenny pointed behind him to the countertop where I kept a row of red plastic canisters. "Let me see, now...this one says 'Flour.' That one there says 'Sugar.' This one says 'Coffee.' And that one says 'Tea.'" He turned back to me. "Tell me. Do any of those jars say 'Money'?"

"No. Of course not."

"So where did this come from, and why is it in the sugar bin?"

I eased past him and set the tumbler in the sink. "I found it. A long time ago. Honestly, I forgot it was even in there. I stuck it there and didn't remember."

"You *stuck* it there," he repeated, making a stupid face to mock me. "Maybe I oughta just stick my fist someplace so you'll remember not to hide money. Don't you think I know what this means?" His voice spiraled up an octave. "Don't you think I know what you're up to?" He lunged, dropping the bill onto the floor. Before I had time to brace myself, he shoved me backward against the counter. With one hand, he squeezed my jaw so hard I thought his fingers would poke right through my skin. Steadily gripping me, he hissed, "Any guy who'd want to screw you would have to double-bag your face first."

Across the room, the pot of boiling jars spewed steam into the air. I needed to turn off the burner before all the water evaporated from my Dutch oven. For some reason, that seemed critically urgent, even more vital than protecting myself from Kenny's imminent eruption.

Kenny loosened his grip. I tried to get past him, but he caught me full-throttle. His forearm struck me across my collarbone, knocking me backward into the stove. Instinctively, I grabbed for the pot handle, but I missed fully connecting with it. My back slammed against the oven door, sending the boiler and jars crashing onto the floor.

I leaped back to dodge the falling threat.

Hot water splashed from the Dutch oven, scalding me as the liquid seeped through my jeans. Screeching, I yanked open my fly and peeled free of my pants.

Kenny tore at my clothing like it was on fire. I thought he was still raging, until he said, "Ohmigod, Renee. Omigod! I'm sorry. I'm so sorry."

Stripped down to my bikini panties and peasant blouse, I stared at the aftermath beneath me. Miraculously, none of the glass had broken.

Kenny used a dishtowel to retrieve two escaped projectiles while I switched off the stovetop and felt along my shins for damage. Only one burn. A red streak about four inches long. Probably wouldn't even blister.

Right then I thought about Sean. What if he hadn't been in his playpen? What if he'd been sitting on the floor beneath me? The horrors of what could have been were too awful to imagine.

Kenny dabbed the towel over the puddle before he looked up and saw my scalded streak. To him, maybe it resembled some kind of roadmap to redemption. He clutched my ankles. Kneeling there in the middle of the kitchen floor, he kissed the burgundy mark he'd caused me to suffer. His lips soothed my sting. As he inched his way up my injured leg, tracing the line well past the point where redness faded to more neutral tones, you could say he found his destination.

It might seem crazy to want to make love to someone who has attacked you. On the surface, it *was* insanity. But I was out of my mind with grief and hurt. I wanted him to take it back, take it all back, through any means possible. And I could see no other way for him to do that.

TEN

I told Kenny that Sean was out of milk so one of us would have to step out and get some. I said it just like that, "one of us," as though it would have been no stranger for the driver to have been me than him. He never even looked at me, kept right on watching *The Rookies* and tossed me the car keys. "I'm timing you. Don't go nowhere but to the store and back."

The only other car I'd ever driven had been Momma's Rambler station wagon, which didn't have much oomph. The Fury, on the other hand, had enough engine power to give me goose bumps. On that muggy winter night, it was just me and the Plymouth for the next fifteen minutes. So I decided to open her up to see how long—like I'd heard so many commercials say—it would take to get from zero to sixty.

After I'd reached fifty-five miles per hour, I noticed a car closing in on my bumper. I slowed to forty-five, reducing my fun to five miles per hour above the posted speed limit. But not in time.

Cherry and blue lights swirled across my rearview mirror. I pulled off onto the road shoulder and waited to see what might be coming next.

A uniformed officer approached my car, his hand on one hip. "Evenin,' ma'am. May I see your license?" As if I could have said no, and he'd have gone on his way to the nearest coffee shop.

I reached for my purse, fumbled with its zippers, and handed the policeman my driver's license. The ID still listed my parents' address and my maiden name.

"Your car's riding a bit low," the officer observed. He'd already begun writing.

"I guess." I didn't know exactly why I felt the need to agree with him. I wondered what the legal limit was. My hands trembled. Grasping the steering wheel, I tried to steady my shakes. Kenny would never let me drive again if I came home with a ticket. "Is this going to take long?"

"You in some kind of rush?"

"Well, yeah...kind of." I looked away and then back at the patrolman. All I could think to say was, "My baby's at home with my husband, and we're out of milk."

"Young lady, driving fifteen miles an hour over the speed limit could make your baby out of a whole lot more than milk." The deputy pushed his pen against the front brim of his Stetson, setting his khaki-colored hat slightly askew. "Step out of the vehicle, please."

I climbed from the driver's seat. "I'm sorry, Officer. But I really do need to get back soon. Could you please just let me go without giving me a ticket?"

He ignored my question, strolled to the rear of my car, and kept scrawling. "Carrying anything in your trunk?"

Good Lord, I had no idea what was in that trunk—probably some soda bottles, tire tools, and maybe somebody else's trash. Kenny had a knack for hauling home stuff he found on the job. I shrugged.

But before I could respond, the officer asked, "Mind if I take a look?"

"No. Go ahead." I stood back to one side of the vehicle, curious myself.

The officer motioned toward the trunk. "Open it."

I slipped the key into the lock and popped the latch.

The policeman shined his county-issued mega-light inside the storage cavity and shook his head. "What do you plan to do with all...*this?* They printing good nursery rhymes in *Hustler* these days?"

I moved to get a better view. Sure enough, there they were: hundreds, maybe thousands, of glandular freaks, women with bosoms so large that they must have had feet like kangaroos to keep from falling on their faces.

From the way it looked, Kenny had been digging those magazines out of trashcans for months. A few of the cover pages had what appeared to be grape seeds stuck to them. The front of one issue pictured a topless blond woman in a pair of unzipped hot pants seductively leaning over a hardened pool of catsup. If Kenny had emptied an adult bookstore, he'd have collected less material than what was inside that trunk. His *wish books* had so completely filled the Fury that, with the rear compartment closed, there couldn't have been more than two inches remaining between the trunk lid and the top layer of breasts.

The patrolman must have been expecting something more or less exciting, depending on how you define that adjective, than what he'd uncovered. He flipped through a few magazines, and then handed me a warning slip before saying he had to respond to a call across town.

At home, Kenny tried to explain away his secret stash. To hear him tell it, he was only being an astute businessman. "Guys pay good money for those magazines. Even used ones."

"So you're telling me you *sell* these things?" Good grief, he'd been running a cottage porn industry from his vehicle. And all I had to show for it was a lone twenty-dollar bill I'd stuffed in the sugar bin.

"Mostly. Get a dollar a piece for 'em, too." He smirked. "Not counting the ones I give Ricky for free."

~

Some mothers record their baby's first milestones in satin-covered books chockfull of candid photos and cute phrases. But I didn't document all that much because I didn't own one of those books and didn't possess a camera. The sum total of what I recall about Sean's first years are that he crawled at age seven months, took his first steps at fourteen months and, despite my best efforts to the contrary, learned to say the word "Daddy" before he could mouth anything else.

Kenny kept right on hauling trash for both the city and his private business while I lollygagged away my days, tending to Sean, dodging Kenny, and looking forward to nothing more than a decent night's sleep. Granny filled in the gaps.

Clomp. Swish. Clomp. Swish. I could hear her out there with her broom, sweeping away yesterday's dusty layers like she did every morning. Maybe that was Granny's way of calling out to me, "Hey, come outside, and let's visit so I don't lose my mind trying to talk to this old fart over here." Unless it was raining, my front door generally remained open, as it was on that October morning, to catch a breeze.

Sean struggled away from my one-handed grip, ran to the screen door, and grunted. Filled with the normal curiosity of an eighteen-month-old, he remained impossible to feed. I caught up to him right as Granny Henderson approached the other side of the screen door. "Mornin', Peanut. You comin' out to help me pick up pe-cans today?"

The only vegetation in our front yard was a mature pecan tree that stole all the sunshine needed to support grass. That was just as well; neither of our two worse-halves would have mowed a lawn, anyway. Proof of that existed in our backyards, where what looked like a hayfield had grown right up to the foundation. I'd worn a footpath through those weeds to access the wire clothesline attached to the house.

"We'll be right out, Granny," I said. "Sean needs to finish his cereal, first." But Sean wasn't about to return to breakfast now that he'd seen Granny. I gave up trying to convince him cold oatmeal was useful only as glue and joined my neighbor outdoors.

"Them damn squirrels 'bout got all our pe-cans today, Sean," Granny huffed. The three of us inspected the front yard, bending and stooping like a flock of bantam chickens. We tossed the few nuts we found into a bushel produce basket Granny had set out for that purpose. "We better hurry," Granny said. "Looks like more rain's a-comin'."

The Hendersons' Chevy had vacated its usual resting place, so Sean stopped to poke his fingers in the water that remained where the car had been parked.

"Old Man gone already?" I asked.

"Left before eight this morning, dressed like he's goin' to meet the Mayor," Granny said.

"Maybe he's got a girlfriend."

"Lordy, girl. If that old devil can find another woman to put up with him, she's more than welcome to him. I wished he could." She walked back to the porch and scooted into her swing. "Don't nobody want a man who won't do nothin' but piss on hisself."

I laughed. "I think I got one of those, now." I set Sean on the steps, next to me. He kicked his feet in front of him and squealed in utter delight over being outdoors.

"Hmmm. You know, you just might. I believe you just might." Granny scratched at her dry scalp, then brushed a loose silver tendril from one eye. "And if you ain't careful, you're gonna end up just like me," she said in a more serious tone.

I kissed the top of Sean's platinum-blond head as he patted at my thighs. "What do you mean?"

"There's two things I never got, but you still can...and if you get 'em, things might turn out different for you. Them's education and a job. You gotta get you some kind of work if you don't want to still be living here when you're *eighty*." Granny stopped to wave at a pickup heading east on Hawk Creek Road. "I know. You tell yourself times'll get better. But they don't, I'm tellin' you. They can't. Not as long as you only know how to make babies, wipe noses, and tend to a man who won't stop gallivanting all over like he's some kind of dandy dude." She looked at her empty driveway and shook her head. "I'd sure miss talking to you and Little Sean but, honey, you'd be better off out there a-workin' so you can have some kind of life."

I was contemplating what Granny had just said when an auto marked, "County Sheriff," pulled into her side of the drive. A deputy stepped from the vehicle and approached us.

"One of you two ladies Mrs. Henderson?" he asked, scraping the mud off one of his shoes onto the sidewalk Granny had just swept.

She looked at the man like he was a ten-year-old who needed scolding. "I am."

"Ma'am, could you come with me to the Sheriff's Office? We believe we may have found your husband's vehicle down off the Hawk Creek Bridge embankment."

~

Folks speculated about what might have happened to poor Old Man Henderson. I had my theory. Granny had hers. I thought he was probably driving with that cane of his, misjudged the distance between him and one of those rock-haulers, and at the last minute swerved to miss the narrow bridge that wasn't wide enough to carry both of them at once. Granny said she believed he was looking at a girlie magazine, the one found inside his car at the scene, and missed the bridge entirely. No matter who was right, I only hoped there hadn't been any grape seeds stuck to that men's journal.

ELEVEN

Judging by the way salesmen kept showing up on my doorstep, someone must have sent Sean's birth announcement to the Lolaville Chamber of Commerce. Either that or I had the same name as a recent sweepstakes winner. Whatever the cause, I was grateful for any interruption that offered a break from my daytime monotony. My life as a stay-at-home mom had become long on habits and short on thrills. I'd read Sean's Little Golden Books so many times that I could recite them without looking at the pages, and I'd come frighteningly close to falling hard for Mister Rogers.

The sales calls began with a guy wearing a seersucker suit and a pompadour hairstyle. He did his best to convince me I needed life insurance. Or rather, Kenny did. "For just fifteen cents a day, you can have five thousand dollars' worth of protection and peace of mind," the salesman enthused. But I didn't need an adding machine to know I couldn't afford his offer. And Kenny's short fuse and frequent outbursts guaranteed I'd never have peace of mind.

After the insurance man dropped in on me, I received a visit from an elderly gentleman who offered to bronze Sean's baby shoes. He said, "As a mom, you'll naturally want to have these keepsakes preserved." I'd been saving Sean's first pair of

Thom McAns in a box I'd set up high on a closet shelf. It had never occurred to me that I should have smothered them first in melted copper. I didn't understand why anyone would want to destroy a perfectly good pair of baby shoes that way or how it made sense to waste precious dollars on what looked like melted pennies.

I had to laugh when the encyclopedia salesman with the earnest look and desperate message arrived. He insisted Sean was at risk. It was his duty, he said, to warn me about what happens to children who don't have good study aids. Considering that Sean's second birthday was still weeks away, and he wouldn't be learning to read for another four years, I wasn't overly worried.

I explained to the encyclopedia guy that Momma had already begun collecting a set of children's reference books with her A & P Grocery stamps. She'd acquired volumes A through M, minus the H. But the store manager had promised to help Momma find the missing copy. I was hoping she'd get it soon because I'd read all the other volumes, from front to back—twice.

Granny marveled at the way I attracted "peddlers." For some reason, salesmen avoided her house. Granny's explanation was, "They know if they come 'round here, they won't get a word in edgewise. I'll talk their ears off."

I knew exactly how Granny felt. There were times when I'd have chatted with an escaped convict for the sake of variety. It wasn't that I didn't enjoy being home with Sean or playing house servant to Kenny on those rare occasions when he was in a good mood. I simply longed for more conversation than I could get from a toddler and an elderly neighbor. All day long, I'd wait for the chance to talk to Kenny. But when he came home, he spoke very little—other than to ask where something was or to order a change of TV channels. After emptying garbage cans for eight hours, he didn't exactly want to discuss his work. His days, I imagined, were even less eventful than mine.

Weekends weren't much better. Kenny spent Saturday and Sunday afternoons riding around in his car, going to no place in particular, burning gasoline we couldn't afford to waste. He'd take a jaunt down by the lake to see what was happening—never much—maybe cruise the city park to see who was there—rarely anyone—then follow some deserted county road until he tired of viewing the same scenery over and over. He could have been working out the answers to some puzzle in his brain. There was no way to be sure because he didn't speak, and probably couldn't have if he'd wanted to. While he drove, he kept one hand in his mouth so he could chew his nails. Often, I asked him to drop me off at Momma's place so I didn't have to witness him gnawing his cuticles and wearing away the last of the Plymouth's tire tread. Besides, I thought it senseless to ride around in circles.

Sometimes at home, I tried to draw Kenny into a verbal exchange. But it was difficult to find a subject, other than sex, that appealed to him. I could have told him about Granny's failed attempts to teach me to crochet or what new curse words Sean had learned to repeat, if Kenny had seemed interested in that kind of news. However, to do that, I would have had to shout over the TV. And I couldn't compete with *Columbo*.

Once Sean learned to speak, he paid close attention to anything uttered with emphasis, especially phrases Kenny yelled at me or screamed during sports programs. When a wheel fell off Sean's toy tractor, I heard my precious darling shout, "Sumbitch!" After that, I asked Kenny to watch his language when Sean was nearby. Kenny just smirked and said, "Watch it do what?"

One afternoon, while I was teaching Sean a nursery rhyme to improve his vocabulary, I heard a knock at my door. Seated in my lap, Sean walked his fingers up my collarbone, chanting, "Teen-sie ween-sie spi-der." I rubbed my nose against his, handed him his Teddy bear, and scurried to the front door.

On my porch stood a fellow who looked to be in his early thirties, with chiseled features and soft eyes, dressed in pressed jeans and a starched dress shirt. He held a thick black binder in one hand and grasped a business card in his other. I eased open the screen door. "Can I help you?" I knew full well I couldn't because I had no money to buy whatever he was selling.

"Good afternoon. On The Spot Photography." He handed me the card. "I understand you're a new mom, so I thought I'd come by to offer my services." The man studied my face. I gave him a welcoming look that he likely mistook for product interest.

"I specialize in children's portraiture. If you have time, I'd like to show you some of my work." He offered his binder for my review.

I looked behind me to be sure Sean hadn't been frightened by the stranger. He seemed disinterested in anything other than the Teddy bear he was nuzzling. "Sure," I said. "Would you like to come inside?"

I never thought about what might follow. I only imagined it would be easier to sit on the sofa and look through his pictures than to make him try and balance that binder while he flipped the pages. The gentleman appeared harmless enough, and I had an hour or more to kill before Kenny came home. I'd already whipped up some tuna salad and cooked fried fruit pies for dinner, so looking at photos seemed as good a way as any to pass the time.

"I'd love to, if you don't mind." He stepped inside and immediately zeroed in on Sean. "Hi, there, buddy. Whatcha got? Is that your friend?"

Sean handed the toy bear to the chatty visitor. "Bo-bo!"

"Bo-bo?" The photographer made a silly face.

"That's what he named it." I sat down on the couch, thankful to have earlier wiped the grime stains from the cracked vinyl armrests.

"Maybe I can take a picture of you with Bobo."

I smiled. "Would you like a fried blackberry pie and some tea?" I'd made the fried pies from some dewberries Momma had picked from the farm fencerows. Not many people knew the difference between dewberries and blackberries, so I hadn't bothered to make the distinction. With enough sugar added, the two tasted pretty much the same.

The photographer sat down on the sofa next to me and opened his notebook. "I'd love a fried pie." He sighed. "My grandmother used to make the *best* fruit pies."

"I doubt mine'll live up to your grandma's, but my husband says they're half decent. Be right back with one." I motioned for Sean to follow me to the kitchen. He tottered behind, dragging his bear by one ear.

From a cabinet, I grabbed two Milk Glass saucers I'd received as a wedding gift but had never found an occasion to use. The plates were too small and "phoo-phooey" for Kenny's liking and too fragile for Sean's active hands. I slid a dessert onto each saucer: one for my guest, the other for me. For Sean, I broke off a piece of my fruit pie and squeezed out the berries so nothing was left inside the pastry but a thick, purplish filling. He dropped his stuffed toy and reached his chubby fingers to grab the fried crust. I hadn't yet taught him how to say "thank you," but his eyes glinted with appreciation.

In the living room, I set down the saucers and backtracked to retrieve two glasses of sweet tea. Already the photographer had opened his binder to display a pair of eight-by-ten photos. I glanced at the perfectly posed preschoolers in their nice, clean outfits. Then I looked at Sean in his Kmart-special corduroy pants and stained T-shirt that, like his lips, were smudged with blackberry jam. My imagination had to stretch far to envision how differently the children in those portraits lived.

"Ohmigod," he exclaimed, "this is soooo delicious." I grinned and sat down next to him, leaving an appropriate distance between us.

The visitor told me how he could photograph Sean using an assortment of backdrops. He flipped through his notebook and showed me examples of each one—various colored screens and props, including a white rocking horse that looked like it had come to life right out of a children's storybook. His photography was crisp and distinctive, and I could tell he had a talent for working with kids. But even more than a portrait of Sean in one of those lavish settings, I wanted my son to have the lifestyle those images implied.

I studied the last pages of what the photographer called his *portfolio.* "What a great prop!" In one picture, a little girl holding a paintbrush stood before an artist's easel. The child, who looked to be about three, wore a royal blue smocked dress with a red painter's palette embroidery stitched to her bib collar. Her hair, pulled up on the sides and fastened at the crown, was accented by an enormous cherry-colored bow.

"That's my daughter."

"She's adorable."

"Yeah, she's a sweetheart." The man's posture straightened. "She wants to be an artist when she grows up, just like her mother."

The salesman quoted his photography rates, which exceeded my weekly rent, and said to call him when I was ready to schedule a session. He thanked me for the pie and my hospitality as the screen door closed behind him.

I'd just settled Sean in front of the television when Kenny came tearing through the living room door in a high-alert mode.

"Who the hell was *that?*"

I looked up at him from the sofa. "Who?"

"That *longhair* I saw pulling out of here." Kenny scanned the room like a detective searching for murder clues. His gaze settled on the coffee table. There remained the two empty saucers, accompanied by two forks and two partially filled tumblers. "You had that man in this house?"

"A photographer. Selling children's portraits." I stood up. Kenny had that look that hinted he was about to go berserk. I'd learned to recognize the flaring nostrils, deepening frown, and raised chin as a kind of personal safety alarm. "Look." I held out the business card the photographer had left behind. "Here's his card."

Kenny fumed like a madman. His face grew so red it looked like it might explode. "I don't give a damn what he was selling. I want to know what he was *getting!*"

"A fruit pie."

"Or maybe a *fur* pie!"

"I don't know what you're talking about." I took a step toward Sean.

Kenny lunged, swinging one forearm like a bat. The blow struck my right shoulder and sent me reeling. I stumbled into the two-by-four top of our makeshift coffee table. The concrete base sliced a gash in one shin as I fell. My head hit the sofa, and my left knee caught one of the boards. The plank shot up and slammed against my mouth. I half expected the ceiling to crash down on me next.

Sean let out a shriek and took off running toward the bedroom.

"You listen to me! Don't you *ever* let a stranger in this house again!" Kenny's words spewed out faster than his mouth could keep up. "I tode you...you can't be talkin' to no men when I ain't around. Don't...don't act like you don't know what I mean." He kicked one of the two-by-fours hard with his steel-toed boot. I dodged the flying lumber. "It means you keep your sorry ass inside this house, and you keep them pussy-sniffin' hounds outside. You got that?"

I nodded, feeling my pulse in my lower lip. A taste of blood. With one hand, I wiped at the split. Something hard rolled across my tongue. I leaned and spit out a piece of enamel. I didn't want to cry, but I couldn't keep from it. It hurt. Every bit of it. The cuts and gouges, the mistrust, the fear of what could happen next. "All right. All right," I whimpered. "It won't happen again. I promise."

"You're damn right it won't. Not unless you want me to ruin what's left of your ugly-assed face." Kenny exhaled loudly. "And there better be some of them pies left for *me*."

~

I couldn't eat much that night, not with my busted lip and shattered spirit. Kenny wolfed down two sandwiches, three deviled eggs, and two fried pies before he left the table to make his nightly escape. When I heard the theme music from *Adam-12*, I knew I was safe for the rest of the evening. Physically, at least.

I pulled Sean's highchair near the sink so I could watch him while I washed the dishes. He tore a Vienna sausage into morsels as he chewed on a single chunk. I wiped his mouth with a dishtowel.

"Woman," Kenny hollered from the living room, "bring me another one of them pies."

I carried the last of my homemade dessert to him, the whole time willing one of those dewberries to lodge in his gullet. He couldn't count on me to give him the Heimlich maneuver if that happened.

Retrieving Sean, I carried him into the bedroom to ready him for sleep. The night chill warranted footed pajamas, so I snapped him into the yellow terrycloth onesie that made him look like a downy duckling. I decided to teach him a new nursery rhyme before bedtime. Seated on my bed, with him in my lap, I hugged his chest to mine.

Sean pulled back, mashed his palms on either side of my face, and peered into my eyes. With one finger, he pressed the bulge in my bottom lip.

I recalled the photographer and what he'd said about his daughter, how she wanted to be like her mother. I'd never desired to be like mine. Yet it seemed I hadn't strayed all that far from her path. Would Sean one day want to be a garbage man—or maybe a wife beater—like his dad? That unthinkable possibility was more than I could stomach. Perhaps he'd look to me for inspiration instead of Kenny. If so, I had little career guidance to offer.

I lifted Sean's hands into a prayer position.

"Mommy!" he said, as though he were answering a million-dollar question.

"Yes. Mommy." I gently poked his soft middle. "Seanny."

"On-nee!"

No matter how dark my mood, Sean could always turn my despair into momentary delight. I grimaced, feeling the tightness in my swollen lower lip when I smiled. "Let's sing a new rhyme tonight." I tried to recall something we hadn't yet rehearsed. "How about this one?" I clapped Sean's hands together, setting a beat. "Pe-ter, Pe-ter, pum-kin eat-er, had a wife and could-n't keep her...." For the first time, I really heard the words I was reciting. What *was* I teaching my son?

TWELVE

Momma arrived, ready to be my chauffeur. I'd enlisted her in what was sure to be, in Kenny's mind at least, a crime. I had to find a job. It was either that or resign myself to a lifetime of poverty and staring at pavement. The prospect terrified me, though. At age fourteen, I'd found my first and only employment at a Tastee-Freeze. And after two weeks of wrestling with the soft-serve machine, I'd been fired for being too generous with my portion sizes.

Neta Sue had already come and gone, ecstatic over the chance to have Sean all to herself for the day. Daddy and Kenny had left for work. It had been a school day for Ricky. So Momma and I darn near felt like Cinderella and her godmother.

I greeted Momma, and then slung my purse over one shoulder, ready for a quick getaway. If Granny Henderson saw us, she would ask where I was heading. And then she might slip and mention it to Kenny.

"You're going to wear *that?*" Momma asked.

I jumped into the passenger seat, slammed the car door, and motioned for her to hurry and climb in. "Wear what?" I surveyed my zip-up-the-front dress, one of the few I owned. The sheath's bold yellow, black, and white vertical stripes made me feel taller than my actual five-feet, three inches. And the dress's deep neckline provided a good focal point to reveal the closest thing I'd ever had to cleavage. I looked *fine*. But I couldn't quite say the same for Momma.

Momma appeared as she always did, her hair a short bob of wiry chestnut and gray flyaways. Her thick eye lenses weighted down her cat-rim frames so much that her glasses rested on the tip of her nose. As usual, her beige cardigan carried enough electricity to power a small appliance, and her turquoise stretch pants had been dryer-shrunk into pedal-pushers. She certainly was no Mary Tyler Moore. And yet she'd instigated a fashion debate with *me*.

"It's a little short for a job interview," she critiqued.

Momma declared anything above the knee burlesque. Once, when I'd been in the ninth grade, at Daddy's insistence she'd lengthened the hemline of every one of my dresses while I was at school. Of course, she'd failed to let me in on the secret, which had caused me to harbor a nightmarish fear that somehow I'd developed osteoporosis at age fifteen.

"No, it's not," I said. "It was either this or a gray miniskirt with metal studs on it, and I thought this was the better choice." Thank goodness, Momma no longer had access to my closet. Otherwise, she'd have disposed of half my clothes.

Momma represented everything I never wanted to be. She modeled what wouldn't work in my life and likely hadn't worked well in hers, either. I'd witnessed her constant duty and had seen the reward—an indisputable amount of premature aging. If I'd gained anything from her instruction, I couldn't name it. Though I needed Momma, inside I resented her for a role I couldn't yet name but felt certain she'd played in my current predicament. The thought of her assisting me now seemed far-fetched. Her highest calling for twenty years had been to remain married to my father. She'd either decided or been trained early on to surrender to Daddy for the sake of peacekeeping, and maybe the Lord. What could she teach me about defiance, when she'd never exhibited any? But I had nowhere else to turn.

~

Keslo Electronics looked more like an army compound than an equal opportunity employer. An eight-foot fence surrounded the parking lots, where a few gates remained open, ready to ensnare those desperate enough to draw close. On that day, I was among them.

Momma drove through an entrance gate marked, "Employment Center," and followed the arrows pointing to the smallest building on the site. "I'll wait here, in the car," she said. Exactly what I'd hoped, given how she was dressed. I didn't want to have to worry about making two good impressions. One would be difficult enough.

I wandered along the sidewalk leading to a mostly windowless building, the entire time entertaining reasons why I might not be employable. My dress was, indeed, too short, though I'd never admit that to Momma. With a little luck, maybe it would distract from my plain face. I couldn't type, and I'd never learned to sew. What employment skills could I offer? I doubted anyone would ask how well I could clean house or take care of a child. Nobody cared that I could shampoo away the worst cases of gray scalp. "No. I didn't graduate from high school," I imagined saying. "But I passed my GED test on my very first try."

Inside the employment center, the main area smelled of stale smoke and fresh paint. A chipper-sounding receptionist sat at a tidy metal desk in the front of the room—an expansive area filled with dozens of applicants, most of whom were middle-aged minorities. "You're number thirty-one." The receptionist handed me a clipboard that contained an application form. "Please have a seat. We'll call you shortly."

My twenty-something-year-old greeter wore an emerald-green-and-white polka dot pantsuit. A solid white neckerchief hung knotted around her neck like a cowboy's bandana, accenting her ensemble. Her long straight locks formed a V in the middle of her back, and her shoulders, erect and square, gave a hint of self-importance. She had her place, a job to do, and the freedom to do it. And good God, I wanted to be just like her.

The task I'd unknowingly applied for, however, wasn't quite the one I'd envisioned. No sprawling secretarial desk. No paintings to brighten my workspace. No chance to say, "Thank you" or "Please have a seat" to anyone. I'd been screened and categorized for assembly work.

My interviewer bore a striking resemblance to my high school math teacher. Over his reading glasses, he studied me as he scribbled. "Date of your last period?"

I froze. No one other than Momma and my doctor had ever asked me such a question. "Huh?"

"I *said*, date of your last period," he voiced a little louder. "You aren't *pregnant*, are you?"

"No, sir. I'm not. "Geez, what did this have to do with the job? "About two weeks ago," I blurted.

That must have been the answer the guy was looking for because as soon as I spoke, he handed me a plastic cup, told me to see the lab technician down the hall, and assigned me a date to report for duty. In the process, I lost whatever had been left of my name's value. I'd been reduced to a numeric identity. I'd become employee number 116901.

~

I didn't immediately tell Kenny about my employment. And when I eventually did, he took it pretty much the way I'd anticipated.

"You *what?*" Kenny set down his plastic tumbler...hard, spilling liquid down its sides.

I tried to hide my fear. "You heard me. I interviewed for a job and got it." I pressed my back into the dining chair.

"But I *tode* you not to!"

Again, I pictured a creature that might give me warts, but I didn't dare correct Kenny's language. Instead, I smiled and handed Sean a buttered biscuit. "Well, I did anyway." I stroked Sean's baby-fine hair. Like most two-year-olds, he was more interested in toying with his food than eating it. He picked at his bread, pulling it into smaller and smaller pieces. None of the morsels made their way into his mouth.

I eyed Kenny. "And they offered me two dollars and ten cents an hour, enough to get us out of this flimsy excuse for a house."

Kenny shook his head and exhaled hard. "Damn it, Renee!"

He'd said my name, "Renee." I couldn't recall the last time I'd heard him use it. Normally, he'd have said "bitch" or maybe "woman."

"Why'd you go and do this?" He squinted and looked at Sean. "Quit playin' with that biscuit and eat it, son."

"Do what?" I asked. "Try and find us more money?"

"You're gonna do just like all the guys tode me you would—run off with another man." Kenny's eyes reddened in their sockets. "And bitch, I'm tellin' you now, you better pray I don't find you if you do!"

Maybe I'd become emboldened by employment. He wasn't going to intimidate me. "We can't live like this forever, you know. And you can't force me to stay home for the rest of my life."

Kenny sprang from his chair. He charged at me, stopping barely short of my face. "We-e-e-l-l, now, Little Miss Hoity-Toity. Don't you think you're smart all the sudden?" He leaned closer. "I can do anything I want to you, stupid. You're my *wife.*" He stepped back. "If you don't like it, then you can...*Suck this.*" He added a hand gesture, in case I'd forgotten where his snake was located, and sat back down.

Ignoring my protective instincts, I refilled Sean's Tommee Tippee cup at the sink and continued. "Just how long do you think we can sleep in the same bedroom with Sean?"

"'Til we get something bigger." With his filthy fingers, Kenny grabbed another sausage patty from the platter before him.

Returning to my seat, I pushed the basket of biscuits beyond Kenny's reach. "And how are we going to manage that?"

"What do you think?" Kenny shot up again, this time with his hands balled into fists. "You think I got some kind of Magic Eight Ball? You think I got all the goddamn answers?"

Sean let out a burst of tears. He raised his arms high in what looked like an act of surrender.

"I don't think you have the answers for anything," I said, standing my ground. "That's why I'm going to work, starting next Monday." I slipped from my chair and angled toward Sean. But before I could reach him, Kenny clenched me by my neck. He forced my back against a kitchen wall and pinned me there.

"Go ahead, then. Take your sorry ass to work," he growled, before releasing his hold on my windpipe. "But don't 'spect me to be any different on account of it."

Kenny hadn't needed to tell me that. I didn't expect him *ever* to be any different. That was why I knew I had to be.

THIRTEEN

I visited Granny to brag about my job and borrow her telephone. I figured she'd be happy to hear that I'd paid attention to something she told me. But it looked as though she'd been sitting on bigger news than I had.

"I been meaning to tell you." Granny nodded at the pile of boxes stacked beneath her wall phone. "My oldest daughter, Stella, wants me to come to Arkansas. Her husband was a logger there. Died in an accident. Good man."

"You're moving."

"Yes'm. Looks like it's time I went on. I've done everything I aimed to do in this life. Even outlived Old Man." Granny sighed. "Stella and me have had our disagreements. I want to make things right while I still can." She limped across her living room and lifted a framed photo of a petite brunette woman from a shelf. "She never forgave me for staying with Old Man. If I'd've been able to leave 'im, I would have."

"What did he do to make her so mad?"

Granny opened her front door to let out some of the hot air. She'd been running her old gas heater too high again. Her place was perfect for baking yeast bread. But right then, it was the two of us cooking. She stared at something far away, past her front door, past Hawk Creek Road, something

107

so distant that it had pushed beyond her point of forgiveness. "He did it to Stella...something a father shouldn't do to his own blood." She set the photo back in place. "And I'll be taking it to my own grave."

I could see she didn't want to draw out the conversation any further, and I didn't need to know the details. Her expression pretty much told the whole story. "When are you moving?"

Granny sat down next to me on her living room sofa. The furniture's overstuffed cushions felt like giant bed pillows. A true granny couch, if ever I'd seen one. The blue floral-print fabric looked like something you'd find in a Southern quilt. She swatted me on one knee with her good hand. "Stella's coming for me the end of next month."

I was about to ask where in Arkansas Stella lived when Kenny hollered through Granny's screen door. "Renee, you plan on feedin' me and Sean lunch today? Or are you leavin' us t' starve t' death while you're over here a yackin'?"

"I better go," I said. "Before Kenny wastes away." I gave a nervous laugh and checked the doorway. "Real quick, let me tell you. I got a job at Keslo Electronics. And I'm starting tomorrow!"

"Oh, that's the best. Yes it is. That's the best thing you could've told me." Granny's toothless grin covered her whole face. "Looks like both our futures gonna be improvin'. Yes, ma'am."

I let myself out through the screen door and said goodbye. Just then, it came to me how I was going to spend my first paycheck. On my *own* telephone.

~

I followed my escort, an older woman wearing a blue smock and a silver badge, to the KE100 Calculator Assembly Area. It felt like we walked about a mile before we reached the glassed-in bullpen situated inside a building large enough to swallow six Kmarts whole. I thought a major rainstorm might cause a roof that big to collapse. But I didn't dwell on the idea too long because I had a higher chance of being flattened by Kenny than I did of being penned underneath my employer's ceiling.

My foreman, Mr. Gibbons, placed me at workstation number one, at the head of the assembly belt. He said that was where he stuck all new employees because, from that position, they couldn't fall behind. That made perfect sense to me. I didn't want to be like Lucy Ricardo in the candy factory. I'd look pretty silly trying to eat trays full of calculators.

Station One set the pace for the entire assembly belt. I liked being first at most anything, so that position suited me. I'd show Gibbons. I'd work faster than he'd ever seen anyone go, and then maybe he'd notice, and I'd get a promotion, and then Kenny and I would buy a house, one with two full bedrooms and a solid cement drive. Maybe I'd work my way up to a position in Keslo Electronics'

Employment Center, where I'd hand out clipboards from my very own private desk.

My task was as simple as counting from one to ten, backward. That was how I had to load calculator keys. When trays filled with calculator front plates entered my station facedown, my assignment was to stuff each template with numbered keys. The girl to my right was in charge of the plus, minus, subtract, divide, and equal buttons, so I didn't have to worry about them. At first, I didn't understand why I hadn't been given *all* of the keys to load. But then I found out. Ten manual moves in a matter of seconds exceeded most people's coordination skills. I concentrated hard and found my rhythm. And in no time at all, the process turned automatic.

Mr. Gibbons floated in and out of the assembly area. Through the glass interior windows on my left, I could see him drinking coffee and talking to another man in the hallway. Gibbons had a baby face and a full head of sandy-colored hair like Robert Redford. I guessed him to be in his mid-thirties. He was slender, I imagined from all his pacing. His short-sleeved pastel-blue shirt didn't quite cover the sailor tattoo on his left arm, but all I could see was the anchor part.

Gibbons reentered the assembly area, sauntered over to me, and said, "Say-ay. You're doin' pretty good there." He gave me a pat on the shoulder. "Can you go any faster?"

I nodded.

"O-kay! Show me what you got." He returned to the opposite side of the glass where he spent most of his time. The way he studied the assembly workers, he might just as well have been a research scientist.

His remark was all I needed to hear. My fingers flew like those digits belonged to some kind of world-class pianist, hands moving at lightning speed. I was doing something well, doing something right. Finally, someone had noticed.

Soon I realized trays of calculators had been pulled off the belt at stations three, five, and six. I'd been going so fast that my coworkers couldn't keep up with me. Gibbons would soon see that he'd chosen the right person to head this production. Already he might be planning my first promotion.

I surveyed the conveyor belt and caught the "evil eye" cast at me by a woman twice my age. She was the size of a professional fullback and looked like she might have already tackled one too many. Over her right eyelid, a four-inch scar cut through her brow at a forty-five-degree angle. "Hey, you," she hollered at me.

I looked away and pretended not to hear the potential assailant.

All around me, electric screwdrivers buzzed. The assembly belt's motor whirred. Women chattered as they snapped cranberry-colored calculator lenses and gold bezels into place. High above my workstation, a symphony of sounds rose, the least of which had been the woman who'd yelled at me from forty feet away. I decided not to look her direction again.

A few minutes later, Scar Face called out again, louder. "Hey! You better look'et me wid dat ugly-hair head o' yours."

Sheepishly, I glanced over at her.

"You better slow your scrawny ass down." The woman wagged one index finger in sync with her head, which gyrated peculiarly from left to right. I glanced at my trays. And then, as any sane person would have, I slowed my skinny ass down.

My face heated with embarrassment and anger. Hadn't I suffered enough torment during high school? Didn't I have enough threats to deal with already? Was this bullying going to continue for the rest of my life? It seemed there was no place I could go to escape it. Mindlessly, I loaded keys. I looked forward to my dinner break. With any luck, maybe the beast with three eyebrows wouldn't corner me in the cafeteria.

The tension around me eased. Once again, the production line hummed with casual conversation.

"You hear 'bout Martha?" one lady asked another.

"G-ir-ir-l. Go on, now. Ever'body done heard 'bout that bitch."

My ears worked like radar. I took it all in and didn't know what to do with any of it. Other than Kenny and his momma and maybe a few show-off schoolgirls, I hadn't ever heard anyone speak that way in public.

A man on the other side of the assembly belt spiced up the night further when he asked, "Have you heard that new Streisand album, *The Way We Were?*" It took me a second to realize he was speaking to me.

I was anxious to make small talk with anyone right then. "Yeah," I answered, despite knowing Kenny had told me not to speak to other men.

"OO-oo-oo," he squealed. Then he rolled his eyes. "I just got it to-day. And every time I listen to it, it makes my nipples get hard."

I couldn't quite put my finger on it, but something seemed different about the guy. If Kenny had met him, he probably wouldn't have even minded me speaking to him. I laughed out loud at his comment. And then I remembered Scar Face and shut up. She'd grown quiet. Maybe she'd caught up and was no longer mad at me. I picked up my tempo, but only a little. 9, 8, 7, 6, 5, 4, 3, 2, 1, 0. 9, 8, 7, 6, 5, 4, 3, 2, 0. 9876543210, 9876543210, 9876543210.

"Say, motha-fucka!" It was her again. I knew that voice, and I wasn't about to raise my head. "I know you know I'm talkin' to *you.*"

9,8,7,6,5,4,3,2,1,0. 9-8-7-6-5-4-3-2-1-0. 9 – 8 – 7 – 6 – 5 – 4 – 3 – 2 – 1 – 0.

"I'm gonna *cut* your ass if you don't slow down."

The assembly line turned so quiet that I could hear the sound of my own heart pounding.

Why didn't somebody take up for me? Couldn't they see I was new? Couldn't they tell I was practically a child? I was only trying to do my job well. Good grief. This might have been my first stop on the way toward independence, but I had no intention of making it my final destination. $9 - 8 - 7 - 6 - 5 - 4 - 3 - 2 - 1 - 0$. $9 - 8 - 7 - 6 - 5 - 4 - 3 - 2 - 1 - 0$.

Gibbons returned to the assembly area. He'd been observing all this through the glass as if we were guppies in his private aquarium. He marched over and whispered in my left ear. "Did you slow down?"

I nodded.

"Well, speed back up." He walked away, leaving me in a quandary. I wanted to do what he asked. But I didn't want that whacko woman to show me her switchblade.

Near tears, I caught up to Gibbons on my dinner break. "Mr. Gibbons, I want to do a good job for you, but—"

"You're doin' great. Doin' fine." He sipped from his Styrofoam cup of coffee and stared down a hallway that seemingly had no end.

"Yessir," I said, trying to be respectful. "But, see, I don't want to *die* over it."

To my surprise, Gibbons knew what had been happening to me the whole time. He simply hadn't realized the woman had threatened to *knife* me. He'd had problems with her before, he said. And from what I could tell, he was as afraid of the brute as I was. To remedy the situation, Gibbons transferred me to the day shift the following week.

FOURTEEN

"I can load keys real fast," I told Russell, my new supervisor. He just looked at me and blinked as if I'd said something unintelligible. His size-twenty-eight jeans and rodeo-prizewinning belt buckle distracted my attention, but I thought I heard him mumble, "We don't do that here."

Russ, as he told me to call him, had a horseshoe mustache that looked like it might overtake his mouth at any minute. His stringy brown hair hung three inches past his collar. And his ears, which poked through his oily mop, caused him to look like he had handles jutting out on either side of his head. I felt sure that if they'd let *him* become a supervisor, I might work my way up to company president.

"You'll start at station twenty-seven." Russ pointed to a small table at the back of a room big enough to park twenty-five cars inside. "I'll put you next to Selma. She can get you started."

I hurried to keep up with him while he walked to where he'd just indicated. His lizard-skin cowboy boots pounded the vinyl floor in a way that hinted he might be fifty pounds heavier than his jeans size suggested.

"Ever use a soldering iron before?"

I'd only used two kinds of irons that I could recall, one on my hair and one on my dresses. "No, sir. What's a soldering iron?"

Russ gave me a sympathetic look. "Selma'll show you."

Selma, who must have been about thirty-eight, spent her weekends singing with a country and western band. She had teased-up, over-bleached hair and wore red-light-district nail polish and matching lipstick that looked like nothing I'd ever seen in any Avon catalog. But I loved sitting next to her. Even the pockmarks on her face interested me. Most days, it was just the two of us soldering next to each other for eight hours, and sometimes a QC, which I learned about two months later stood for "Quality Control" worker. We talked about worthless husbands and priceless children, which didn't stray all that far from the songs she liked to sing. Once, I even told Selma about David Lassiter, my first boyfriend. She lent her unsolicited advice and said I should call him up sometime.

Occasionally, a QC gal we called Bird would strut over in her mustard-colored smock and say, "Got any solder-bridges for me?" Then she'd pick up the last few PC boards and lead-frames I'd just assembled and hold them underneath a special light she used to find flaws.

Selma told me that Bird had earned her name from being a little dim and from wearing her hair spiked so that it stood up like a cockatoo's feathers. But I thought maybe it had more to do with that beak on her face. She had a *schnoz* like a toucan, and she was always poking her bill where it wasn't welcome.

"Did you see the new nightshift supervisor?" Bird asked Selma.

"Nope. Is he cute?"

"Gives me pea-nut butter legs." Bird widened her stance and swiveled her hips. "Easy to sprea-ea-ea-d." Her gaze shifted to me. "How 'bout you?"

My face grew hot. She was all but asking me if I'd have sex with Mr. Gibbons, the man who'd been kind enough to get me transferred to day shift. He seemed more like a father figure than a sex symbol to me. I couldn't even think of him the way she was suggesting. "I'm married," I said, indignant, and then I went right back to soldering.

Bird snorted. She gave a knowing look to Selma. "So am I. And so is Selma. You think that means anything?"

I stopped soldering and stared at her. "Yes, I do. I think it means a lot." She'd pushed a self-righteousness button I never knew I'd possessed. "I think it means you don't mess around with other people."

Bird slapped the table with the flat of her hand and sneered. "How *old* are you, anyway?"

"Nineteen," I said, not knowing why I felt compelled to answer her, or for that matter, why I'd let her get my goat. "Almost twenty."

"Well, shug, let me tell you something." Bird said this like she was some kind of wise owl instead of the pullet I knew her to be. "While you're sittin' here being all high and mighty with me, your husband...don't he work nights?" She glanced at Selma but didn't wait for confirmation. "Your husband's out there humpin' somebody else."

I turned to Selma, expecting her to jump to my defense. But she only nodded like she was listening to a Sunday sermon aimed directly at her. She reached over her soldering iron holder and wrapped her long scarlet nails around my left wrist. In a consoling voice, she offered, "It's okay, Honey. They *ah-ahll* do it. You just haven't caught him yet."

Most women wouldn't want to hear that their husband was having an affair. However, I decided if Kenny was involved with someone else, it must be Christmas because that was the best gift I could ever receive.

I could see the opportunity in that situation. I'd catch him, find out about his mistress, and act outraged over his betrayal. Truth be told, I'd be dancing a little jig behind his back. His temptress would likely be younger than me, big-breasted, and blond, but I wouldn't care because then no one, not even Momma and Daddy, would fault me for leaving him. I'd be free of Kenny at last. He'd be the *perp,* and I'd be the victim of his tomfoolery. I'd be the wife he didn't have sense enough to keep, instead of the one he'd driven bonkers. Adultery was one of the many *Thou shalt nots* I'd read in the Bible, so no one could argue with that. I remembered one verse said it was even wrong to lust after your neighbor's wife. But I couldn't recall any that spoke against being mean to your own. Maybe that one got left out. I didn't know. All I understood was that a woman needed to have a terrible tale if she wanted any sympathy for leaving her spouse. And I didn't think Kenny's name-calling and shoving would be enough to do the trick.

~

A few nights after Bird had deposited those first seeds of doubt, I decided to check up on Kenny. I peeked in at him to make sure he was asleep, first. Then I slipped into the bathroom, opened his wallet, and surveyed its contents: a five, two ones, his driver's license, a social security card, a photo of his momma, and what looked like a stub from a carnival ride ticket. We'd taken Sean to the County Fair a few days before.

There'd been no leads in there, after all. Possibly Kenny had enough intelligence not to hide evidence in his billfold.

Kenny would slip one day, though. And when he did, I'd be there waiting like a bobcat ready to sink my incisors deeply into him. I'd stalk him without calling attention to my suspicions, something I'd failed to do the day I'd accused him and he'd pushed me to the ground. Next time, I'd spring from nowhere. And then I'd drag his sorry self all the way to divorce court. I'd tell everyone what he'd done, too.

Maybe even the District Attorney, since the girl he'd be seeing would likely be underage. If Kenny so much as tried to stop me from leaving him, I'd have Daddy drive over with his twenty-two and set him straight. Momma would tell me, again, how under special circumstances Jesus forgives people whose marriages don't work out. And within a few months, Sean, being only two years old, would forget all about Kenny. I'd find a new daddy for him, someone who could teach him how to be a gentleman instead of a monster. Someone like David Lassiter. And then we'd all live happily ever after in a brick home with lots of zinnias, marigolds, and crape myrtles in the front yard.

Sheets rustled in the bedroom. Kenny called out, "Renee? What the hell? You comin' to bed tonight, or are you waitin' up for the Tooth Fairy?"

"Be right there!" I set Kenny's wallet on the bathroom sink and crept back to the bedroom. Leaning across Sean's twin bed, I kissed him lightly on one cheek. He stirred, clutched his Teddy bear, and became still again. Soon I'd have him sleeping in his own room, a whimsical place where toys would dance from painted wooden shelves and superheroes would fly across his windows.

After I slipped under the sheets and joined Kenny, he said, "I've been waiting for you to come scratch my back. It itches." His voice was so loud that no one would ever suspect he shared the room with a sleeping toddler.

121

"Where?" I whispered, hoping he'd take the hint. I raked my nails down both sides to find the offending spot. The quicker I hit the mark, the sooner he'd shut up.

"All over. Just keep scratching 'til I tell you to stop."

I pictured that wildcat again, tearing muscle and fat away from the bones of an animal twice its size. "I'm tired. I'll scratch it tomorrow."

Raising his voice another notch, Kenny ordered, "No. You'll do it *now.*"

"But Ken-ee-ee-ee—"

"It's time you did *something* for me. You shouldn't of gotten a job if it makes you that tired."

My job wasn't open for debate, so I sank my nails in deep. Maybe I could shred the top three layers of his hide, strip off the hardened exterior that prevented him from regarding anyone's needs but his own.

"Mm...hmm. That feels good. Rea-ea-l-l g-oo-d."

I had to distract myself, so I contemplated the burgers I planned to cook the next day and the chain lamp I'd placed in lay-away at the furniture store last week. Then I thought of Granny and remembered she'd soon be moving. She'd said she had something to give to Sean. I wondered what it was.

~

I didn't how to act when Granny gave me the gun, seeing as how I'd never once held one. I was more scared than grateful. "Belonged to Old Man," Granny said before she instructed me to keep the prize for Sean. "Don't give it to him 'til he's old enough to be responsible. Meanwhile, you never know when you might need a little protection."

Considering the way Kenny handled that rifle, I questioned whether Sean would survive to see his teen years.

Right off, when he saw the Remington, Kenny cracked the gun apart and stared down the barrel. Snapping the firearm back together, he used my head for a sightline. "Ain't nothin' in the chamber," he said, as if it would have mattered to him if there had been. "Now I've got me somethin' to keep you in line."

"What?" I asked, all but daring him to repeat himself.

"Oh, don't be so goddamn serious. I'm just kiddin' ya."

"Did you notice I'm not laughing?"

"You don't laugh at nothin' no more." He brought the rifle back to a vertical position. "I'll be back in a minute. Gonna ride up town and get me some shells."

FIFTEEN

Memorial Day was exceptionally quiet. The gravel trucks didn't run on Hawk Creek Road because of the holiday, and no one came to visit us. Texas summers combined with a lack of air conditioning tended to deter all but the most determined guests.

I'd been avoiding Neta Sue, like always. She worried me with her warped ideas about child rearing. Why would I listen to her, anyway? Her son was proof enough of her parenting skills. Still, I'd let her take Sean to her house for a few hours. In such a short time, I figured she couldn't do too much damage. Besides, I needed a break. Now I had the afternoon all to myself because Kenny was off someplace with a friend, supposedly shooting water moccasins.

I sat on my gold chenille bedspread and let our window fan tease my hair. My mop was impossible to brush, too wavy. But then I remembered the new hot comb Momma had bought me. "It's supposed to tame frizzy hair like yours," she'd said. I'd tossed it in a drawer and forgotten about it until just then. After years of pressing my hair with an iron, rolling it wet onto orange juice cans, and later oatmeal cartons, I'd pretty much given up on smoothing my locks. What worked for others seldom suited me. But since I was in the doldrums, I decided to experiment.

That wasn't the first time I'd had the urge to revamp my appearance. I'd been near stir-crazy the day I'd plucked my eyebrows, a decision I'd not once regretted. But the blond-in-a-bottle hair-color job I'd later done on myself had been a huge mistake. It had taken nine months and two layer-cuts to get rid of the yellowish straw I'd been left with. Only the ends of my shoulder-length hair remained brassy. I'd squeezed lemon juice on the rest, to make the colors blend together better. A little straightening might further improve the total effect.

When the first strands of my hair dried to a silky finish, I just about cried. I'd never looked this way before: normal. My tresses neither frizzed nor waved. They were as smooth as Cher's! I did my makeup and wrapped myself in a slinky halter-top. Next, I squeezed into a pair of low-rise jeans. Standing in front of my closet mirror, I was stunned by my own reflection. Could this be the same person who'd walked her high school hallways in fear of being seen? Why, I'd had nothing to be ashamed of—nothing at all. I had simply needed better hair-care products, along with a little eyebrow tweezing. Of course, it hadn't hurt that I'd added a few beauty products to enhance my facial features. I'd outgrown that gangly appearance I could see had been only a temporary stage. Thanks to Sean, I'd gained the necessary weight to fill out my size-six hip-huggers. Damn, I actually looked all right.

I swayed my hips, wondering if someone like me could be alluring. What would David Lassiter have thought if he'd seen me? I'd like to show him a few of the new tricks I'd learned from Kenny. They'd likely be twice as much fun with a man who truly appreciated me. Someday I vowed to find out.

The front screen door slammed, announcing Kenny's arrival. "Renee! You need to get your son. He's asleep in the car."

I stepped out from behind the closet door and acted as if I'd been putting away laundry. "Oh, you're home."

He stopped cold in front of me, his eyes scrolling my body, his head tilted to one side. In one hand, he gripped the Remington, and in the other, he held a grocery-size paper bag. "What the shit?" He set the sack down on the bedroom floor. "Where the hell do you think you're goin' all done up like that?"

"I ain't going nowhere. Don't be silly."

Kenny stared at me through squinted eyes. "Then how come you're all fixed up? What'd you do to your hair, anyway?"

I turned a pivot to show off my new *do*. "I straightened it with a hot comb. Don't you like it?"

"It's okay." He gave me an accusing glare. "You tryin' to impress somebody with those little tits of yours?"

Little tits. That was exactly what the boys in school used to say to me. "You're tits are so tiny you got to wear falsies," they'd scream loud enough for everyone on the school bus to hear. One day, David Lassiter's voice had been among the hecklers. It must have been one of his darker times, a day when he was desperate for peer acceptance. But he'd gained it at my expense. And I'd been furious. With my head held high and my chest thrust forward, I'd walked, expressionless, down the bus aisle and then stopped in front of him. "Give me your hand," I'd said. And when he did, I directed his open palm underneath my shirt and slipped it inside my bra cup. I let his hand linger there for about as long as a firefly lights up, time enough for him to confirm what he was touching was authentic breast tissue, but too short a stint to bring him any real kicks. "Feel like a falsie to you?"

But this wasn't high school, and there was no part of me that Kenny hadn't felt. I had little to offer in defense. "Of course not." I frowned. "Why do you say things like that to me?"

"You wanna know why? I'll tell you why." Kenny stared at me with what felt like X-ray vision. "'Cause if you ever screw around, I'll hunt you down like an animal and shoot you in the back." He pointed to the rifle he'd dropped on the bed. "Don't you think I won't, neither. And while I'm at it, I'll save a couple shells for your boyfriend."

SIXTEEN

The worse Kenny acted at home, the better I liked working outside of it. He graduated from daytime garbage removal to nighttime street sweeper operator the same week I moved from evening assembly to daylight inspections. For a couple with only one car and no money for childcare, I considered our alternate work schedules a good fortune. I could have been happier only if I didn't have to see Kenny's mug for that hour every weekday between our work shifts' start and stop times.

After I'd learned to prevent solder bridges, those accidental connections that caused calculator brains to short out, Russ promoted me to the testing center where I received the white-glove treatment. I had to wear a pair of those mitts every day. Russ said the gloves were necessary to keep my nails from scratching the micron-plated gold bezels that accented those fine plastic calculator cases. "We don't want any oily fingerprints on the lenses," he explained. "Keslo Electronics prides itself on shipping only products that meet the highest standards."

My new friend Pearly worked directly across the table from me. From time to time, she'd bend her head and look under the bright factory lights that hung low between us. Her work gloves made her dark hands looked like they'd been dipped in marshmallow cream. She was about the friendliest and most talkative woman I'd ever met.

"You got kids?" Pearly asked.

"One," I answered. "A three-year-old son."

"Damn. You too young to have chil'ren yet." Pearly laughed. "And here I is, almost too *old* to have any." She rolled her eyes wide. "Ain't right."

"What do you mean, too old?" Pearly didn't look a day over thirty to me.

"Thirty-five. Married nine years and never used birth control. Look like it ain't going to happen for me." Pearly swiped a cotton-covered finger across a calculator lens. Checking the display, she punched in several numbers. "Say, did they tell you where they's movin' you when they brough'cha here?"

"Nope. Just said, 'Follow me.' So I did."

Pearly passed me the calculator she'd been inspecting. "Turn it upside down." She studied me carefully.

I stared at the lit numbers and read, "7734." The display looked fine to me. It didn't appear to be a *reject*. That was what we called the products that failed our inspections. At home, that was what Kenny called me. "You're a total reject, Renee."

"You got to turn it *upside down*," Pearly repeated.

I spun the unit 180 degrees and looked at the display again. I could see what she'd been trying to show me; the lens displayed the word, "*hELL*."

"You got to entertain yo'self someway around here," Pearly said.

I liked her right from the start.

Like me, Pearly didn't have much formal education. But she knew more about dieting than anyone I'd ever met. In fact, she was on a new one every few weeks: a grapefruit diet, a breadless diet, a beef jerky and cheddar cheese diet,

129

a lettuce at every meal diet, and a sugarless diet, to name a few. And nothing irked her more than to watch me down a king-size chocolate bar and Dr Pepper during both our daily fifteen-minute breaks.

"Damn, if you don't eat that shit and still have a skinny ass," she'd tease. Her outspoken ways didn't bother me because she was good-natured and laughed about most everything. But she didn't joke much about kids. She wanted one badly, worse than she wanted to lose weight. And it didn't help that Rosemary, the woman who sat to my left, had six of them, at least one of which was always sick with strep throat or tonsillitis. Rosemary was a walking billboard for birth control pills, an invention she'd obviously never been introduced to. Because of her large brood, Rosemary needed work more than the rest of us. So whenever overtime was offered, Pearly and I let Rosemary have first chance at it. The two of us had husbands. And unlike me, Pearly was fond of spending time with hers.

"G-ir-ir-l, my *hus*-band done made me the *best* apricot cake," Pearly bragged one Monday morning.

I about fell out of my work chair. Kenny would sooner have missed *Saturday Night Wrestling* than to have been caught playing Betty Crocker. "Your husband bakes cakes?" I fought the urge to snicker.

"Wha'choo mean? You don't think I'd marry me a man who can't *cook*, now do ya?" Pearly patted her rotund belly. "A man's gotta work as much as I do, if he wants to stay around *my* house. I don't put up with none o' that laying up and acting crazy."

Pearly's husband, Jarnell, commanded a beer truck all day, and to hear her tell it, drove Pearly all night. For

130

someone married nine years, she was having way more fun than she should have been. Well, if she was telling the truth, which I prayed she wasn't. Otherwise, my life was short of even more than I'd imagined.

~

I wouldn't win any mother-of-the-year prize for saying it, but I enjoyed the eight hours a day I spent at work. I did miss Sean. And I envied the time Kenny and Neta Sue could spend with him while I focused on consumer products I had no use for. However, the best part of my day didn't occur at work or home. Those moments happened when I sat in the driver's seat.

Kenny's disregard for auto care aided my plans to acquire a personal vehicle. He showed his Fury the same respect he gave me, which might explain why the Plymouth blew her engine.

Neta Sue loaned us the thousand dollars required for repairs. But she said she didn't have a solution for how Kenny or I would get to work during the week the Fury would have to stay at the mechanic's shop. We'd run her plum ragged if she tried to chauffeur us back and forth for different work shifts. Certainly, she'd have missed the beauty sleep no one could deny she desperately needed. So Kenny and I had bummed rides home on Friday, and now we had two days to devise another plan.

I thumbed through the Penny Saver News looking at the auto ads. "Maybe we should get a second car," I said, as if I'd just inherited a million dollars.

"Maybe we should go to Disneyland, too," Kenny taunted.

"No, really, I'm serious. We can't be left like this every time the Plymouth breaks down." I'd found a chance to work on what little existed of Kenny's reasoning. "We could use our tax return for a down payment."

We'd received a $200 refund check that neither of us had felt obligated to confess to Neta Sue. If she had a grand to spare, she didn't need her loot half as much as we needed ours. For that reason, we'd accepted her money and kept quiet about our own.

Kenny scratched his scalp. "We can't afford nothin' fancy."

That was all I needed to hear. Within less than an hour, we were stubbing our toes against tires.

At a used car lot, I eyed a cream-puff Monte Carlo that I could imagine riding high inside. The Chevy's baby blue body and sugar-white vinyl top practically screamed my name. But the sticker price said something more like, "Mayor's daughter."

Kenny pointed to a jeep that might have been used last by military, possibly in Vietnam. I gave him a have-you-lost-your-marbles stare.

Eventually, we settled on an older model Mustang, its twelve hundred dollar price painted in shoe polish on the windshield.

"How do you want to title this?" the salesman asked.

Before I could speak, Kenny blurted, "In *my* name."

The sales dude scrawled something on triplicate carbon paper. "Just you?"

"Just me," Kenny confirmed.

I let him have his big moment. I had my car, so it didn't matter what anyone wrote on paper. Kenny could put his name on the title and all over the note, too, if doing that made him feel like a winner. But I intended to be the primary driver of that Mustang, and I would pilot it as if it had wings.

~

At last I could make my winter commutes by myself every day, with all the windows rolled up. For an extra reward, the likes of Kenny's music—Black Sabbath and Jethro Tull—couldn't interfere with my more Manilow-like daydreams. I could even stop on my way home and pick up some candy for Sean when I had a little leftover from the lunch money Kenny gave me.

Most days while I drove the two-lane country road leading home, I'd entertain thoughts of what awaited. Mentally, I'd compare the scene I'd like to find against the one I expected to encounter. Once I'd discovered Sean's Big Wheel parked on our porch, its back tires punctured with holes from where earlier he'd been spinning out in our gravel driveway. Imitating his dad, I suspected.

When I'd asked Sean about the Big Wheel tires, he'd floored me by saying, "I been thinkin' of tradin' it in, anyhow." Where would a three-year-old ever get such an idea? I chuckled as I recalled Sean's remark.

Home, I parked my car in the driveway next to Kenny's and drew a deep breath.

Ten steps inside the entry door, Kenny sat sprawled across the sofa watching Sean drag the last of his toys into the living room. On the coffee table were two dirty, cereal-crusted bowls. Yesterday's clothes, empty soda cans, cookie bags, and moon pie wrappers decorated the floors. In front of the TV, a spill of grape soda formed a sticky pond that already had claimed one of Sean's socks.

"'Bout time you got home." Kenny said, looking at his watch. "Sean's hungry."

"So why didn't you feed him something, then?" In no mood to hear his sorry excuses, I sauntered past Kenny and into the kitchen. From the looks of the place, he'd plowed through every snack food item on hand. I opened the refrigerator.

"Be-cause you ain't been to the grocery this week!" Kenny yelled.

He knew there was plenty of food inside the cupboards. There just wasn't anything in there that he could fix without turning on a burner. I pulled a carton of eggs from the fridge and set them on the stove. Egg salad sounded good to me. I'd make some right after I cleaned up the purple lake in front of the TV.

Passing through our bedroom, I mentally noted every hazardous item within Sean's reach. There stood the Remington in the corner next to our bed. No doubt, the rifle chamber was full.

"Is this gun in here loaded?" I shouted.

"Of course it is," Kenny said. "You expect me to shoot an intruder with an empty gun?"

Most evenings when Kenny left for work, I was ready to throw him out the door. But I never did. In our marriage, Kenny was the one who did all the shoving. I only thought about tackling him the way some folks dream about climbing Mount Everest or winning the Olympics.

Every evening after Kenny made his highly anticipated departure, I'd straighten up the place, turn off the television, and put Sean in my lap. Often we'd grab the Sears catalog and look at toys together while Sean pointed out what he next wanted to receive from *Santy* Clause.

After Sean went to bed, I'd listen to some Moody Blues and Seals & Crofts albums and flip through the catalog some more. Sometimes, when I listened to my favorite song, *Hummingbird*, I could feel myself flying, soaring to a place where picket fences instead of dangerous roads and active railroads bordered every yard, to where friends and family gathered, to a fictional location where love, instead of fear, kept us all connected.

Someday my real mate, the one I should have had, would arrive to rescue me. Whoever he was, he'd conquer Kenny with kindness instead of brute force. I didn't know what he'd look like. David Lassiter, perhaps. Or maybe Burt Reynolds. Or possibly Jesus.

I spent hours inventing fantasy lovers. Sitting alone at night, I imagined every detail of their appearances. The Wish Book came in handy then, too. Particularly helpful was the men's underwear section.

By the time Kenny arrived home in the wee hours of the morning, I'd usually fallen asleep. Often I dreamt about making love to a guy I hadn't yet met. I succumbed to my make-believe partner fully, in ways I'd never give in to Kenny. I lived for this man, endured for him, waited patiently for his appearance. And I would wait for all eternity before I would resign my destiny to Kenny.

~

I told Pearly, "I'm going to leave him as soon as I can save up enough money."

She turned out to be more sympathetic than I'd expected. "Can't say I blame you, shugah. Been me, I'd done shot his sorry ass."

I thought about the rifle Kenny kept next to our bed. Repeatedly, he'd warned I'd better never try and leave him. Any time Kenny felt he was losing face or ground, he resorted to violence. "He's probably going to shoot my butt, if he finds out," I said.

Pearly pursed her lips and thought for a second. "You just tell me when you're ready. Me and Jarnell will bring his truck over, and we'll get you outta there." She seemed over-enthused to get in the middle of something that at best could be dangerous and, at worst, fatal. If I'd had half her gumption, I'd already have been a free woman. But then again, if I'd had Pearly's fortitude, Kenny would have been a dead man.

On our way to lunch, I grabbed my purse and followed Pearly out the door. "You better put that pay raise you're getting in the credit union," Pearly directed, as if she thought I knew something about banking. What few bills Kenny and I couldn't take care of in person, we paid with money orders. Kenny cashed my paychecks before I even had the chance to look hard at them.

"Kenny'd find out," I said, already feeling defeated.

"How's he gonna find out?" Pearly looked at me like I was twelve instead of twenty. "Your pay ain't gonna go down none, if you do this right. Have your statements mailed some place 'sides home."

Pearly was the most headstrong woman I knew, other than maybe Neta Sue. She could plot and scheme better than a soap opera villainess. "Come on. Follow me," she said. "I'll show you where to go to open an account."

I followed Pearly inside a room marked, "Keslo Electronics Credit Union," and at her insistence signed up for automatic payroll deposits. She showed me how to hide ten dollars each payday from Kenny, money he'd never miss. After I'd finished filling out the paperwork, I said, "We'd better hurry, if you want to eat today."

"Girl, I ain't missin' a meal over *this*," Pearly said. But after seeing what she had in her lunch bag, I had to wonder why not.

"What the hell is that?" I eyed her sandwich with disgust—two split weenies and some hot mustard stuck between a couple slices of white bread. "What kind of diet are you on now?"

Pearly's eyebrows arched. She gave me an indignant look. "I'll have you know it's a diet that *works*. I done lost five pounds. And my Ontie lost twenty." She pulled two boiled eggs and a banana from her sack. "It's called the egg, weenie, and banana diet," she explained really serious-like. "You eat nothin' but weenies the first day. The second day, you eat nothin' but boiled eggs...all you want...and the third day, you eat nothin' but bananas." She retrieved an overripe piece of monkey fruit from inside her bag. "And on day four, you can eat all three." Peeling her banana, she volunteered, "I'm on day four," though she failed to explain the bread.

"That'll work." I giggled at her expression. I didn't want to make her mad, seeing as how she'd gone out of her way to be helpful to me. But I felt I had to point out the obvious. "You could eat anything that way and lose weight. You're not taking in enough calories for it to matter what you're eating."

"Aw, hush. You don't know nothin' 'bout dietin', no way." Pearly pointed to the package of chips I'd just opened. "I don't know why I even talk to you about it."

"Why do you want to lose weight so bad? Especially since *your* husband loves *you* just how you are." I popped a handful of corn chips into my mouth and chased them with a swig of soda pop.

"I know he does. But I don't like being this size. And I don't like the way people look at me when I go places, like they think I'm gonna eat up all the food in the buffet 'fore they get to it." Her voice broke. "But the worst thing is when people asks if I'm pregnant."

I could relate to that part. "Oh, I know all about that. Strangers used to say to me, 'You *can't* be pregnant! Why, you're still a *child* yourself.'"

Pearly clapped her hands together and belted out a laugh. "I know tha's right!"

We were an unlikely pair, Pearly and me. The one thing we both had in common was our struggle to accept a fate we'd failed to accurately predict.

Nothing could have dampened my mood that day. I'd taken the first few steps in a thousand-mile journey, and I felt invigorated. I didn't get mad at Kenny later that afternoon, not even when he told me that, when he hadn't been looking, which didn't narrow things down too much, Sean had broken my Seals and Crofts album. The *Hummingbird* one.

SEVENTEEN

While I'd been only dreaming of flying away, Daddy had actually done it. Now I knew whose defective genes I'd inherited. I'd been afraid of what he'd think of me if I left Kenny, worried about his appraisal of me as his daughter, too embarrassed ever to admit the truth of my situation. Come to find out, all that time, my morals had been higher than his.

As soon as I heard the news from Ricky, I rushed over to Momma's house. I found her sitting in a dining chair looking like somebody had let all the air out of her body. Kneeling before her, I waited for her to bring her gaze level. She didn't tell me the whole story, but Ricky had already clued me in on the worst of it.

"How could he do this?" She blew her nose on one of Daddy's embroidered hankies.

"Are you sure?" I shook my head. "I mean, did you call Brother Sontag? Did you ask him if he was missing anything...like, maybe his wife?"

That must have been the wrong response because Momma let out a bawl.

I patted her on one knee, doing my best to take back my remark. "Okay. Okay," I said, uncertain which of us I wanted most to reassure.

Momma's eyes appeared focused on something far ahead, way off in the distance. "What am I going to do? They were already in California when he called." She let out a wail. "California! How is that possible?" She gave me a dumbfounded look. "I never even knew he liked *avocados!*"

I tried to ignore the twisted logic behind her statement. "Apparently, there's a lot more you didn't know. Nobody would think Daddy would do such a thing. It's crazy. It's selfish." I searched for more descriptive words. "It's plain...wrong."

Momma folded and refolded her handkerchief. "I'm nobody's wife, now. And if I'm nobody's wife, then who am I?" She didn't wait for me to answer. "Nobody."

That was too much for me to hear. I leapt to my feet. She'd just identified the crux of the problem. If she'd regarded herself more highly, maybe Daddy would have, too. I wasn't sure how, but it seemed to me that Momma's attitude had maligned more than her marriage. "Don't say that. You're my mother, and you're...you."

Momma shook her head. "Without Jesse, I'm nothing, Renee." She sat up straighter. "I'm not like you."

I hadn't come here to pick a fight, but it sure felt like one was brewing. "What do you mean by that?"

Momma refused eye contact. "You've always been so..." She appeared to search for the perfect word. "*Independent.*" The way she said it, it sounded like a curse word. But I accepted it as a compliment.

141

~

"I don't *freakin'* believe it," I said to Pearly. "He left Momma just like that, after twenty-five years of marriage, and after she'd lived damn near her whole life treating him like he ruled the roost."

Pearly peered at me over her safety lenses. "See there. That's why you don't let 'em rule the roost." She wagged one index finger in the air. "'Cause you can't count on 'em to be there the next mornin' when it's time to crow."

But Momma had depended on Daddy. She'd expected him to do what she'd always done—make do with what was on hand. She simply hadn't identified that what was available included the minister's wife.

It crushed me to think my daddy would do something like this, that he could so easily abandon his family for another one. I guessed he'd have the daughter he'd always admired, the one he liked to describe as a *natural* beauty. If he couldn't produce one himself, he'd steal somebody else's. But I wasn't about to give Janice Sontag a free pass. She'd been equally at fault. Her prayers had conjured up more than the Holy Ghost in Daddy's heart.

"He went testifying on Wednesday evenings," Momma had said, trying to recreate the crime scene in her head. "I knew Janice went with him. But as far as I know, that's the only time they could have been together, alone." Momma was looking for the road signs she'd missed, the ones that had been marked, *Adultery Straight Ahead.*

"All I can say is, Daddy must have been witnessing more to his own needs than to others'."

Momma burst into tears.

In hindsight, I realized I didn't possess the most sympathetic ears Momma could have bent. Our thoughts were traveling in different directions. She was dying over the idea of losing her marriage, and I was living for the day I could break free of mine. Mostly, I was mad at Daddy for pretending to be somebody he wasn't and angry at Momma for forgetting who she was.

~

Neta Sue and her big mouth had plenty to say about Daddy's disappearance. Even on holidays, she couldn't restrain herself enough to be civil. "You know, some folks got more sex hormones than's good for 'em," she spouted. "I hear you can inherit that. Maybe you got it from your daddy."

I wanted to run over and snatch that fake copper hairpiece of hers right off the top of her half-bald head. How dare she link Daddy's extramarital affair to my teen pregnancy? I'd been sixteen when I made my mistake. And I hadn't done it with someone else's spouse.

"I doubt hormones had much to do with it," I fired back. "Daddy's forty-six years old."

"Like that means anything." Neta Sue waved off my comment and wandered into her seldom-used kitchen. "Kenny's father ain't found his way home yet from wherever he's laid up. And he's fifty-two," she continued from the next room.

Anson Murphy had been missing for years. Or so Neta Sue claimed. She said he'd gone off one day on one of his many three-day drunks, and simply failed to return. And even now, at Christmastime, she rarely made mention of him.

But I knew Momma was sitting home thinking plenty about Daddy and about everything she'd lost. She'd had to sell the farm because she couldn't afford to keep it. Now she and Ricky lived in an apartment in the city. Christmas for her would never again be the same. Family traditions that had once brought comfort now summoned her grief. Even the standard tree ornaments seemed out of place hanging from a four-foot, tabletop tree inside Momma's sparsely decorated apartment. Thank goodness Momma had Ricky to be with her on Christmas Eve. I'd see her tomorrow.

I pulled a chair away from Neta Sue's dining table. Before I could get my caboose in the seat, she barked, "Don't sit *there*. That's where I set Kenny's plate. You can sit over there." She indicated another chair. "Next to Sean."

Kenny's painted dishes from childhood never failed to make their way back to Neta Sue's dining table whenever we visited. It was the most ridiculous thing I'd ever seen—a grown man eating his food and drinking his tea from his toddler plate and tumbler. I wouldn't have been surprised to see her set out his baby fork, too.

After we'd all filled our plates, Neta Sue said, "Mm, mm. I cooked that turkey right good, if I do say so myself." She'd dived right in before we had even said prayer. "Pays to work for somebody who 'preciates you." She pointed with her fork to the free bird she'd received from Jumpin' Janitors, where she worked. "I even got a canister of popcorn someone left 'side their desk. Had a sign on it that said, 'For the cleaning staff.'" She puffed up like an inner-tube making contact with an air compressor. "People 'members those whose work's important."

I'd received a free calculator and an extra half-hour lunch break on my last day of work before the holiday. And Kenny had been given a brick of cheese and a ten-pound ham. Unlike Neta Sue, I didn't feel the need to brag on it.

Sean stood up in his chair and leaned across the table. I tugged at his corduroy britches, pulling him up short of his goal. I didn't want him to get burned on Neta Sue's candle centerpiece. The outer globe displayed a glass-beaded likeness of the Virgin Mary. "I wanna blow it out," Sean whined. Earlier, I'd told him today was Jesus' birthday. So I could see how he'd connected those dots.

"No, honey. You can't have Grandma's prayer candle," Neta Sue scolded. She moved one fat forefinger like a pendulum, flashing her fake nails the way she always did when she was trying to show them off. "I'm burnin' that so God'll help me win next week's twenty-five-hundred-dollar bingo pot."

Kenny burst out laughing. "You ain't gonna win no twenty-five hundred dollars playin' *bin-go*, anymore than you ended up on *The Price Is Right* the last time you burned one of these things."

"You shut your mouth." Neta Sue gave Kenny a hostile look. "It worked for Charlotte Kilpatrick. She burned one to get a new car, and her loan was approved the next *day!*"

Sean sat down squarely in my lap and shoveled dressing with a plastic spoon. I let him go at it while I cut the turkey and jellied cranberries I'd layered onto my plate.

"I wish you'd look at that." Neta Sue nodded toward Sean. "That baby must be starvin' to death. Poor thing." Then she cut her eyes at Kenny. "Notice you been lookin' a little poor lately, too."

~

The sounds of gunfire pierced the cold night air. I snuggled further down under the bedcovers. "Hope those idiots don't hit our house," I said. Bullets being cheaper than fireworks, the week between Christmas and New Year's Eve could be dangerous.

Kenny leaned back onto his pillow and folded his arms behind his head, unconcerned. "Too far away."

"Make any resolutions yet?" I asked.

"Yep. Gonna buy a twenty-one-inch TV." That was the extent to which Kenny's dreams traveled.

"How about a bigger place to live?" I suggested, hoping to raise his priorities.

He turned his head to study me. "Like a yacht, too?"

I waited for his mood to settle. "I been thinking..."

"Your first mistake—"

"—about going to college."

"You ain't going."

"Wouldn't cost us nothing, 'cause Keslo has a tuition assistance program that would pay for everything, even my books."

Kenny punched his pillow to fluff its contents. "You ain't going to no damn college."

I propped up on one elbow and turned toward him. "I want to learn to write. Teachers said I had a talent for it."

Kenny tucked the covers tight around his middle. "Then write yourself a note. College is for smart people who think they're better than everybody else. And you ain't going."

An hour later, the gunfire ceased. My thoughts about higher education, however, did not.

~

After the holidays, I went back to work. But Ricky must have felt he had more options because he refused to return to school. "I gotta take care of Momma," he'd said when I asked him about dropping out. "She needs me more than school does." But from what I could tell, he hadn't found work or done anything that would have prevented him from graduating.

I let the sore subject slide until late January, when I broke down and asked Momma, "What's Ricky doing these days?"

"He's fixed the neighbor's TV set and made twenty dollars this week," Momma said, citing the sum of Ricky's work efforts. Momma knew how to inflate Ricky's practically inert status to make him sound almost industrious. Once she'd told me that Ricky was working at a recycling plant. Later, I'd learned he'd only been picking up cans along the roadway and selling them for scrap aluminum.

A draft sent a chill over the assembly area. My work gloves would serve dual purpose today. I shivered and checked a lens for scratches amidst the room's eerie silence. It sounded as if everyone's body had returned to work without their minds. I glanced across the worktable where Pearly appeared engrossed in filling out a final inspection form.

"Look like nothin'll ever become of my brother Ricky," I said. "He's probably gonna end up on some assembly line like us."

Pearly gave me a stupefied look. "There's worse places to be, you know. Like the pen, or maybe the cemetery."

I snickered. "Or living with somebody who makes you feel like you're in both."

"How much you saved now?" she asked.

I thought for a second. "About two hundred."

"Girl, tha's rent for a month. You almost there."

EIGHTEEN

Sexual desire can motivate a person to do about anything, I guess. It can make you crazy enough to rip off your underpants in a Winn-Dixie parking lot and, at the same time, it can make you feel like you're damn near bulletproof. I'll be the first to admit, that's pretty much how Anthony affected my thinking.

His real name was Antonio Salazar. But he said I should call him Anthony. We met during one of my short coffee breaks, when he was standing behind me at the soda machine and I was searching for enough change to do the job. "Aw, shoot," I said, cleaning up my language for the sake of strangers.

"Need some coins?" Anthony asked. He extended his hand and opened his fist to reveal an assortment of nickels, dimes, and quarters.

I'd been short a dime, so I searched inside his open palm to locate one. Then I glanced up at his deep-set eyes, handsome grin, and perfect teeth, all of which had been more than I'd expected to find. I felt myself blush. *Great*, I thought, *now he knows I think he's good-looking*. "Thanks," was all I could manage.

I didn't know what caused him to follow me back to the break room bench. Maybe my pupils dilated really large or my jeans hugged my rear a little too tightly that day. Whatever was responsible for his initial attraction, Anthony stuck to me like white on rice.

Pearly was waiting for me on the other end of that four-seat platform. When Anthony approached, she scooted her broad behind to make room for him to sit next to me. As she did, she gave me an accusing, yet hilarious, stare.

"I see you here all the time," Anthony said, allowing his right thigh to brush against my left. "What area do you work in?"

"That one, there." I pointed to the catty-corner modular walls.

"Huh." Anthony chuckled. "You're building what I'm fixing."

Anthony spent his days around the corner from me, working as a technician, trouble-shooting integrated circuitry with a group of men to whom I'd never paid much attention. Generally, when our break times were over, the men went one direction and the women disappeared in another, a kind of corporate segregation. Break time reminded me of the way, after Thanksgiving dinner, my father, brother, and uncles all used to get up from Granny Goodchild's table and move into the den, leaving all the gals inside the kitchen to do the cleanup.

Anthony stole a glimpse at the break room clock. "What time do you go to lunch?"

"Eleven-thirty," I said. "I go early." Checking my surroundings, I noticed that most of the other employees had returned to their workstations. Pearly had left without even speaking to me, which wasn't like her.

"Me, too." Anthony deposited his empty soda can in a nearby trash receptacle. "Maybe I'll see you there."

"Maybe."

I'd little more than turned the corner before I saw Pearly waiting for me. She punched me with one elbow as we hustled to return to our group. "That man's got the hots for you. And you workin' it, girl."

"You don't know what you're talking about. I ain't doing nothing but being polite."

"Mm, hmm. Politely stupid." Pearly opened a door marked, "Authorized Personnel Only," and we both stepped back into joint reality. "Just 'cause you got a car now don't mean you can act reckless," she continued.

"Not being reckless. I'm just thinking hard about what I want someday, same way I got my Mustang."

~

I wasn't sure whose spirit I was channeling when I agreed to have lunch with Anthony. I heard myself say the word "yes," but it didn't feel like that answer had come from me.

Over a plate lunch that could have been mule feed for all I cared, Anthony looked at my left hand and said, "I take it you're married."

"Yes, I am. Just not happy about it."

I studied the thin gold band that had cost Kenny thirteen dollars at Kmart. What did it mean? A band of eternity, but eternal what? I wondered. Anthony gave me a sympathetic smile. He was gorgeous to look at, even better than those guys in the Sears catalogs. His body smelled manly, but in a good way. "If you want to expand on that, you can," he said.

"Some other time, maybe."

We ate in silence for what felt like forever before he asked, "You ever think about leaving him?"

I blotted my mouth with my napkin, borrowing time. "Hardly a day when I don't think about it." I stared off, away from Anthony's piercing gaze, to keep from crying. "But it's kind of like climbing Mount Everest. You know?"

Anthony tilted his head to one side. "What's holding you back?"

"A Remington."

"The western painter?"

I had no earthly idea where that came from or to whom he might be referring. "The western rifle maker," he said.

"How about you?" I asked, shifting the subject to something more interesting. "Are you married?"

He flashed the backside of his left hand at me. "Not yet. My girlfriend works here in the personnel center. You might have seen her."

153

Girlfriend? Oh, no. I didn't want him to have a love interest. "The one with the long black hair?" I prayed I'd guessed wrong.

"Darlene. That's her. Yeah, I know before you say it. She's pretty. Everybody tells me that."

~

Simply knowing that someone like Anthony would speak to me sent my confidence soaring. That meant that if, under the right circumstances, I met another nice man—say, one without a gorgeous girlfriend—that he might find me interesting, too. For right now, it was enough that I had a name and a face to attach to the man I'd previously only known as "the underwear guy." In my sleep, I imagined our steamy trysts. And when I'd awaken, I could hardly bring myself to look at Kenny. I hadn't broken any wedding vows, but my X-rated thoughts disturbed me. Clearly, my daddy and I had more in common than I wanted to admit.

"We don't get to talk all that much at work," Anthony said one afternoon. "Maybe I could call you some night when Kenny's not home...to keep you company. I spend lots of evenings alone myself."

It began that innocently, with harmless phone conversations. Really. We just talked about layoff rumors and Anthony's engineering classes. Sometimes I'd tell him what Sean had done that day that was cuter than anything I'd ever seen.

And Anthony would mention that Darlene was away, visiting her sister or mother for the evening.

Pearly said I should have known things would get complicated.

One night, Kenny's street sweeper broke down and he became stranded inside the City's break area for several hours. The pay phone there had gone on the blink, and it was letting everyone dial out for free. Either out of boredom or suspicion, Kenny suffered a mental flash to call me.

"What the hell?" he screamed, when he finally got through. "I've been trying to call you for over an hour. Who you been on the phone with this late at night?"

"I haven't been on the phone," I said, trying to think fast. "Sean must have knocked it off the hook. I noticed the receiver was crooked, so I jiggled it into place and it rang."

"You better not be lying to me. I might come home *early* and find out."

That conversation had been enough to put a gun-load of fear back into me. So the next morning, during my morning break, I informed Anthony, "You better not call me anymore."

"Why not? Don't you want to talk to me?" He looked like I'd stolen his last ounce of joy. But actually I'd squashed my own. In my instant awakening, survival had trumped any thoughts of happiness or pleasure.

How could I make him understand I was married to a crazy man who wasn't above using

155

both our skulls for target practice? If Kenny found out I was talking to Anthony, he'd go berserk. And if Anthony ever learned what Kenny was capable of, he might decide to relocate to another continent. "Of course I want to talk to you. Our conversations are all that keep me going. I'm just afraid Kenny or Darlene will find out and get mad."

Anthony slipped his hands over mine. "You can quit worrying about Darlene. I sent her packing a few days ago."

I wanted to register disbelief, but it was all I could do to keep from shouting, "Praise God!" Though I was pretty sure the Lord had little to do with that.

Those dark circles underneath Anthony's eyes had been explained. "You kicked her out?" I wanted to hear the good news one more time.

Anthony sighed. "Found out her sister wasn't who she'd been seeing. Let's leave it at that. Okay?"

~

"Damn!" I said. "Have I got news to tell *you!*"

"You finally left him?" Pearly guessed.

Darn if she hadn't found a way to steal the better part of my enthusiasm. "No, not yet," I replied at half-power. "Darlene's gone."

Pearly clucked her tongue and gave me a look of disapproval. "Mm, hmm. Girl, trouble's 'bout to start. You better get yo'self outta there, whilst you still can."

I passed a plastic tub filled with calculator units to the woman seated next to me so she'd get to work and quit listening to my not-so-private discussion. "Here. These are ready for you," I said to Miss Nosey.

I turned to Pearly, picking up where we'd left off. "I'm going to. But I don't quite have everything worked out."

The look on Pearly's face told me she knew better. "You been tellin' me that forever. You been tellin' me that for more'n a year. You ain't never gonna leave that man. But you 'bout to start playin'. And playin'll getcha hurt. Getcha hurt bad."

"You act like I'm sleeping with him. And I told you I'm not. Not even planning on it—at least not while I'm still *married*."

Pearly bent her body below the table surface and lifted a few more units from the tub next to her chair. She popped up like a hound chasing a rabbit through a wheat field. "I know you think I'm jiving. But I been 'round enough to know how playin' starts. And you're doing it *now*."

I checked to see who else might be listening. "Well, it ain't a sin unless I'm sleeping with him. And you can't fault me for *thinkin'* about it."

"'Course you is thinkin' 'bout it. Any woman in your shoes would be." Pearly's facial features softened with her tone. "All I'm saying is you gotta get out, first. Then you can play all you want, even find that drumma fella—"

"David?" I chuckled.

"Tha's right." With her screwdriver, she tightened the back of a calculator into place. "You can have him and Anthony and two or three more while you is espermintin'. But not while you's married." She set the unit aside. "You don't want to go actin' like yo' crazy daddy, now do ya?"

~

Daddy's first letter arrived about three months after he divorced Momma. Why he'd never called, I couldn't say for sure. Maybe he thought writing was a safer form of communication, a better way to announce his latest love, the one he'd dredged up after Janice Sontag had tired of him and returned to her former family. He wrote from someplace he called Silicon Valley. Sounded like a community full of women with breast implants to me. From the photo Daddy enclosed with his letter, I suspected his new gal had some of those synthetic cones herself. On the picture's backside, Daddy had written, "I can't wait for you to meet my new partner, Celeste. She's an intelligent, funny lady I met at a New Age church in San Diego."

I had no idea what he meant by "new age," but the woman in that photo looked like she hadn't lived half my momma's years. Maybe that's why Momma cried so much when I showed her that picture.

"He's never coming back, Renee. He's never coming back, is he?" Her chest heaved as she sobbed. I didn't have the heart to ask why this hadn't occurred to her earlier, like maybe when she'd signed those divorce papers.

That same afternoon, Momma gave me Daddy's black leather Bible. "Doesn't look like he'll be back for it." She dusted its cover with one hand. "I guess I been hanging on to it because it reminded me of him and what else he threw away along with me." She sighed and then gave a lighthearted laugh. "I always figured I was in good company. But you might have more use for it."

I clutched the zipper-bound Scriptures to my chest, fighting back my emotions, and then I promised to read the Bible again as soon as I found time. But in my heart I didn't think it would do me much good. The way I had it figured, the Holy Book hadn't kept Daddy at home with Momma any more than it was going to make me stay with Kenny.

NINETEEN

Pearly sat next to me, a pink sponge roller dangling from her bangs, waiting for the starting bell to signal us from the break area. She looked like she might be having a rough morning, so I decided to keep quiet.

I stretched out my right hand to admire my costume ring.

"What kind of jewelry is that?" Pearly asked.

I pushed my new accessory closer for her inspection. "It's a mood ring. Turns blue when you're calm, purple when you're happy, and black when you're mad or stressed."

"Why the hell can't it turn *black* when you're happy?" She rolled her eyes. "And why you need a ring to tell you what kinda mood you're in, anyway? You white folk kill me...paying good money for something can't even be pawned."

"I sure don't need a ring to tell me *your* mood today," I said, withdrawing my hand from her view.

Pearly searched through the vinyl tote at her feet, pawing her way through the clutter inside. She removed her foam house shoes and stuck them into the bag, trading the slippers for a bottle of Geritol. Brandishing the medicine, she let out a hoot. "If that Jarnell ain't crazy. Man's been telling me I need to take this for iron core blood."

"You mean iron *poor* blood," I corrected. Pearly always made me laugh when I least expected it. I chuckled at her botched slogan.

But she continued, unfazed by my ribbing. "Yeah. That could have been it. Silly fool don't know I's just tired 'cause o' my tumor."

"You mean, you haven't told Jarnell?"

Pearly looked at me as though I'd asked her to divulge her current weight. "Course not. He'd worry me to death. And I's worried 'nough for bofe o' us." Ever since she'd lost down to a size fourteen, Pearly had said that she hadn't felt quite right.

"How do you know it's a tumor if you haven't been to see a doctor?" I asked.

Pearly removed her sponge curler. "I just know. I can feel it moving all around in my stomach. Bound to be a big ol' cancer."

"More like a big ol' fart."

The buzzer rang its obnoxious tone. Time to start our day on the clock.

Pearly stood and raised one hand as if she was testifying. "Yeah, go on and laugh. Gone be a race to see which one of us goes first. You got plenty to worry about yo'self. Too crazy and fast to know it."

Inside our work area, Russ, our brainless supervisor, stood on one leg and braced himself off the other with a crutch. He'd injured himself, again, riding bulls. I guessed herding factory employees around all week wasn't enough to keep him satisfied. Regularly he showed up for work on Monday mornings sporting some new rodeo injury.

Reading from a slip of paper he held in one hand, Russ announced, "Effective May first, all overtime hours have been suspended until further notice. All work hours exceeding eight hours a day or forty hours a week will be considered voluntary and shall be worked without pay." After that brief, but clear message, he hobbled back to his cubicle at the rear of the assembly area.

"There goes my va-cation," a coworker said.

Rosemary, the gal with six dependents, spoke up. "Va-cation? Who are you kidding? I got to have overtime to feed my kids."

It might sound silly, but killing mandatory overtime made more people mad than happy. A low mood took hold as the assembly hummed at a muted volume, the kind typically reserved for funerals. Only, what had died had been a bunch of folks' chances to survive between paychecks.

Rosemary looked like she might burst out crying any second. Seated next to me, she swabbed at a calculator as though it might be a baby.

I felt sorry for her. "Hey," I said. "They're offering typing classes after work on Tuesdays and Thursdays in the cafeteria. Maybe you could sign up." She didn't look at me until I added, "The school district's putting them on for *free*. If you could type, you could put in for a higher-paying job here, and then you wouldn't need to depend so much on overtime."

Pearly gave me a funny look. "*You* takin' them classes?"

I shifted in my seat. "Thinking 'bout it." Pearly didn't need to know that the thought had right then entered my mind for the first time. I'd seen a sign posted the prior week. Maybe I'd gain a new skill that would lead me to a better job, one where I could toss my hair and inspect my nails instead of staring at busted gadgets all day.

"Girl, you betta do more than think about it," Pearly said. "'Cause you gone be a single mother soon yo'self."

Rosemary ignored Pearly's comment. "Where do I go to sign up?"

"The poster I saw said to register at the employment center," I said. "I'll go with you if you want, and we can do it together at lunch." I studied Pearly. "Do you want to take typing with us?"

"No use, girl. I don't 'magine it would do me no good." She stared out the interior windows next to us at something I couldn't see. "This tumor's movin' more and more ever' day."

~

For the next six weeks, Rosemary and I left work on Tuesday and Thursday afternoons a half-hour before our scheduled quitting time. Our typing instructor somehow convinced Russ to let us go early. So for an hour every class day, we sat together in a room filled with twenty typewriters and a dozen other young women determined to find their way out of assembly work. None of us knew where we were headed next. But it would have been difficult for any move to set us in a wrong direction.

On our last day of typing class, our teacher told us we could compose a letter or do anything we wanted, as long as we typed. For some reason, I decided to bang out a letter to Daddy in San Diego.

There's probably nothing you can do about it from where you are, but I think you should know that Ricky quit school and I suspect he is smoking pot. Also, I've met a man named Anthony and I'm thinking of leaving Kenny, like you left Momma. I thought I'd tell you first since you're more likely to understand.

I don't know why I felt the need to tell all that to Daddy, other than maybe I wanted him to feel bad. It wasn't fair that he'd escaped his marriage and family obligations without suffering major loss. It hadn't worked that way for the rest of us. And I wanted him to have to face the damage he'd left behind. I could have told Daddy about the new clerical job I'd bid on or Momma's employment at the Get-N-Go. But I didn't.

~

A week after I mailed my letter to Daddy, I received an offer for a new position. My promotion to Marketing Secretary threatened to split Pearly and me apart before her tumor did. But as it turned out, her self-diagnosis had been a tad misleading.

One Wednesday, right after I'd given Russell my two weeks' notice, Pearly said, "Gir-ir-l, you ain't even gonna be-*lieve* what I's about to tell you!" Grinning like a coyote, she thrust out her chest and squared her shoulders. "I's five months *preg-nant!*"

"What?" I thought I must have heard wrong. "Pregnant? You said you couldn't get that way."

Pearly beamed. "Couldn't. Not whilst I was overweight and *anemic*. Look like all that dietin' and Geritol done me some good." She stood and reached behind her, pulling her blue lab coat tight across her front. The inflated tire she normally carried had pushed out into a bubble. Spinning sideways, she displayed her telltale profile. "Five months! Can you be-lieve it?"

"I can't believe you didn't *know* it," I said. "Don't you know what it means when you miss your period five times in a *row?*"

Pearly waved off my comment with one hand. "I done missed so many periods, I'd'a thought I's dyin' if I had one. But let me tell you, Jarnell never been more happy in his whole life."

I forced a smile. That was good news, but for some reason I couldn't find my cheer button. "What are you going to do, now? You gonna keep working here?" The answer I both hoped for and feared would mean I'd lose touch with her entirely.

"Oh, no. You know better than *that*." Pearly chuckled. "Jarnell said he'd work *four* jobs, if need be, so I can stay home." She smoothed her work smock down over her belly. "Gonna raise *this* baby decent."

I didn't know how to properly respond because Pearly's circumstances were different than mine had been. When I'd found out I was pregnant with Sean, most everybody I knew had cried. And not from happiness. Momma didn't speak to me for three whole days, not even to tell me when it was time for supper. And Daddy sort of stepped around me, giving me a wider clearance than normal. He probably felt that if he got too close, he'd lose his temper and pound me the way he'd pulverized the lawnmower.

For the next two Sundays, my folks stopped going to church altogether. They made up some kind of story about Daddy having a respiratory problem. And no one bothered to say that it was his daughter's condition, and not his own, that had caused his impaired breathing.

TWENTY

During one of my many nighttime telephone conversations with Anthony, he said, "Since we don't work so close together anymore, we can take the same sick days, and nobody'll suspect anything." I was glad, right then, that he couldn't see my face.

"And do *what?*" I asked, as if I didn't know what he had in mind.

"Whatever we want. Maybe go to the lake or something."

I let out a nervous laugh. "The only time I ever tried that, I got caught by a truant officer."

"A truant officer?"

"Yeah, it was one of those harebrained schemes teenagers cook up. Skipping school. Last week of the year, too. I didn't see any harm in it. We'd all left at lunchtime and gone to the lake. And before we'd even roasted our first weenie, we got caught."

Anthony snickered. "I think we're a little too old to worry about truant officers."

"Yeah, I suppose. But I still have a husband to hide from."

For a second, we both reflected on that statement before Anthony spoke. "If you weren't married, would you do it?"

He'd cornered me, and I had to decide. Already I'd earned the title of Fornicator. I didn't need an Adulteress tag to go along with it. I might not have always chosen correctly between right and wrong, but that didn't necessarily mean I wanted to continue my moral vacation. The sins I'd committed hadn't shaken my belief in monogamy. Contrary to Neta Sue's opinions, I was *not* like my daddy.

"If I wasn't married, I'd do *lots* of things. You'd be surprised."

The line grew dead quiet. Maybe the connection had been broken. I waited to hear a dial tone.

Anthony's voice broke the silence. "Then why do you stay with him? Why don't you leave?"

How many times would I need to hear this question before I found an acceptable answer? "I'm leaving him soon...as soon as I save up enough money."

"Good God, Renee." Anthony's voice went high. "Is *money* all that's keeping you from doing it?"

My gaze shifted from a watermark on the ceiling to my sleeping child. "Yeah, money and thinking about Sean."

"I've got cash, right now," Anthony said, his speech accelerating. "How much do you need?"

I sighed. "I don't know." I realized I truly didn't have any idea. How much would it take to live normally, with adequate space, standard utilities, and a super-strength deadbolt? "Enough to feel safe."

If I left Kenny, no amount of money would protect me. I knew that, but didn't say it. Kenny would hunt me down and shoot me, as he'd threatened multiple times. That stern realization kept me from accepting Anthony's offer, but it had zero effect on my lustful desires.

I said I had to go before the conversation heated up any further, and my shorts caught fire.

I pictured myself sitting in a boat next to Anthony, our bodies rocking gently in time with the lapping waves. I could feel the sun warming my skin, sense its searing rays heating me through. Anthony's imaginary kisses sent a white heat burning deeper inside me. "Burn me up," I said to no one. "Let me smolder into ashes that the winds will carry far from here."

~

A severe drought and repeated whirlwinds freed the white rock dust to travel for miles. The summer of '76 tested the perseverance of every living plant and creature within the bounds of our powder-coated community. I could practically hear the weeds in our yard choking for breath.

By late June, our lawn had ripened to pale hay. Corn ears roasted in place in the fields, singed beyond any hope of harvest. Area well and lake levels fell so low that you couldn't drink a glass of water until you'd first set aside the liquid and waited for the silt to settle.

Due to the weather conditions, Limestone County proposed outlawing fireworks for that

Diana Estill

year's Fourth of July festivities. Considering what my empty-headed husband accomplished with a Roman candle, it was a crying shame local government didn't follow through. Townies were to blame. They kicked up such a ruckus that the fireworks stand was permitted to open in its usual place—ten feet past the White Rock city limits sign.

I looked forward to Independence Day because the holiday reminded me of the stock from which I'd come: determined people, idealists, folks willing to fight for their freedom and confront the unknown. Somewhere, if only I could look back far enough, my ancestors had included fearless men and women who deserved to be celebrated.

Momma probably had ulterior motives for doing it, but she agreed to orchestrate a July Fourth shindig of sorts. She'd use any excuse she could find to gather what was left of her family. "Ya'll bring little Sean and we'll have a picnic," she suggested. So after the town parade was over, we collected at the park behind Momma's place next to the public landfill. The only apartment units in White Rock hadn't exactly been built on the choicest of lots.

"Looks like we got lucky," Kenny said, sniffing. "Wind's out of the right direction today."

I turned my head and giggled. What a joke. There wasn't any wind. Besides, Kenny's smeller had quit detecting those odors a long time ago.

Underneath the shade of an ancient cottonwood tree, we choked down bologna and cheese sandwiches and guzzled old-fashioned root beers. Sean insisted on playing on the merry-go-round, but the darn thing was too hot to touch, so I kicked around a medicine ball with him instead. Kenny and Ricky wandered off down by a dried-up creek bed, probably to go smoke pot. More often than not lately, Ricky had those incriminating bloodshot eyes, a droopy posture, and an I-don't-give-a-damn attitude about most everything. Mentally, Kenny and Ricky were the same age. Both their IQs combined would come up short of a triple-digit number.

It didn't take long to reach a consensus that it was too hot to be outdoors. Regrouped inside, we hoped to pour the last of our sodas over some of Momma's homemade vanilla ice cream. She'd churned the dessert for hours, but when we opened the container its contents looked like regular milk.

Momma stared inside the ice cream freezer the way a child might study a broken toy. "I can't imagine what happened," she said, her hands resting on her hips. "I ran out of rock salt, so I used a little from the shaker." Momma pointed at a ceramic hen on the kitchen table. "You don't think that would have done it, do you?"

"Naw," Kenny said. "In the winter, we use table salt all the time at work. Breaks up the ice real good." He burst out laughing, and Ricky hee-hawed. They were obviously high.

Momma looked dismayed.

Kenny and Ricky were still snickering about Momma's freezer failure when they left to go buy fireworks. "Don't spend all our grocery money," I called after them, fully expecting Kenny to ignore me. Stoned, he thought he was a millionaire. Sober, he suspected I was a thief.

Anytime Kenny couldn't account for money that he spent, he'd shout, "Goddammit, Renee! You've been in my wallet again. Where's the twenty I had in here?" Then he'd find my purse and empty its contents: a brush, lipstick, some gum wrappers, and sometimes a few hairy pennies he'd leave in pile on the floor.

Momma and I sat at her oak dinette, a gorgeous piece she kept hidden underneath an ugly tablecloth. "It's not practical to eat right on the wood," she'd explained. Maybe not. But the gingham checked vinyl cloth Momma had thrown over the table hid its beautiful wood grain patterns. For all anyone knew, that furniture could have been made of cardboard.

Sean played on the shag carpet beneath our feet. To keep him occupied, I'd brought along some of his MatchBox Cars. I didn't want him listening to what I was about to tell Momma. Now was the perfect time for me to fess up, to admit how much I wanted to ditch my marriage and find the kind of release Momma had gained but resented.

Daddy had been gone for over a year, yet divorce remained a touchy subject. Possibly Momma was too ingrained in religious doctrines to hear me out. I'd have to be delicate with the facts when I told her what a creep Kenny was. She'd want the precise details of my dissatisfaction. Then I'd have to explain why, if Kenny was all that bad, I'd remained with him for nearly five years. I hoped she'd be sympathetic.

Before I could begin, Momma asked, "Ya'll been doing okay financially?"

The perfect opening.

"Better...now that I got this new job. But Kenny still spends way too much on stuff we don't need."

Momma frowned as though she'd expected me to say I'd opened a college savings account for Sean. "Oh, yeah? Like what?"

"Like *fireworks* and eight-track tapes and twenty-two shells and dual mufflers." I shook my head. "And here Sean is, don't even have his own bedroom. And he's not ever gonna have one if we don't start saving somethin'."

"Oh..." Momma's mouth hung open. "So that's why you're having your credit union statement sent here? You're trying to save money without Kenny knowing it?"

I felt a catch in my throat. "Please don't say anything about that in front of Kenny." If she ever divulged that account, Kenny would think I'd been violating more than his billfold. And he'd make me pay in ways too horrible to imagine.

"Said I wouldn't, and I won't." Seemingly annoyed, Momma left the table and strode into her kitchen. From inside the top drawer next to her

173

sink she withdrew an envelope. She dropped the packet onto the table in front of me.

I opened the letter and checked the statement balance: $520.00. With one hand, I slid the form across the table. "Just file it with the rest of them."

Momma scooted her chair forward. "You heard from your daddy lately?"

Once again, our conversation had taken a turn in the wrong direction. How did she do that every time? Momma had a knack for centering any discussion on her pain, her loneliness, life's unfairness, and Daddy's fall from grace. No wonder I never told her about Kenny's terrible temper. She never gave me the chance.

I sucked on my straw. "Not recently. But can I tell you something?"

Momma nodded vigorously, probably thinking I meant something about Daddy.

There was only one way for me to say it. I leaned forward onto my elbows and blurted, "I'm thinking of leaving Kenny."

Momma's body stiffened. Her chin jutted out. "You're leaving him?" She loosened the paper towel underneath her drinking glass and pressed it to her mouth. "I knew it! Your daddy's corrupted you." She shot me a disapproving look. "You think what he's done is okay, don't you? Think it's perfectly fine to shun responsibility, throw away God's law and make your own."

She'd done it again, circled right back to Daddy, the way she always did.

"What Daddy did was different. He didn't even have a reason for leaving. But I've got about nine million. Wanna hear 'em?"

Momma set down her damp towel. "No, I don't." She drew her lips into a tight thin line. "Divorce is wrong, Renee Ann. Wrong, wrong, wrong. Says it right there in the Bible—"

Momma was not the person to appeal to for help. In her opinion, unless a man was cheating, stealing, drinking, or gambling away everything he owned, a wife had no justification for ending a marriage. That was why she'd stayed with Daddy for so many years, despite the demands he'd put on her and the lashings he'd given me and Ricky. Several times Momma had watched Daddy take his belt to us, open-ended, as if he were whipping buggy horses. She'd stood there and looked on in silence with the same indifference she now showed me. I would never make her understand how much my heart hurt to be loved by someone—anyone—how my ribs ached to be hugged, how I longed to be held in something other than a chokehold, to be kissed by a clean-shaven man who saw me through adoring eyes—someone who listened to me as though I could offer something of value, other than a place to park his penis.

"You mean, divorce is wrong, even if your husband beats you?" I squawked.

175

Momma stared at me, dead on, the way Daddy used to do whenever I questioned his authority, which, to be perfectly honest, wasn't all that often. "You're telling me Kenny beats you?"

I could see she didn't believe me. Already she'd drawn a dividing line, and I was standing on the wrong side of it. "Yes."

She folded her arms in front of her. "Then how come you never mentioned it before now? How come—"

Momma's apartment door swung open. In like a crazed posse marched Ricky and Kenny, their arms loaded with fireworks. Kenny boasted, "We done got us a fu—a shit-load of explosives!" He plopped down onto Momma's maple sofa, spilling out a grocery bag full of bottle rockets, Roman candles, sparklers, and Black Cats. But all I saw scattered across Momma's scratched coffee table was our next month's grocery budget.

Ricky dived for a fistful of bottle rockets. "Can I shoot these here ones?"

"How many you got?" Kenny asked, considering Ricky's request.

"Maybe four dozen."

Kenny squinted like he was working hard to recall something. "Yeah. I reckon. I bought a gross of those."

I gave Momma a sidelong look. "Guess we'll be eating with you next week."

Kenny heard me. "Now don't start. I didn't *buy* all of these, Re-*nee*. That stupid U-*bang*-ee down 'ere gave me extry."

Someone had done something nice, given Kenny free merchandise, and here he was calling the guy degrading names and insulting his intelligence. Kenny was lower than the current water table. "Ever think maybe he was just trying to be *nice*," I said.

Kenny double-blinked. "Naw, I doubt he was being sweet on me."

By nightfall, Kenny and Ricky had conjured up an extra-long list of excuses to step outside: they had to get more bottle rockets from Kenny's car, needed to see where that smoke in the park was coming from, wanted to see about a car Ricky's friend's brother had for sale. Each time, they returned smelling like a potpourri of dried alfalfa, bark chips, and smoldering pine needles. I figured they'd blown through Ricky's entire stash of pot. But as it turned out, Ricky had an ample weed supply and Kenny still had plenty of Roman candles to burn.

Glimpsing the remaining fireworks, Ricky suggested, "Let's shoot 'em off the balcony!"

Momma acted like she hadn't heard Ricky's temporary flash of brilliance. Either that or she was too engrossed in the evening's televised festivities to pay him any mind.

Sean slept, draped end-to-end across both our laps, exhausted from all the running around he'd done that morning at the parade and then later in the park.

Kenny and Ricky each grabbed a Roman candle and proceeded through the sliding glass door that lead to Momma's apartment balcony. "Aren't you supposed to butt those things into the ground?" I asked. If either of them heard me, he didn't respond. I saw little use in repeating myself. I was too busy weighing out Momma's strict interpretation of my marriage vows.

It looked like I'd have to wait for God to intervene before I could break my ties to Kenny. 'Til death do us part. Maybe his demise would come quickly and he'd blow himself to smithereens with some of his fireworks. Possibly, Kenny might get zapped by lightning, run over by a semi-truck, or fall victim to some industrial catastrophe. Or perhaps the Lord would look down on me with pity, the way He had favored David in that Bible story, and grant me victory against an oversized goon.

I was reviewing all the causes of premature death I could think of, when a ball of fire swooped through Momma's living room. It happened so fast, I didn't register Kenny's Roman candle had shot backwards from the wrong end. All I saw was a green globe of light, like some kind of UFO, whiz by me. The glowing ball bounced off Momma's recliner and then tumbled out of sight, leaving behind a burned trail of singed shag carpet.

I leapt from the sofa and stomped along the streak of smoldering yarn for all I was worth. Then

I ran to get a pitcher of water from Momma's kitchen, but she'd already beat me there.

"Move!" she yelled, jolting past me. "Gotta pour this on the floor before it's too late." However, her carpet was the least of her worries.

"Holy shit! Sonofabitch!" Kenny yanked at the curtain rod over his head. "Get the other side," he hollered at Ricky. "Get it down! Now!"

Dark smoke billowed up from the bottom of the gauzy curtains framing the patio door. The Roman candle's misfire had caught the edge of the panels, setting blaze to one of them along its hem. Within seconds, the window treatments flamed waist-high, smoke swirling up to the textured ceiling. In no time at all, the air turned a tobacco color.

Kenny tugged at the curtains, shattering the rod, while Momma splashed three quarts of cold water onto the sheers. Her aim being less than perfect, she managed to spray her Zenith TV, too. On the screen, televised fireworks burst into 3-D. Instead of putting out the curtain flames, Momma had extinguished her television.

I looked on in silence, my feet locked into place beneath me. Sean sputtered awake and sat up wild-eyed.

In all the commotion, I couldn't think what to do next: seize my child and run for our lives, or grab the phone and call the fire department. As strange as this might sound, a part of me wanted to simply stand there, the way a farmer might monitor a stubble fire, and watch those curtains flame brilliant against the night sky.

~

Sometime around midnight, I placed Sean on the sofa in our living room. His eyes fluttered open like a doll's before he dozed off again. I covered him with a lightweight sheet and switched on a fan. Tonight I was extra-thankful for the oscillating propeller noise.

Closing the bedroom door, I gave Kenny a glare that must have alerted him to what was coming next.

"Don't say a goddam word," he warned.

Now, if I had any good sense about me, I might have kept quiet. But Independence Day had a carry-over effect. The more I thought about my gutless response and the damage Kenny had caused, the angrier I grew. I didn't know who I detested more, Kenny or myself. I'd stood there like a deaf-mute while the village idiot had set fire to my mother's residence.

Ready for sleep, Kenny pulled off his red, white, and blue muscle-shirt. I stared at the words "Spirit of 1776" emblazoned on the fabric. Had that war been fought by folks like me, I felt sure we'd all be celebrating Queen's Day instead the Fourth of July.

I couldn't keep my tongue still another minute. "Damn it, Kenny! Have you lost your mind altogether? How could you do such a *stupid* thing?"

His eyes dared me to continue, but I kept going.

"You smoked up Momma's apartment, burned up her curtains, and cracked her sliding glass door. For chrissakes! You even melted the knobs off her *TV*. And now you're going to come in here and act like it never happened? Just go to *sleep*?" I tugged out of my jeans, stomping the waistband flat against the floor. "If you and Ricky hadn't been so busy getting *high*, none of this would have happened."

"Shut up. I don't have to listen to this. Heard enough already." Kenny swaggered past the end of the bed and over to my side, where I remained standing. Leaning close, he all but dared me to hit him. "It was an *ac*ci-dent. Kind'a like your face, you know? An accident." He howled into the air. "You're one ugly-assed dog. You know that?"

"So help me, I'm sick of your pure ignorance and your name calling." If he said another word, I might find a new use for the butcher knife he'd left on the nightstand. He'd employed the blade as a fingernail cleaner. But right then it looked more like an equalizer to me.

"Who you calling *ig*-norant?" Kenny grabbed me by one arm and held me in a tight claw. "Huh? You calling me ignorant? It's time I took you down a few notches." His eyes darted from me to the corner where he kept his rifle.

I clenched my teeth and pushed back against him, trying to break his hold. "Let go of me, you pig!"

Kenny dragged me back to where the gun stood upright against the wall and shoved me facedown onto the bed. I felt his knees sink into the mattress on either side of me. With one hand, he pinned my head down, and I knew he was reaching for the rifle with the other.

"*Pig*? Who you calling a *pig*?" The gun's steel barrel ground against my spine. From behind, another hard object threatened further harm. "How 'bout you lay there real still, now, so I don't *accidentally* shoot you?" Kenny sank his teeth into my right shoulder. "'Bout time I taught you some *re*-spect."

I took what he had that night, took it all without so much as making a sound. This animal was not my husband. Though he held me forcibly, he did not possess me—and he never would. He proved he could overpower my body, but that meant nothing. My mind was untouchable, beyond his vicious grasp. And my heart was even farther out of range. He could pull that trigger, for all I cared. I'd be better off. At least death offered some promise of relief.

~

"Baby?" Kenny checked my eyes to see if I might still be asleep.

I wasn't.

I'd been lying there for more than hour listening to the window fan churn and the birds call to each other. Cardinals. By their high-pitched chirps, I could tell them apart from all the others. Sean snorted from the living room sofa, turned over, and sighed. He'd be awake and padding into our bedroom soon.

I didn't want to hear whatever Kenny was about to say. But I couldn't help noticing the odd way he'd addressed me. Not exactly the kind of pet name you'd expect to hear from someone who'd raped you the night before. I refused to make eye contact.

"Baby, please look at me." Kenny sat upright on the mattress, now bare from where he'd wrestled off the fitted sheet. His thick, calloused hands caressed my shoulder. He kissed me lightly on my neck. "I know you're mad. Got ever' right to be." Each word sounded as though it was being squeezed from him. Maybe he was about to cry. I didn't feel the least bit sorry for him. I wouldn't ever forgive him for what he'd done.

"I'm no good," he professed. "Never gonna be one of them guys with a suit and tie. Never gonna be anyone to anybody." He hung his head over my torso and wept. "I need you to love me, Renee. I *need* that. I'm sorry. I go crazy sometimes—thinkin' you *don't.*" His tears fell moist against my naked breast, his sobs echoing in my left ear. I had to turn and face him, if for no other reason than to salvage my hearing.

With a tug, I covered my nude body with the top sheet. I didn't want to let his eyes fall across any of my soft parts. Those were mine to deny him now. With utter detachment, I took pleasure in watching him wallow in his misery. I wouldn't give him what he wanted, wouldn't offer my forgiveness. Not this time. I'd seen that act before. Through repetitious exposure, I'd grown impervious to its intended effect.

"What can I do?" Kenny begged. "Just tell me...anything, I'll do it. I promise. I'll do anything to make it up to you."

Using the wall for a headboard, I propped myself up on my pillow and stared through him. I had nothing to offer. The only way he could make things better would be to take his ass and all his clothes and drive off to someplace far away, like his daddy had, and never come back. Now that I thought about it, maybe Neta Sue hadn't received such a bad deal after all. When it came to loving a woman, Kenny's father had likely been no better than his son.

Kenny stroked my hair, combing his fingers through it. "Baby, I was the one who loved you when no one else did. Remember?" He smoothed a few locks into place, twining them behind my ear. "Didn't run away when you got pregnant, the way some guys do. I married you and gave our baby a

name...even worked as a garbage man to feed us."
Kenny shook his head. "I know I ain't always done
what's right. Not even close, sometimes." He'd quit
crying and now sounded woefully earnest. "But I
always *wanted* to."

"Wanting's not enough," I said, choking on
my own regrets.

TWENTY-ONE

One hot, airless night in August, Anthony finally said the words I'd been warned would come twirling out of his mouth. Pearly had predicted it. "Them words gone spin like a twista headin' straight fo' yo' house." I'd hoped that I'd be separated and living elsewhere, when and if that ever happened.

But I wasn't.

"There's got to be *some* way for us to see each other," Anthony insisted. "I can understand why you don't want to call in sick on your new job. But don't you have some weeknight or weekend when you can slip away by yourself? Don't you ever go *anywhere*, alone?"

"Not really. Unless you count the grocery store or Washateria."

Anthony ignored my remark. "Babe, I just want to take you to a nice dinner and talk someplace where there's no fluorescent lights or mystery meat specials on the menu...and no shop foreman staring at us. Come on, whadda ya say?"

That sounded like a scene from one of my few G-rated fantasies about him: an image of the two of us seated at a table covered with starched white linens, one set with lots of extra forks and sprigs of lilacs, inside the kind of place I'd only seen on TV—or while driving sixty miles per hour past their storefronts.

"If we went somewhere in Dallas, Kenny wouldn't ever know it," Anthony said, plotting his way through the deed.

I snickered, thinking about Kenny's travel range and friendship circle. "If we went any place other than the taco shack, no one Kenny has ever *met* would know it. Kenny thinks going anywhere past Lolaville is adventure travel."

Anthony cracked up. "Don't worry. I can do better than that. Besides, if I wanted to feed you Mexican food, I'd make it myself before I'd take you *there*." His voice took on a more serious note. "Will you at least think about it?"

I couldn't stand it. Desperate to keep him in pursuit, I blurted, "That's *all* I'll think about 'til I figure out how to make it happen."

As soon as I said that, I realized I couldn't take it back. I'd done it. I'd crossed the threshold and become what Pearly called a *player*.

Over the next few days, my thinking turned downright strategic. What I came up with was pretty clever, considering my inexperience at direct deceit. A new Winn-Dixie had opened near Keslo Electronics. I told Kenny I wanted to take advantage of their grand opening sale while he babysat Sean. Already I was aware that he'd planned a boy's night out, which for Kenny was practically every Saturday night, at a baseball game.

"Me un the guys are gonna drink beer, eat pork skins, belch, fart, 'n watch baseball," Kenny argued. "Cain't do that with no four-year-old around." He propped his feet on a couple of two-by-fours suspended over a matched pair of concrete blocks—our coffee table. Poring over the evening's TV schedule, he asked, "Why can't you go during the afternoon?"

I was already a step ahead of him. "I'm helping Momma. Remember? I promised I'd help her bake for her church bazaar?" I thought quickly. "I might could save a few cookies back for you and the boys, if you'll take Sean to the ballgame with you...just this once."

"Chocolate chip?"

"Mm, hmm. With *pe-cans.*"

He folded his arms behind his head. "Turn on Channel Eleven. Wrestling's about to start."

I spun the dial. So help me God, I silently swore, if I ever got rid of this man, I was never again going to function as anyone's remote control. "Well?"

"What the hell's the matter with you?" Kenny eyed me suspiciously. "You meetin' somebody at that grocery or something?"

I squeezed my pelvis tight to keep from wetting my pants. Had I said something to give myself away, tipped him off somehow? "Right. I've got a hot date with the produce manager. Didn't I tell you?" I gave my best pretend laugh and twisted at my wedding band. I couldn't tell if he really thought I was on the make or if he was simply trying to get out of taking Sean to the ballpark.

Kenny stared through me and grunted, "Save me some of 'em."

"So you'll take him with you, then?"

"Didn't say that." He craned his neck to see around me. "I just said *save me some.*"

"I'll have to bake extra. And I won't have time, if I gotta do all the grocery shopping between when I get back from Momma's and when you leave."

A television announcer shouted, "And now, *live*, from Dallas Sportatorium—"

I thought fast. "Besides, don't you want Sean to grow up natural? You don't want him to spend all his time focused on *women's* stuff, now do you?"

"Oh, awright." Kenny scowled, probably wishing I'd shut up so he could hear his show. "But I'm not doin' this every weekend. So don't go astin' me to."

It was that simple.

Anthony and I had planned all along to meet at an inconspicuous place, like maybe a grocery store. That grand opening couldn't have been better timed. We'd go to dinner in Anthony's car, leaving mine in the Winn-Dixie parking lot in case Kenny got ambitious enough to drive by. And later, when we returned, we'd hug and kiss goodbye right before I drove home with my car trunk filled with bottles of soft drinks, boxes of macaroni and cheese, and tubes of toilet paper. With any luck, Kenny wouldn't know how long I'd been gone. He and his friends would spend hours whooping it up at the ball fields.

I felt jittery all the same, partly because I knew what Kenny would do if he caught me, and somewhat because I was afraid of what Anthony might do, given the chance. Fooling around wasn't on my agenda. We were simply going to have a romantic date, something I'd never experienced. And that alone, I thought, would sustain me until I found the strength to leave Kenny for good.

Unfortunately, my predictions were never as accurate as Pearly's.

~

Anthony waited for me right where he said he would be—on the east side of the parking lot. I pulled in three spaces over from where his black Trans Am idled. Every vertebrae in my spine tingled. My muscles jumped like a hooked trout. I drew a deep breath and stepped from my Mustang, strutting on air. No longer a fantasy, my first ever real date with Anthony was about to begin.

Anthony hustled to open the passenger-side door. "I didn't see you pull in."

"I was trying not to call attention to myself." I grinned and brushed my short skirt smooth.

Anthony laughed as I stared dreamily into his mouth at the tongue I wanted him to flick against my own, feel him slide wet across my skin.

My lips ached. My breasts stood at full attention. At any moment, I half-expected smoke signals to rise from underneath my skirt.

Anthony's eyes scrolled my body. "Then you better go home and change clothes. 'Cause in *that* outfit, nobody's going to miss seeing *you!*"

I skimmed my hands over my breasts and noted my nipples were rigid. My red knit shirt was tied together with a spaghetti strap on one side. Opposite the bow, my other arm and shoulder peeked out bare. It would have been senseless to wear a bra, but now I felt somewhat overexposed. I folded my arms high across my chest and asked, "So what do we do now?"

"Depends." Anthony stared at the single tie holding my top together. I knew what he was thinking. And the answer was yes. If he pulled that string tie apart, my shirt would fall to my waist. "How long you got?"

"That depends on what you have in mind," I said, torturing him with my eyes. "But somewhere along the line, I *do* need to pick up some groceries."

He pointed to the sprawling store. "Sign says it's open 'til ten. How much time do you need to shop?"

"I brought a list." I patted my purse. "It won't take me very long."

The black hair peeking out from under Anthony's open collar caught my attention. He looked like a male model in that body shirt. The silky fabric shimmered in the light and clung to his sculpted biceps. Beneath the purple and navy print, I could see his taut muscles, imagine touching them. I wanted to nestle my nose in his soft chest hairs, breathe in his masculine scent, and trace my tongue along his lips. "Uh, it's getting a little warm in here," I said. "Maybe we ought to get going."

"Okay. But can I give you a quick kiss first?" Anthony's eyes had found my face. I could see his heart beating right through his form-fitted shirt. He nodded at the solid brick wall in front of us. "We're parked out of view."

To be honest, I wanted to straddle that console and tear him free of his clothes. But somehow I restrained myself enough to say, "I think it would be best to wait until after dark, when no one can see us."

~

Other than maybe school or work, Spaghetti Junction held more people than I'd ever seen in any one place. Anthony had driven a half-hour to find somewhere remote enough for us to be seen together. Downtown Dallas was a good choice because Kenny and his pals avoided that area as diligently as they dodged adulthood. None of them wanted to risk being hassled by the Dallas police.

Anthony set down his menu. "Would you like a glass of wine? They have a nice Chianti, I see."

I had no idea what Chianti might be. I'd never before sipped wine. Would one glass of it make me stupid? Maybe I'd look really lowbrow if I didn't have one. I didn't want Anthony to think I was too much of a country hick to take to a nice restaurant. Though I'd turned twenty-one, it hadn't occurred to me that I could legally drink. "What are you having?"

"The house Chianti sounds good. But feel free to have anything you like."

"I'll have the same thing, then." I figured I could always take a few sips and leave the bulk of my glass untouched. But when the drinks came, I timidly tasted mine and admitted, "I've never drank anything alcoholic before."

"You haven't?" Anthony seemed surprised. "Well, why didn't you say so? I could've helped you pick something better. Do you like the Chianti?"

I took another taste, savoring the bittersweet liquid as the moist heaviness slid down my throat. "Better than sex."

"Depends on who you've had sex with." Anthony smiled like he expected to change my opinion soon. "If you mean sex with people like Darlene and Kenny, you could be right."

"Well, I never had sex with Darlene." I laughed. "And Kenny's the only man I've been with, so—"

"You never had a guy in your life before Kenny?" Anthony's eyebrows peaked. He stared at me as if I was some rare species long since thought extinct.

I glanced around the room to see if anyone might be listening to us. "Not really. Unless you count my first boyfriend, David Lassiter. And we never went any further than kissing."

"That's *it?*" Anthony chortled.

It seemed he was making fun of me, treating me like some prudish schoolgirl who'd just confessed to not knowing how babies are born. "I was *fifteen* when I met Kenny. *Sixteen* when we married. When would I have had a chance to be with anyone else?"

The possum-grin Anthony had been wearing disappeared. "Sorry. I forget." He twirled his spaghetti with his fork.

I studied the stringy pasta, the way it spun on the tines, and thought about that tornado Pearly had forecasted. "One day, girl, it's gonna blow the roof off yo' whole house." From what I could tell, that day had arrived.

~

It would be easy, though mostly unfair, for me to blame what happened that night on our waitress. That pesky woman in a skimpy outfit kept asking, "Would you like another wine refill?" So finally, to make her go away and leave us alone for more than five minutes, I said yes. Later, I could see how that might have factored into my downfall. By the time I'd finished my third glass of Chianti, I no longer cared who was listening to us. In fact, I'd even stopped worrying if Kenny was waiting for me back at the Winn-Dixie. However, I was sober enough to feel relieved when I saw that he wasn't.

At the grocery store, Anthony and I drew the attention of a few curious spectators—possibly because of the way we staggered through the frozen foods section, my nipples winking at all the stock clerks. I'd been looking back at Anthony, instead of ahead where I was steering, when I caught the corner of my buggy on a stacked display of cereal boxes. Dozens of Corn Flakes cartons crashed to the floor, thudding and echoing against the cheap asbestos tiles.

Giggling like a pair of delinquent teens, Anthony and I ignored the spill and hurried to the next grocery aisle. As Anthony shuffled behind me, he playfully pinched my bottom.

From an end aisle, a few feet over from breakfast foods, a store clerk stopped to spy on us. For a few minutes, we tried our best to look like normal shoppers. But once the gawking man left, which was pretty quickly, I launched a single-roll of toilet tissue into the air. "How 'bout a game of supermarket football?"

Chasing my wobbled toss, he ran long for the pass. He caught the spiraling cylinder in midair and then lobbed it into my grocery basket. "Touchdown!"

By then most everyone was staring at us, so I paid for my groceries and left.

Melting into my Mustang, I felt as giddy as a junior high student, and every bit as hormonally challenged. For two weeks, I'd been dodging Kenny's advances. Due to that bout of celibacy, an accidental buzz, or maybe both, my sex drive had shifted into high gear.

Anthony climbed in the seat next to me and, without warning, kissed me. My skin felt prickly all over. My lower half quivered. I wondered how far he thought we could carry this. We were sitting in a parked car, in plain view, even if the area *was* poorly lit. Surely he didn't expect me to do anything right there in the Winn-Dixie parking lot.

I had to leave soon. If I didn't, Kenny would start out looking for me. I didn't want him or some straggling patron to find me there, in a compromised position. "I don't know if now's the best time for this," I cautioned.

Anthony fondled my nipples through my shirt. "Feels to me like it is." His hands trailed up to the hollow of my neck, the pads of his fingers smooth and promising. "God, Renee. You're beautiful. If that crazy husband of yours won't take care of you, I will."

Before I knew it, he'd slipped one hand inside my panties. I thought I'd let it linger there for only a minute. One quick, forbidden touch. But something went wrong. He found that spring release button of mine, the one that instantly converts my legs into a Y.

"I better start the engine," I said, realizing we were going to suffocate if I didn't turn on some air.

"I hate to tell ya' but your engine's been running for a while," Anthony observed.

I'd gone mad with lust, aroused beyond hope of return. I couldn't help it. Like those black holes I'd learned about from watching public television, I wanted to draw in everything around me, drink in the darkness, and absorb all the energy.

Anthony pleaded, "Oh God, Renee. Don't make me wait any longer."

So I didn't.

TWENTY-TWO

My bedroom didn't look the same after my night with Anthony. I wanted to deny ownership of that squalid space, reject my connection to it—to Kenny. Staring at our double bed, I tried to remember when, if ever, I'd felt loved by the man I'd married. It seemed as though I'd used up the bulk of Kenny's affections before I'd made it out of the backseat of his car. Because of that, I'd been compelled to do unspeakable things in the front seat of my own.

Would Kenny detect the scent of another man in my hair or on my skin? I sniffed the air. Smelled like I'd been swimming in someone's frog pond. He'd know I'd become a parking lot whore for sure if he came home before I bathed.

Glimpsing the rifle against the bedroom's far wall, I thought to hide it. But Kenny would notice it missing right away, I suspected. If nothing else, though, I could empty it. Too bad I didn't know how.

I'd rather be dead, anyway, than to have sex with Kenny again. My body felt sacred, for the first time, because someone who loved me had entered it. I couldn't keep swallowing vinegar after I'd tasted wine.

Anthony's touch had awakened every part of me. He was the man I should have been with all along, a lover who knew how to make me feel desired.

198

In his arms I felt sexy, even attractive. How had I let Kenny convince me that no one else would ever want me, that he was the only man charitable enough to have sex with me? His bad magic act would no longer work; I'd seen how the stunt was performed.

I noted the time on the bedroom wall clock, a Budweiser sign Kenny had found in someone's trash. Ten past ten. He'd return home any moment, if only to bring Sean inside and then leave again. I raced to the bathroom and turned on the tub faucet, hoping to rinse away my foreign smells—and maybe a little guilt.

"Adulterer!" my conscience shouted. That was what I'd become, regardless of my intentions. But I didn't have time to listen to my moral half; I had to concentrate on saving my skin.

Kicked back in the bathtub, my head reclined against the cold porcelain ridge, I savored the details of my evening escapade. The soaked washcloth I layered on top of my breasts soothed me with its liquid warmth. I recalled the tranquilizing wetness of Anthony's lips, the satiny hairs of his beard, and the tickle I'd felt when his face brushed against mine. He'd moved, slow and gentle, held me as if we'd had all night instead of a few stolen moments. I wanted to be with him, to make love to him for the rest of my life—however brief a time that might be. I didn't care about the consequences. If I died at that very instant, at least I'd die knowing what love felt like.

After I'd finished bathing and regained some of my composure, Kenny stumbled into the house. He entered the living room, seriously looped, carrying Sean, who was groggy but not quite asleep. Without a word, Kenny passed Sean off to me. And then, as if he'd suddenly been struck dead, he crashed, fully clothed, onto our bed.

Sean looked up at me, his eyes barely open. "Daddy lemme bartend. Why you didn't go with us?"

Bartend? I couldn't wait to hear what he meant by *that.* In the morning, I'd be sure to ask. I tucked Sean into his single bed. With a tug, I pulled the chain on the light that hung where there should have been a headboard. Perfect, I thought. Kenny had said that illuminated beer sign would go well with our bedroom clock. The juke joint remnant displayed a team of galloping Clydesdale horses that probably preferred water to beer. Because Sean was afraid of the dark, we used the backlit advertisement for his night-light. For a second, I could have sworn those horses were sniggering at me.

Sean blinked, still waiting for me to explain my evening absence. "Mommy had to shop and do a few things," I cooed. I ran my fingers through his feathery blond hair. "Be a good boy and go to sleep."

I kissed Sean's forehead and handed him the monkey Momma had made out of a pair of Daddy's old socks. "Had to find *some* use for 'em," Momma had said when I'd marveled at her creativity. The chimp's red mouth grinned fiendishly from where Daddy's feet had once resided. Sean clutched the toy by its rosy bottom. It was odd, I considered, what could be made into a monkey's butt.

I slipped into bed and drew a sigh of relief. There'd be no fighting with Kenny that night. At a minimum, I was guaranteed a reprieve until morning. Maybe by sunrise I'd find the guts to do *myself* in. It was true; I was nothing but a whore, just like Kenny had always said. Tonight, I'd confirmed as much.

"Nighty-night," Sean whispered.

"Night, Seany."

I left Kenny lying there on top the bedspread, thankful I didn't have to feel his beer-bloated belly pressed against my back. What a pathetic sight. His plaid shirttail hung wrinkled over his flare-leg knit pants. He'd molded those sweaty feet of his into a pair of broken-down, fake-leather loafers. No socks, of course, because he refused to wear any.

Kenny moaned, turning his face away from the drool that already had begun pooling on his pillow. He'd been too loaded to see anything other than a soft place to fall when he'd come home. For all I'd gained from it, his intoxication had an alarming downside. He'd been driving drunk with my child in the car, one more reason I needed to get away from him.

Crickets hurled themselves against the window screen next to Sean's bed. The bugs clamored like a church congregation beckoned to follow the light.

Those serenading fools didn't realize the glow they vigorously pursued was artificial and luring them closer toward death.

I lay there speculating about insect behavior and gunshot wounds, entertaining thoughts like: How much would it hurt if a bullet pierced my skin? Would there be a mess? What if I didn't die right away? How long would I suffer? Would the noise alert anyone?

I breathed through my mouth, sucking in the stifling air, listening as my heart ticked like a stopwatch. Right then, I wanted to die.

Or maybe I just wanted my fear of dying to end.

What would Kenny say when someone found me? Would the police examine my body, find traces of Anthony, and link him to my suicide in some way? Would they think I'd been sexually assaulted? I *had*, but that had been two weeks earlier—by my own husband. Maybe Anthony would confess we'd had an affair. If he did, would Kenny kill him? My loose ways, I hated to acknowledge, had placed more than *my* life at risk.

In the corner next to the bed, I could see the rifle's evil barrel silhouetted against the room's shadowy walls. Kenny would likely use that gun to murder me, if I didn't kill myself with it first. It was a matter of time, perhaps a limited amount. Tomorrow? Maybe next week? As soon as he found out about Anthony, I imagined. But right then, the sheets felt like they might suffocate me before

Kenny had the chance to do me in. I kicked out from under the cotton layers and hiked my gauzy nightgown to my hips. A faint breeze cooled my bare legs. Nothing hotter than August in Texas, except maybe Hell. Best I could tell, I was lying in both.

In the darkness, my head swooned with criminal thoughts. How many .22 shells did it take to kill a person? The chamber was full, I knew, because Kenny kept it that way. My palms itched; my hands trembled. If I positioned a pillow over his head, would it muffle the sound? Could I hide the blood? Would I awaken Sean?

The rifle whispered to me, "Kill or be killed. Those are your choices. Shoot him first, and you'll be saving several lives." If I splattered his drunken brains while he slept, I could possibly call it self-defense. Only one story to tell: mine.

There had to be some way out of this situation without a loss of life, though I couldn't think of such a solution. If I remained with Kenny and never saw Anthony again, I'd be as good as dead. Stuck in this marriage, my spirit would wither to nothing. I'd be little more than an empty carcass. And if I left, Kenny would turn me into a bullet-ridden one.

"Go ahead. Do it now," the rifle whispered. "Do it now, while you've got the chance. If *you* don't, *he* will."

"No," I silently replied. "Not tonight."

I needed more time to entertain all the possible outcomes. All I wanted to think about right then was Anthony and the rhapsody I'd experienced in his arms.

~

By sunup, I'd made a decision. I'd follow through, right after I carried Sean to Momma's apartment. I didn't want my child to see the bloody remains of a marriage that had gone fatally south. Already he'd been exposed to enough. Where I'd find the strength to pull that trigger, I didn't know. But somehow, I reassured myself, I'd do it—because I had to.

I didn't want to take my own life. And I didn't want to wait and wonder when Kenny might aim for me or Anthony, something I knew would happen soon unless I took immediate action. I couldn't hold Kenny off forever. He'd be demanding sex or raping me to get it any day now.

Though I hadn't yet figured out how it would unfold, change was coming because I'd decided to take action. I didn't know how I'd avoid being tried for murder. But I had a pair of those cotton gloves from Keslo Electronics, and I thought they'd work into my plot pretty well. No fingerprints, at least. Fuelled by my instincts for self-preservation, I set my scheme into motion.

When Kenny finally awakened, I said, "I'm taking Sean over to Momma's for a while. Got to return her cookie platter." Before he could say a word, I added, "Besides, ever since she started working at the Get-N-Go, she hardly ever has a chance to see him."

Kenny rubbed his eyes. "Don't talk so goddamn loud. I ain't in *Mex-i-co.*" He shucked out of the shirt and pants he'd perspired in all night and raked his knobby fingers at his bare crotch. "You coming straight back?"

"No. I'm going to stay a while and visit."

"Be back by lunch. And bring me a Belt Buster, with mayonnaise, and some fries, too." Freeing his wallet from the crumpled heap at his feet, he pitched me a ten-dollar bill. "Get whatever you want."

The Dairy Queen was a block from Momma's apartment. Kenny couldn't drive past it without suffering a sudden hunger urge. It only seemed right that the DQ folks would prepare Kenny's last meal. I wondered if I could get him some arsenic to go with those taters.

"Sean's staying at Momma's for the night. I'm picking him up tomorrow morning." I knew that would put Kenny in a good mood, as he'd interpret that to mean he'd be getting more than a burger this afternoon.

Kenny kept clawing at himself. I felt like telling him if he'd put on some underwear once in a while, he might get over that jock itch. But soon enough he'd find himself beyond scratching at anything.

"Got something planned?" he asked, a sly smile spreading toward one ear.

I knew what he meant, and I surely did. But it wasn't what he had in mind. "As a matter of fact, I *do*."

"Mee-maw, Mee-Maw," Sean recited. He might have been the only person in the world who looked forward to Momma's cooking. Sean thought fried bologna and spam sandwiches, cheese puffs, and cream sodas were nothing short of gourmet.

"Yes, we're going to Mee-Maw's," I said. I stuffed the ten in my purse.

By the time I loaded the car with Momma's platter, my bag, and a few of Sean's toys, I'd begun to feel sorry for ever being born. I pulled my car onto Hawk Creek Road and steered blindly toward White Rock. For some reason, I thought of Granny Henderson. "God puts us all here for a reason," she liked to say. If that was true, what was my purpose? Must not have been much.

Sean bounced in the front seat next to me, excited by this spontaneous outing. Nearing a stop sign, I automatically braced his soft middle with the backside of my arm. That was when it dawned on me; perhaps *Sean* was my purpose. Simply bringing him into the world and encouraging him to be different from Kenny might be all that I'd been sent here to do. But seeing as how Sean was already bartending at age four, I appeared destined for failure.

Unless something changed drastically, Sean had little hope of becoming anything but a lazy, beer-guzzling, wife-beating, no-count. He would have been better off having no father at all than having Kenny for a daddy.

But if I ended up in jail, then I'd never get to be with Anthony. And Sean might wind up with Neta Sue, the very person who'd raised Kenny. If that happened, it wouldn't matter if Kenny were dead. Sean would still turn out exactly like him. And I'd have wasted my life for nothing. I'd sooner shoot myself than live to witness such a tragedy.

Maybe suicide *was* the better option. I had to face the fact that I was never going to *like* Kenny, let alone *love* him. Not after all he'd done to me. I also knew I'd never again refuse Anthony. He'd become my addiction. I had to have him. I lived for that man. So where did any of that leave me? I wasn't so crafty or slick that I could escape being caught. Even if I successfully managed to run away, eventually Kenny would find me. What if, when he did, he didn't confine himself to firearms? What if he decided to take a crowbar to my face, instead? I imagined the crushing blows to my temples, the caved teeth, gaping flesh, and blinded eyes. Permanent disfigurement, to the point that no one would ever again want to look at me. No. Better to die on my own terms than on those.

~

"Are you okay?" Momma asked. "You look a little pale."

"I'm fine. That time of the month, I guess."

207

Ricky sat at Momma's kitchen table, repairing a portable radio. "On that note, I think I'll leave," he said. "Come on, Seany. Let's me an' you go back here. Us men don't belong in *that* conversation."

I caught sight of an entertainment magazine Momma had left on her kitchen countertop. The front cover headlines announced a local tycoon had been accused of hiring someone to snuff out his wife. I leaned my elbows onto the bar counter and asked, "Momma, you ever thought about killing Daddy for what he done to you?" I said it just like that, like I'd asked her if she'd ever considered purchasing a wrinkle cream or shaving under her arms.

"Why land alive, No! What would make you think such a thing, Renee? Do I look like a mankiller to you?"

"Of course not. I just wondered if you ever got that mad at him, seein' as how he shamed you like he did."

"Well..." Momma looked like she was straining to recall. "I suppose I did think about it once. Not seriously, I mean. I did wish him dead once or twice." Momma studied my face. "Why? What's Kenny done *now?*"

"He's been Kenny. I reckon that's enough."

Momma shook her head and grinned. "He's done *one* thing right."

"Yeah? What's that?" I couldn't think of a single praiseworthy accomplishment he'd achieved.

She pointed toward Ricky's bedroom. "He produced that precious grandson of mine."

Momma acted like I'd had nothing to do with Sean's birth. Nothing at all. "Hmph. Produced one life, destroyed another."

Momma screwed up her face as though she was struggling to decipher my comment. I didn't waste any effort trying to explain. Later, my energies would be needed for a better use.

~

The drive home from Momma's gave me more time to assess my decision. Somewhere between the Dairy Queen and my driveway, I partially regained my senses. At a core level, I didn't really want to *murder* Kenny. I simply didn't want to live with him anymore.

If Kenny aimed to shoot me, as he'd repeatedly blustered, then he'd better do it *now*, I decided. Because I'd reached that point where dying looked better than living like a hunted duck. Given the choice of staying with Kenny or being murdered by him, I planned to go down staring into the coward's beady yellow eyes. He wouldn't surprise me from behind, the chicken-shit way. I would face him, openly defy him, and tell him I was leaving. If it came to such an end, I would hold my neck stretched high and my chin proudly cocked forward, and I'd take those slugs one by one. Whether he shot me or let me go free, either way, there'd be an improvement.

With the grace of a homecoming queen, I breezed through our living room. Kenny, partially clad in a pair of briefs and believing himself irresistible, joked, "Whadda you want first? That burger...or me?"

I set the DQ bag on our coffee table and wandered, zombie-like, into the bedroom. I could hear Kenny fingering the paper food wrappers. *If there's a God in Heaven, maybe He'll intervene now and let Kenny choke to death.* No sooner had I thought this than I noticed Daddy's Bible. It was sitting on top of a box filled with old photo albums Momma had given me months earlier. Suddenly, for reasons I couldn't explain, I felt like praying—on the outside chance there might really be such a thing as Divine Intervention. I'd never seen any evidence of it, but I hadn't exactly given up the idea.

I lifted the Bible and unzipped the cover, dislodging a bookmark. I grabbed the marker as it floated down, catching the laminated cardboard before it hit the ground. Staring at the keepsake, I read, *"The Lord is my light and my salvation; whom shall I fear? The Lord is the strength of my life; of whom shall I be afraid? Psalm 27:1."* Those words cloaked me, resonated through me, and brought me comfort. I stood there, my eyes brimming with tears. Yet some part of me felt oddly elated, almost superhuman, as though I could rise above every challenge I'd ever had. Here was my proof.

God *must* exist. I felt Him inside of me, right then. He'd delivered His message, right when I'd needed it, dropped it into my very hands. I had nothing to fear. Not Kenny, and certainly not death.

I set down the Bible and bookmark, exchanging them for the gun.

Like some kind of apparition, I floated into the living room where Kenny sat finishing off the last of his fries. Ghostlike, I stood before him.

Because I'd broken the sightline between him and the television, he noticed me right away.

He squirmed from a partially reclined to a fully upright position, his eyes transfixed on the Remington. "What the fu—"

"I've got something to say to you," I said, my voice unwavering. I felt calm, sure of myself, even courageous. "I'm leaving you. Right now. This minute. So I've brought you your gun." I held the weapon at arm's length, pointed toward the heavens. "Here." I shoved the rifle closer to him.

Kenny seemed paralyzed by my words. I tensed, waiting for him to rip the gun from my grip. But he made no effort to take it from me.

"If you mean to shoot me, then I'm ready to die," I said, blinking back my grief. "I've thought about it. I'd rather be *dead* than to live one more minute with *you.*"

For the first time in my life, I felt powerful, mightier than any force Kenny could launch against me. I was leaving him. He couldn't stop me. All he could do was assist me in the process. He could either let me go or blast me to smithereens. Either way, I was on my way out.

Kenny eased the weapon from me. His face contorted. Gently, he set the gun on the sofa. As if he'd been only a reflection in a funhouse mirror, the giant before me morphed into a pint-sized image. The monster I'd feared had disappeared.

Kenny dropped to his knees. "Oh, baby, don't leave me. I swear I'd never shoot you. I never meant that. I only said that to keep you here. I love you, baby." He clutched my thighs like a frightened toddler. "Please don't *leave*. You *know* we can work things out."

"Nothing to work out. I want out. Out of this hopeless marriage. Away from you." I looked over his bent body and into his empty recliner. "And as far as I can get from that disgusting, hideous chair."

TWENTY-THREE

I wasn't thrown off-course by Kenny's instant personality change. Matched against his need for control, I could almost guarantee his remorseful state had no staying power. Like one of those childhood bubbles I used to puff through a make-believe pipe, at any second his mood was subject to burst and dissolve. Though I'd initially been awestruck by Kenny's premier attempt at honesty, I held fast to the knowledge that I remained one false step away from total destruction. If Kenny sensed his amended ways had no bearing on my attitude, if he thought I might never return, he'd no doubt resort to direct combat. Therefore, to discourage Kenny from reversing his strategy and using my head for a trophy, I told him I wanted only a trial separation. You'd have thought he would have known better, considering I'd already found an apartment and revised Sean's childcare arrangements. But I guessed Kenny wanted to believe me as much as I wanted to believe him.

On Saturdays, when I pretended to already be a single woman, Sean stayed overnight with Kenny. That kept Kenny's temper in check and Sean from telling anyone about the man who made Mommy smile so wide she showed all her teeth, even the chipped one. I couldn't wipe that grin off of my face for anything, except when Kenny came around. Then, you'd have thought I'd just put down the family dog or worse. But of course, we didn't own a pet. I could barely afford *our* food.

With my hair mussed and flattened against one ear, face striped with yesterday's mascara, and my body sheathed inside a pair of baggy sweat pants, I'd greet Kenny at my door. "Wha'choo doin' tonight?" he'd ask.

Having memorized the TV schedule, a skill I'd perfected while living with him, I'd rattle off a list of programs I planned to watch that evening. Sometimes, though, I'd say I'd made arrangements to see Pearly. In reality, I hadn't spoken with her in a couple of months. She and Jarnell had stopped by to visit once, right after I'd moved into my apartment. Other than that, we checked in with each other by phone from time to time.

For the most part, my fake schedules were enough to nix Kenny's requests and send him on his way. Occasionally, though, he'd assume a forlorn look and say, "Why don't you come with me and Sean? It'd be good for ya."

It hadn't been good for me for years, was what I wanted to tell him. But I didn't. Instead, I'd scoff and say, "And do what? Hang out at Neta Sue's all night? No, thanks."

I wondered what he thought I'd do if I ever agreed to go with him. Sit inside his momma's living room, mentally noting all the stuff she'd stolen from me? If I had to bet my last dollar, I'd wager that Neta Sue hadn't let the fat on my hamburger congeal before she'd shown up with that borrowed livestock trailer. Twenty-four hours after I told Kenny I was leaving him, Neta Sue had arrived to claim all of what I didn't want—and most of what I did. I saw her there when I'd sneaked back to nab the rest of my belongings. I'd noticed the pipe-rail trailer filled with furniture, including my childhood bedroom set. The manure-crusted contraption was parked in our front yard. Inside the hauler, my chenille bedspread had been thrown carelessly to protect a few worthless items: a fifties-style nightstand, Sean's broken baby chair, and a rusted-out set of metal shelving. Our joint assets.

I'd driven over that day expecting to retrieve the last of my personal things while Kenny was at work. But after seeing a Jumpin' Janitors truck hitched to that doublewide horse trailer, I looped around and then swung back by from the opposite direction. In the process, I decided that if I never again had to fall victim to Neta Sue's hissy fits, despite what I might forfeit, that would be a good trade.

Those first few weeks Sean and I lived in our apartment at Jewel Gardens, I thought I'd never stop pinching myself. I decorated Sean's premier private bedroom until it didn't look one bit adult. I even covered Sean's single bed that one of Momma's neighbors had sold me—mattress and all for twenty-five dollars—with a Superman spread. Ricky gave me an old light fixture that somebody had thrown in the trash and he'd repaired. The antique car lamp fit squarely on top the double milk-crate nightstand I positioned next to Sean's bed. Inside the plastic bins, I neatly arranged Sean's plush toys: Bert, Ernie, Big Bird, and a stuffed parrot doll. It wasn't exactly designer. But sometimes, when the light was just right, I stood in the doorway and took in his room, thinking how it could be the bedroom of almost any five-year-old.

The rest of my apartment remained spare. I didn't own a dining table. And my bedroom had no contents whatsoever. I slept in my living room on a sofa I bought real cheap.

Daddy mailed me a check for a hundred and fifty dollars; out of guilt, I supposed. He said he wanted me to use the money to get reestablished, which was mighty big of him considering I'd written and told him I thought Celeste looked like a flower child. Anyway, I used Daddy's money to purchase an ultra-modern couch. It wasn't much other than a couple of oversized corduroy cushions, one stacked on top the other, with two L-shaped bolster pillows forming the sides and back. At night, I threw the bolsters to one side and used the base to sleep on. But I viewed this as a temporary arrangement. In the near future, I'd have a queen-size bed to sleep in—and Anthony, my soon-to-be next husband, to share it with. The fact that I hadn't yet legally divorced Kenny was immaterial. Our marriage, like some kind of prehistoric beast, had fossilized a couple billion years earlier. All that remained were the faint impressions.

~

One Saturday night in September while I was getting ready for a date with Anthony, I heard sounds coming from the other side of my bathroom wall: the neighbors. I stood at my sink, smudging a glob of turquoise eye-shadow across my lids and thinking how lucky I was to have a couple move in next door to me. As I primped and groomed, inspected my blush color, and inventoried my facial flaws, what I'd previously thought to be idle chatter escalated to an audible brawl. From the opposite side of the drywall, a woman shouted, "Get out of here! Go ahead, asshole. Leave! See if I care."

A thud shook the mirror in front of me.

A man's voice boomed, "Wha'cha say, now? Huh?"

Silence.

"You wanna get messed up, do ya?"

The woman screamed. "You goddamn bastard! I'll call the cops if you touch me again—"

My reflection vibrated. Then something hard, like maybe an elbow or a skull, knocked against the wall. I heard crashing sounds. The woman yelled, "Stop! You idiot! Help—"

I dropped my mascara wand in the sink. Inside my veins, I could feel adrenaline coursing. I knew what it was like to be the woman on the other

217

side of that wall, how degrading it was to be attacked physically by your closest relation, to suffer blows and bruises from the man whose children you'd borne, whose body you'd once lovingly accepted into your own.

Should I call the cops? They'd arrive an hour from now, especially once I gave them the location: Jewel Gardens. It was one of those subsidized housing projects where the police get summoned so often they might as well open a precinct on the premises.

I could call the after-hours security number. What were the chances of an unarmed, minimum-wage-earning security guard intervening in a domestic disturbance? Zip. Nada. No, I'd have to take a different approach.

Fastening my jeans, I shoved my feet into my denim platform sandals. Maybe, I decided, he'd stop hitting her once something distracted him. I sucked in my breath, exhaled deeply, and marched next door to protest the noise.

"Stay back!" I heard the man say to the woman inside. For her sake, I prayed she wasn't married to this jerk.

The neighbor's apartment door opened to reveal a surly Neanderthal in his mid- to late-twenties. His stringy shoulder-length hair looked like it had been brushed with an eggbeater. A paunch hung over his grease-stained blue jeans. I'd seen this guy once before, I recalled, on the sidewalk, repairing a motorcycle.

"Yeah?" he grunted. "What can I do you for?"

"Uh...I...uh...heard a loud racket and wondered if everything was okay over here." I shifted my weight from one leg to the other.

"Racket? He turned and looked over his shoulder. "Linda Gail, this here neighbor lady says she heard something...some kind of loud noise. You hear it?"

A female voice said, "I think it came from next door."

He shrugged. "Hmph. She thinks it came from somewheres else. We'll follow up on it, if we hear it again."

"Sorry to bother you," I said, backing away slowly. He stared at me as if my forehead might be see-through and my thoughts readily divined. The bruiser held his door open and continued standing there, watching me as I turned to leave. I could feel his eyes sizing me up as I walked away. He could gawk all he wanted because already I knew more about him that he'd *ever* know about me.

For the first time, I noticed the dim corridor lights and wished they were brighter. I thought how, under the haunting glow of those yellow bug-proof bulbs, the man next door had resembled a mass-murderer whose photo I'd seen on the nightly news. Strutting back toward my apartment, I was determined not to let the bastard intimidate me. I owned a phone, and I was literate enough to dial 9-1-1 if he caused any more trouble.

Behind me, in the breezeway, I heard footsteps. *Geez*, I prayed, *please tell me that overgrown ape isn't following me.* I picked up my pace.

Almost there. I had plenty of time to lunge inside, away from whoever was on my heels. My hand reaching for the doorknob, I dared to look over my left shoulder.

Kenny.

The caveman I'd just confronted closed his door.

"Renee! Wait! I wanna talk to you," Kenny hollered.

Safely inside my living room, I stopped and braced my partially open entry door with one foot. "Kenny," I said, still riled from my encounter with Mr. Manson. I did my best to sound calm. "What are you doing back so soon? Where's Seany?"

"He's *home*, where he b'longs. And where *you* b'long, too." He'd acquired that bully tone again, the one that implied he owned me. "What the hell you doin' over there?" He gestured toward the adjacent apartment. "Is 'at where you go ever' night? You go slippin' out like that, all dressed up?" He scowled, his face a radiant red. "Whadda ya trying to do, screw every man in the complex?" He continued shouting accusations as he wedged a size-ten loafer past my threshold, extending one arm against the door. Any second now, his next move would be to force his way inside.

I stepped back, offering no resistance. In a surprise twist, using both my hands, I thrust my full weight against his chest and shoved him backwards. As soon as he'd cleared the doorjamb, I slammed the steel-reinforced barrier into his unprotected toes. No socks, as usual.

Kenny hopped and howled with pain. Inflicting further injury upon himself, he kicked the door once, hard.

I listened until I heard him limp away.

He wouldn't go far, I guessed, probably not past the parking lot. There was nothing to do but wait him out. If I left home, Kenny would follow me. Or worse.

Breathless, I lifted my kitchen phone receiver and dialed Anthony's number. "Omigod! You're not going to be-*lieve* this!" I said when he answered. "He's *in-sane*, I'm telling you. He's out of his *mind!*"

"Who?" Anthony asked.

"Kenny! Who do you *think?*"

Anthony's sentences all ran together. "Is he *there?* Are you *okay?* Tell me what's going on."

I gave him a recap. "He's probably still sitting out there waiting for me to leave." My hands shook so badly I could hardly hold the receiver.

I could hear anger and disappointment in Anthony's voice. "What's his *prob*-lem?" He sighed.

Kenny had destroyed the evening for both of us. We'd planned a casual night of take-out pizza and dine-in romance. But now I couldn't risk driving across town. And Anthony certainly couldn't chance being seen at my apartment. We'd have to meet each other another time.

"He must have been stalking me," I said, thankful Kenny's timing had been slightly off. "Man, it's a good thing he caught me talking to the creep next door instead of *you!*"

"You got a goddamn right to speak to anybody you want to! Who does that *prick* think he is, anyway?"

I'd never before heard Anthony use words like that. Kenny had a way of bringing out the worst in anyone. Chances were good that Kenny had been thinking exactly what I'd led him to believe, that I hadn't yet severed my connection to him. How could I explain that to Anthony? "He thinks...well, you know...that he's still my husband," I said. "But he won't be for very much longer."

TWENTY-FOUR

I discovered that attorney services, like so many other needs I couldn't afford to buy outright, could be purchased on installments. It said so right there in the TV schedule ad. *Easy Payment Plans.* So with money I'd pulled from my meager savings account, I put a lawyer on layaway.

I told Zachary Swindle that I'd pay him a hundred dollars a month until I'd paid him the five-hundred he charged to handle a "no-fault" divorce. No telling who dreamed up that term, *no-fault.* To me, there was no such thing. More like maybe a "can't-get-anyone-to-accept-the-blame" divorce. Anyway, I had no idea where I'd get the rest of the money to clear my debt.

Swindle took pity on me, accepted my deposit, and agreed to file the necessary paperwork to start my divorce process. "Long as there's no property and you can agree on custody issues, I can do it for that amount." Leaning back in his worn, split-vinyl chair, he clasped his hands behind his head. He eyed the hundred-dollar bill I'd handed him like it might be counterfeit. "You have any children from this marriage?"

"One," I said. "A five-year-old son."

Swindle canted forward and grinned. "That's about all it takes to provoke a custody battle."

I wondered what about that comment amused him, though I wasn't overly worried. No judge in his right mind would grant custody of a child to Kenny. In fact, I couldn't wait to itemize Kenny's faults to someone who'd be my advocate. No longer did I feel powerless in this relationship. For once, Kenny would have to listen to me—because I had a lawyer.

Swindle took the bill I'd given him and sandwiched it between his calendar pages. "What are your living arrangements with this child?" He stared at me as if that might have been a trump question. "Does he live with only you? Nobody else?"

"Mostly." I fidgeted one foot against the rolling casters attached to my chair. "He stays with Kenny a lot on weekends," I clarified.

The lawyer scribbled on a ruled yellow tablet. "Anybody else live in your home?" He didn't give me time to answer before he continued, "Home or apartment?"

I replied fast before he could throw another question on the pile. "Apartment. And it's just the two of us there."

"And your husband? Where's he live? Anybody else live with *him*?"

Now we were getting somewhere. "He lives with his *momma*. And they live in *her* house, in Lolaville."

Swindle canted forward, squinting. "Does she *work*?"

He was beginning to annoy me with all his quizzing. What did Neta Sue's profession have to do with my divorce? "Yeah. She cleans office buildings."

"And when does she clean them?" Swindle crooned with excitement, as if we were playing Clue and he'd right then identified the correct killer.

"At night, when they're empty." For an educated man, he didn't seem too swift. Already I wondered about this guy's courtroom capabilities.

Swindle lit up like the Town Hall Christmas tree. "Ah...you said Mr. Murphy works nights? Right?"

I nodded.

"That means that no one can be home in the evenings with your son."

"Right!" I mirrored his sudden excitement. But then I remembered that a week earlier Kenny had mentioned something about requesting a transfer to the Water Utilities Department—working dayshift. When I shared this update with Swindle, he looked like maybe he'd lost an erection.

"Okay," he said, collecting himself. "You work, I know. What about your evenings? Are you home at night with the child?" He twirled his fat pen the way he might have held a fine cigar, if he'd had one.

"Yeah, pretty much." I marveled at his oversized writing tool and his pudgy bulldog face. If he'd been on *Perry Mason*, he could have easily played the part of a mobster.

"What do you mean? Are you gone part of the time?"

He was getting a bit testy for my tastes. "I just signed up for a few college classes." Why was I suddenly feeling defensive? How else could I ever make a decent living to support my son? "I go on Tuesdays and Thursdays, from six to eight."

"In the mornings?" Swindle's words sounded more baritone than before.

"No. *Evenings.*"

"And your son? Where's he while you're taking these classes?"

Where the hell did he *think*? In an alley? On a bridge? Playing at the city swimming pool? "He's at daycare. Where he stays every day while I'm working. They have an after-hours program." I folded my arms across my chest. "Why? Does that make me *unfit* or something?"

Swindle shook his head. "No. No, it doesn't." The man could shift moods faster than Kenny. "But Mr. Murphy might try to say that, because you work *and* go to college at night, you're not available to meet your child's needs." Swindle put down his pen and looked at his watch. "We'll cross that bridge when we get to it."

~

Two weeks after he'd been transferred to the Water Department, Kenny received the notice of divorce. Unfortunately, his new position must have offered ample phone privileges because, in the middle of the afternoon, he had no difficulty calling me at my job to let me know how he felt about being served with those papers.

"What the hell do you think you're doing? You said this was gonna be a temporary separation! You lyin' bitch!"

I pushed aside my pink message pad and swiveled my secretarial chair to face the wall behind me. "I never said for sure, Kenny. I never said that I wouldn't file for a divorce. I just wanted some time to think about it. And I've thought about it. This is what I want and—"

"What you *want* don't have nothin' to do with what I'm talking about," Kenny blustered. "You remember what I *tode* you, Renee?"

I could practically feel the heat of his breath seeping through the telephone. Of course I remembered. How could I forget?

Kenny didn't wait for me to respond. "You'd *better*. 'Cause you're *not* divorcing me! You hear me?"

My heart felt like it might leap onto my desk calendar and land smack on today's date—December 2. At any minute, my bladder would release and cause me to pee in my chair. I couldn't listen to him talk to me like that any longer. Using something my coworkers called secretarial discretion, I disconnected his call.

Instantly, one of my other two phone lines rang.

Reluctantly, I answered.

"You goddamn bitch! Don't you dare hang up on me again!"

I forced myself to speak. "You can't call me here at work. It's against company policy," I said, as if that would throw him off track. "Goodbye."

The third square phone button lit up. I watched it flash and listened to the buzz until whoever was calling hung up.

Right after the lines grew quiet, Mr. Wilmot, my boss, called out from his corner office. "Not answering the phones today, Ms. Murphy?"

"Yessir. It's just that my husband's been bothering me. I think that last ring was probably him again, so I didn't answer."

Wilmot ambled over to my desk. I noticed a strange knot inside his lower jaw. "And what if it *wasn't* him, Ms. Murphy? Did you ever stop to think it might have been someone important? Someone I needed to speak to?"

"No, sir." I cowered. For a split second, I didn't know who he was. The men in my life were all beginning to look alike: my daddy, my husband, my attorney, my boss—everyone but Anthony. Each seemed dedicated to reminding me that I didn't measure up in some regard, couldn't do things right. "I'm sorry. I didn't think it through, I guess. I was so upset."

Wilmot leaned over my trash receptacle and spit out a wad of chewing tobacco. "Well, see to it that you answer the phones from now on. And stop letting your personal life interfere with your work."

~

After he learned of Kenny's telephone threats, Swindle recommended something called a restraining order. During my temporary hearing, which I presumed was some kind of practice run for the lawyers, Kenny's attorney agreed to Swindle's request for this legal restraint—provided the order was mutual. Maybe someone ought to have told him Kenny was the one with the gun.

All in all, Swindle said the hearing went well. But since I wasn't awarded any child support, I wasn't sure what he used for criteria. "There's a few logistics to work out with child visitation," he said, pausing inside the courthouse lobby to wave goodbye to his opponent. "It may take some time to resolve those." He faced me again. "And, of course, that'll require some additional fees."

I dug into my purse and handed him the fifty dollars I'd managed to save from my daycare budget. By taking my vacation at Christmas, I'd been able to stay home with Sean during the last week of his school holiday break. Kenny had kept him during the first week, so I'd saved nearly a hundred dollars. But I'd already spent part of that on Sean's Christmas presents.

I was short on the full hundred I'd promised Swindle, but he said not to worry. "Maybe you'll get a tax refund," he observed. And I fully expected I would. However, I'd kind of hoped to buy a bed with it.

My living room sofa wasn't big enough for both Sean and me to sleep on. Ever since I'd insisted that Kenny stop retrieving Sean from my apartment, Sean had refused to sleep in his own room. Though his transfers between households went much smoother for Kenny and me now that they took place in the Dairy Queen parking lot, for some reason, Sean didn't adjust well to the change. Steadily, he grew more vocal about his new routines and contacts, including his daycare workers, who he said made him take too many naps. "They won't even lemme get up or talk," he whined.

Time and again, in the middle of the night, I awoke to find Sean sneaking into bed, or should I say "into sofa," with me. More than once, in a state of confusion, instead of shuffling to the restroom, he slipped off the couch and peed in the kitchen trashcan. He'd walk, more asleep than awake, following the same pattern he'd taken to get from his bed to the bathroom in our old duplex. But since he was sleeping in my apartment living room, that path led him directly into the kitchen.

The rapid adjustments I'd inflicted upon Sean had been more than his five-year-old mind could handle. As much as I hated to acknowledge it, Sean had enjoyed his prior lifestyle and Kenny's daily companionship. I realized, though somewhat after the fact, that what had invigorated me had been excruciating for my little boy.

"Momma, I want to sleep in here tonight," Sean said late one January evening. "It's dark in my room." He stood before me, hugging his pillow and wearing his Superman pajamas, though he'd removed the cape. Before I could protest, he wedged one foot under my blanket and climbed in.

Great. I could hear it now. Some social worker would likely take issue with Sean's sleeping habits. I expected a visit from Family Court Services any day. The court-ordered social study to evaluate Sean's living arrangements was required, Swindle said. Truth be told, that social worker would try and determine which of us, I or Neta Sue, best favored June Cleaver. That was the equivalent of asking which most resembles apple pie, mincemeat or pumpkin. But what was I supposed to do? I'd tried every gimmick I could think of to encourage Sean to sleep in his own bed.

"Seany, what about that new night-light Momma bought you? Doesn't it help make your room brighter?"

"Nuh-uh." He shook his head hard, his baby-fine locks falling forward into his eyes. He carefully situated his pillow, rooted his head under my neck, and squeezed my waist.

I forgot all about becoming a model mother. Caving to his request, I kissed the top of his head.

"When's Daddy coming back to get us?" Sean asked, his voice a whimper.

"Oh, sweetie, Daddy didn't leave us. This is our new home, now. And Daddy has his own...with Grandma Murphy." How could I make the idea of a grown man living with his mother sound completely normal? "I left Daddy because I wasn't happy living with him anymore. Daddy hasn't left you." I brushed a lock of hair across his forehead. "I took you with me because I didn't want to leave you either."

"But I want you *and* Daddy."

"I know you do, Seany. I know. But Mommy and Daddy don't get along anymore. So we're not going to live together." I folded the blanket across his shoulders and snuggled up to him. "Now let's get some sleep."

At two o'clock in the morning, a flash of light startled me awake. I checked the pillow next to me and noticed Sean missing. The sounds filtering from the kitchen were the unmistakable noises of someone opening the refrigerator door.

By the time I'd risen, Sean had dropped his drawers, grabbed his privates, and sprayed his hose like a fireman.

"No-o-o!" I yanked an empty cup from the countertop behind me, hoping to deflect the stream. But it was too late. He'd already whizzed half the fridge's contents.

~

I straightened my desk and removed my sweater from the back of my secretarial chair. Spying me, Wilmot jaunted from his office to catch my attention. In his hands he held a ruled tablet, his expression one of urgency. "I need to get this memo out today," he announced.

I checked the wall clock to see if maybe I'd misread the time.

Five after four.

Nope, I hadn't.

"It's already five after." I pointed to the official timekeeper. I couldn't deal with his procrastinated efforts today. With regularity, Wilmot would bound out with some last-second, critical need at the close of my shift. If you asked me, he needed to take one of those time management classes advertised in the brochures he received.

Wilmot continued toward my desk. "I'll pay you overtime. It shouldn't take you more than thirty minutes, but I'll pay you for a full hour."

"I'd like to help, and I could use the extra money—"

"Good." He set the tablet on my desk.

"But I can't stay tonight," I finished.

Before I could explain, he yanked away his ruled pad and stormed back to his private office. He slammed the door behind him.

Even if he'd given me a chance to explain, I doubted he'd have behaved any differently. It wouldn't have mattered to him that a social worker would be visiting me that evening.

After I retrieved Sean from daycare and arrived home to prepare supper, only an hour remained until my appointment. Instead of the canned noodles we normally had every night, I'd sprung for poultry I'd found on sale the week before. But I'd forgotten to thaw the packaged meat until that morning.

I placed two, partially-frozen chicken breasts in the oven and prayed for a miracle.

"Sean, did you put on the clothes I laid out for you?"

"Uh-huh," he answered from his room.

Tonight I needed to look like the world's best mother. Given my upbringing, I didn't know exactly what that entailed. But I'd watched enough *Lassie* reruns to formulate an idea.

Step One: Children should be clean, clothed, and well fed.

Step Two: Offspring should be taught to respect and obey.

Step Three: Moms should periodically examine their brood for adherence to Step Two.

I set Sean's tumbler on the kitchen counter and skittered into his room.

With one hand, Sean rolled a small metal car back and forth across his bed surface, mussing the formerly neat spread. From behind, his clothing appeared equally disheveled.

"Sean?"

He turned to face me. The buttons on the shirt I'd meticulously ironed the evening before peeked at me from the wrong buttonholes. As directed, Sean had tucked in his top. But he'd done so with such gusto that the front of his pants had migrated to where a side seam should have been.

I scrolled down to his feet. The new white socks I'd purchased had been pulled on in reverse, with the heels bunched atop his ankles. His shoe toes pointed in opposite directions.

Thank goodness, I'd remembered Step Three.

~

When Ms. Platt arrived, I was especially grateful for the bedroom furniture I'd been given only the week before: a double bed and an accent table made from one-hundred-percent walnut-grain-printed cardboard.

"Be prepared to demonstrate that Sean and you each have your own room and that he has plenty of clothing," Swindle had advised beforehand. I'd laundered all four pairs of Sean's Toughskins jeans, his only dress shirt, and six long-sleeve T-shirts and hung them in his closet for inspection.

A light tap on my apartment door announced my evaluator's arrival. "Hello. I'm Helen Platt, Limestone County Family Court Services. Are you Mrs. Murphy?" asked the petite woman with a moon face.

"For a bit longer. But you can call me Renee."

The woman who looked to be in her early fifties entered my living room, scanning the bare walls. I hadn't hung any pictures. It was hard to justify framed artwork, I wanted to explain, when you're struggling to pay for childcare, groceries, and a divorce. "We haven't been here very long," I said, apologizing for the uninviting décor.

Platt looked into my empty dining room. "Where shall we sit?"

"Oh, how about here?" I pointed to the corduroy couch that was better suited for sleeping than entertaining. I had to sit with my legs fully extended on the extra-wide, twin-mattress-sized seat cushions if I wanted to lean against the back pillows.

Platt situated herself on the free-form sofa, masking any discomfort she might have felt. She looked like a decorative doll perched on top of a bed, her stubby legs outstretched. Nevertheless, she acted as if she sat on such contemporary furnishings every day.

Sean played in his room while we talked about his care, my work, and both our schools. That woman could write faster than any human I'd ever seen. She must have been an expert in shorthand. Her burgundy leather folder remained tilted so I couldn't see the pages her pen speed threatened to set afire.

Checking the time—six-thirty—Platt asked, "So, do you *normally* eat dinner about now?"

I didn't think it wise to tell her that we usually had reheated canned foods or grilled cheese sandwiches, meals that required much less time to prepare than roasted chicken. Excusing myself, I double-checked the oven temperature. "Yes, actually, we do," I said when I returned. "But this chicken seems to be taking longer to cook tonight than normal."

When Sean rejoined us, Platt said she wanted to speak privately with him in his room. She closed the door so I couldn't hear what was being said. But I imagined she might be asking where the rest of Sean's apparel and toys were hidden.

An hour later, after I'd finished piling two plates high with chicken, boxed dressing, and peas and carrots, I heard Sean's bedroom door creak open. He and the woman assigned to judge my parenting skills waltzed into the living room together like best friends. Sean assumed his standard position at the coffee table, where we ate most of our meals.

"I'm finished with my interviews, so I won't keep you two any longer." Ms. Platt glanced at the chrome and glass table surface, probably eyeing the generous portions I'd served up. "I can let myself out. Thank you for your time."

"What did you tell that lady?" I asked Sean, after Platt departed.

Casually, he spooned a mound of dressing into his mouth before he answered. "She asked me if I ever got in trouble and got spanked. And I told her, 'Uh-huh,

Wunst..." He took a slurp of milk from his Incredible Hulk cup. "When I colored your bookmark."

Why hadn't Platt asked *me* about that? I could have given her the whole story. It wasn't like it sounded.

I hadn't punished Sean for something as petty as coloring a bookmark. I'd been up at three forty-five that morning, cleaning urine from milk and egg cartons, packaged lunchmeats and, thankfully, *closed* condiment jars. Having missed so much sleep, I'd been late for work that day. And Wilmot had written me up for it.

Exhausted and worried, when I'd returned home that evening, I asked Sean to play in his room quietly so I could rest for a short while. I hadn't planned to fall asleep, only to shut my eyes. But sometime during the six o'clock news, I dozed off for fifteen or twenty minutes.

When I woke up, I found Sean had colored in his coloring book, along four feet of wall next to his bed, and all over the bookmark I kept inside Daddy's Bible. In a fit of frustration, I'd smacked him across the back of his legs and cried, "What's wrong with you? Can't you do *anything* right?"

Now I realized that I was the one destined to eternally screw up.

TWENTY-FIVE

A more insightful person might have seen it coming. But I didn't. And it was hard for me to describe the feelings I had when that sorry, no-good, sheep-dung for balls Wilmot fired me, though I can tell you they weren't good ones. What got me most was the way he'd done it: right after Kenny had called me three times in a row, screaming like a banshee. And somehow that moron Wilmot thought *I* was the one who was causing trouble. He said, "Ms. Murphy, I've warned you before about disrupting the workplace. This is *your* divorce, not ours. I don't think the entire staff needs to suffer for your bad decisions. We've tolerated this long enough."

He dismissed me just like that, after I'd done everything but wipe his ass for him for the past ten months. And now all of the sudden, he found it "intolerable" to listen to a few of my noisy phone conversations? Without a job, how did he think I was going to pay for my divorce? Or for that matter, pay my rent? That cud-chewing ox didn't care.

I'd been a good secretary to Wilmot. He couldn't deny it. With perfect diction and a pleasant voice I'd learned to say, "Good afternoon. Marketing. How may I direct your call?" No one would ever guess I was a former assembly worker. But none of that mattered.

"You can carry this down to Personnel. They'll take things from here." Wilmot handed me a typed memo that detailed the grounds for my termination. And *termination* was a good word for it. I was as good as dead. It would have served him right if I'd keeled over then and there.

I feared I'd have to go back to working on some assembly line. With nothing but a GED and a couple of college classes to show for an education, I'd likely have to start at the bottom again—if anyone would even hire me after I'd been fired.

Lord knew, I had neither the looks nor the coordination to take up exotic dancing.

The journey from Wilmot's office to the human resource center left me short of breath but not rage. I followed the familiar passage that snaked through two buildings connected by an enclosed walkway. Plodding the distance, I had plenty of time to think about all the things I wished I'd said to Wilmot, ample opportunity to regret that I'd never gotten even with him for spitting all that chewing tobacco into my trash can. I used to have to hide my waste paper basket underneath my desk to keep him from mistaking it for a spittoon. How many times had I thought to throw a used tampon in his wastebasket, to see if I could equally gross him out? Why hadn't I done it? All he could have done was fire me. In the end, he'd let me go anyway.

I knew I'd lose custody of Sean, for sure. By costing me my job, the only positive attribute I had,

Kenny had already won. Would there ever be a way for me to escape that maniac? It seemed as though our divorce proceedings had only given him another weapon to use against me, one that extended his reach so that he could strangle me with someone *else's* hands.

I trudged through the corridor, envisioning new ways for Kenny to become a fatality. An unlimited number of industrial accidents came to mind. Maybe he'd get decapitated by a faulty fire hydrant, now that he worked in the Water Department. More appropriate still, perhaps he could die from something sewer-related. He might get eaten alive by a bunch of Norway rats. Indiscriminate ones, that is. I imagined rodents gnawing at his crotch.

Poetic, but unlikely.

No, he'd be more apt to fall into one of those massive vats at the waste treatment plant. That would make for an equally fitting end. I begged God to, however He chose to do it, take Kenny's mortal life before the tyrant ruined the rest of mine.

Once Kenny learned he'd managed to get me fired, he wouldn't stop there. Like a hawk, he'd be sure to make another pass. With those long talons of his, escape would be next to impossible. I was as doomed as a rabbit in a freshly mown field.

Inside the covered walkway leading to Personnel, the floor tiles, modular wall panels, and ceiling grids all merged into one massive tunnel of gray. One vast sewer drain. I could almost hear the flushing sounds. And the human waste being disposed of was me.

I had the bend in sight, the one that led in one direction to the parking lot and in the other to my final destination. Maybe I'd bolt for the outdoors instead of progressing toward my official exit. I could see it in my mind's eye, visualize getting into my car and simply driving away. I'd roll down my windows and let the wind rip through my hair while I headed south. To where, I didn't know or care. When the gas tank neared empty, maybe I'd hit the accelerator and speed until I flipped my Mustang end over end.

Naw, that plan wouldn't work. I could end up hurting someone else. Better for me to drive the speed limit, follow those white lines pointing to nowhere in particular, drive until I simply ran out of gas and then had to stop. Yeah. I could do that. I'd likely end up somewhere in the Rio Grande, where I'd take up working as a migrant tomato-picker. Kenny wouldn't bother me then. I'd make myself so invisible that even a skilled predator like him couldn't find me.

I pictured that warm burrow in the sand, the one I'd hide in, the one with an opening so narrow that nothing could crawl inside. Nothing but me. Its umber walls would cradle me, its shadowy hollows lulling me into a peaceful sleep. If only there might be such a place. If I didn't have Sean, I might have really done it.

But I did have Sean. And he needed me, and I loved him.

I opened the door leading to Personnel and faced whatever waited on the other side of unemployment.

~

After I'd been escorted from the building by a security guard, instead of heading due south, I drove to get Sean from daycare. By the time I reached him, I'd had a good bawl and wiped my eyes dry.

Sean marched out to the reception area to greet me looking like he'd just been pronounced World's Best Kid. He ran to my arms, same as usual.

Later that night, when Sean asked me why he had to go to bed before *Happy Days* came on, I told him it was on account of me being sick, which wasn't exactly a lie. I'd never felt worse in my whole life. I was sick of struggling to survive, fed up with fighting for what should have been free, and terminally tired of men in general.

Ever since I'd confessed Kenny had been stalking me, Anthony had been seeing me less and less. He still called me, but now, when I most needed him, he seldom came around.

I climbed into bed and swathed myself inside my peach floral-patterned bedspread, muffling my sobs. The quilted layers smelled of spring-scented fabric softener. I breathed through the covers, staining them with wet mascara. Staring at the patterns, I thought how they were the closest thing to fresh flowers I would see for a while. Unless I got lucky enough to attend Kenny's funeral.

No one ever gave me flowers. Anthony had given me a long-stemmed rose, once. But I didn't count that. A woman dressed in nearly nothing but the top half of a tuxedo had all but embarrassed him into buying it for me. If the truth were told, he'd probably done it to please her more than me.

When I next heard from Anthony, I'd tell him about Kenny's threatening phone call and what it had cost me.

"You worthless slut!" Kenny had screamed through the phone. "Who'd you sleep with *last* night?"

I'd become smarter over time and begun parking my car in a different space, one partially hidden by a commercial dumpster. Probably, Kenny had steered through the apartment complex and hadn't seen my vehicle. From there, he'd allowed his demented mind to drive him nuts.

The telephone on top of my cardboard side table rang several times before I answered it. I prayed it wasn't Kenny.

"Hi. It's me," Anthony said in that deep measured voice of his. "Just calling to tell you about the interesting day I've had." He sounded different than normal, possibly because tears had pooled inside my ears and I was hearing him through water.

"Mm-hmm, me, too," I said, as if maybe I'd blown a tire on my way home, locked myself out of my apartment, or seen Elvis in the Laundromat— but not in any way that would have suggested I'd been fired from my job.

"You feeling okay?" he asked. "Sounds like you're a little stopped up or something."

I sniffed once. "No. I'm okay. Go ahead."

"You're not going to believe *who* called me today." He paused and waited for me to respond, but I was too tired to guess. I could barely remember my own name, let alone his list of oddball friends and previous lovers. If he'd heard from Darlene, I didn't care.

"Kenny," he said, identifying the mystery caller.

"What? Omigod!" I gasped. "How'd he get your name and number?"

"Funny, I was going to ask you the same thing."

Anthony sounded suspicious. Surely he didn't think I'd tell Kenny about him or our Saturday night rendezvous?

"Maybe he trailed me to your place last Saturday night." My fears cycled uncensored from my brain to my mouth.

That slip of the tongue undoubtedly led to what followed.

"He's going to hurt somebody before this whole thing's over with," Anthony predicted.

"Did he threaten you?"

"No, he threatened *you*. He said, 'If you want your little girlfriend to stay pretty, you better stay away from her.'" Anthony coughed once, like he had something lodged in his throat.

The obstruction might have been his balls.

"Renee, look...I'm going to keep my distance for a while, at least until after your divorce is final. This hothead needs time to cool down."

I didn't even try to catch the receiver as it slipped from my hands, fell to the floor, and bounced a few times. I left the device dangling by its thin, curled cord and numbly listened to the dial tone.

Like everything else that had happened to me that day, I didn't have any say. To rid himself of *Kenny*, Anthony had made up his mind to sacrifice *me*. In that respect, he was no different than Wilmot. So he could go ahead and say goodbye, if that's what he wanted. I no longer needed him.

Perhaps I never had.

TWENTY-SIX

My divorce hearing took place on April Fool's Day, at the Limestone County Courthouse. Inside the building, massive columns supported a cathedral ceiling accented with ornate moldings. The interior woodwork was nothing short of impressive: hardwood floors, solid maple congregation pews, and an elevated, hand-carved judge's bench with a distinctly lower witness stand. It was the kind of place that, depending on your circumstances, could make you either want to thumb your nose or find religion.

From the looks of Kenny's attire, it must have had the latter effect on him.

Kenny wore a gray western sports coat and bolo tie that I suspect he borrowed from one of his honky-tonk friends. Probably his attorney had advised him the same way mine had clued me in on what to wear.

Swindle had directed me to be extra-conscious of my appearance. "Wear a dress, something like you might wear to church," he'd suggested. I hadn't attended any religious services since Kenny and I had married, but I'd chosen one of those out-of-style getups Momma had made me about a hundred years ago, a floral print of muted mauves and pinks with a pointy Pilgrim collar. I felt pretty sure that, in that getup, I didn't look the least bit slutty.

"All rise," I heard a voice command. I wondered how I'd find the strength to lift my weight from the chair that supported me. Swindle nudged my left elbow as the judge, a sixty-some-odd-year-old man with a face like a cowpoke, took his seat atop what looked like gallows to me. I'd seen the man before, only a few months earlier, when he'd fully lived up to his reputation for being unfair. He hadn't even flinched when he'd granted Kenny temporary visitation privileges that included Sean's entire spring break.

Given the outcome of that earlier hearing, I had no reason to trust that steely-eyed bastard on the bench or the system that threatened to relieve me of my only reason for living.

If I lost custody of Sean, I couldn't imagine what would happen to me. My reputation, from what I could tell, had been ruined already. I'd become the wayward daughter of a defrocked deacon, a harlot whose son had to be protected from her cheap ways. At least, that's what Kenny had stated during his prior testimony.

All those grandiose plans I'd made with Anthony had faded into the nothingness from which I'd conjured them. I'd been left with only public humiliation and private regrets. I would never again be viewed as a good mother or a decent wife. Not after this. In fact, I was the same homely, immoral, and worthless person I'd been at sixteen. Nothing had changed. And Neta Sue, Kenny, and his attorney, Douglas R. Thornton, III, were present and ready to prove it.

Thick with the devastation of crushed dreams, the air around me smelled foul. I glanced to my attorney's left, to the table opposite the one where Swindle and I sat, and spied Kenny scribbling away on a canary-colored tablet. Thornton appeared to be paying little attention to Kenny's sudden interest in becoming a scribe. I suspected the lawyer knew he had a deadbeat for a client. Loser or saint, Thornton likely figured the fees generated by either one could pay his Brooks Brothers bill.

Neta Sue sat behind them, her hair pinned into a coil, wearing a dress Andy Griffith's Aunt Bee would have liked. The white patent leather pumps into which she'd wedged her fleshy feet looked like they'd been purchased at a swap meet. Given her outfit and her daily disposition, I assured myself she'd fool no one. Her face, like her heart, had suffered severe freezer burn. Waiting amid the silence, arms folded across her chest, she maintained a due-center, don't-tread-on-me stare.

With a nod, the court reporter indicated her readiness to record what certainly would be a dismal account, one that any sane person would want to avoid reading:

Girl meets Boy.

Boy gets girl pregnant.

Boy does responsible thing and marries girl.

Girl isn't satisfied.

Girl leaves Boy so she can find a new boy.

Boy's heart is broken.

Boy wants Child.

With only a few minor variations, the same story probably played out between those walls on a regular basis. Why record it hundreds of times? All anyone needed to do was create a standardized form and fill in the blanks with the appropriate names. From what I could tell, that must have been the method Swindle had used to ready himself for the hearing. It took all of fifteen seconds for him to reveal he'd arrived unprepared.

"Ms. Murphy, is it your testimony today that you've been the primary caretaker of Sam for the past...uh...the past..." Swindle hastily thumbed the pages of his legal pad and then, settling on one sheet, continued. "Uh, five years, essentially ever since he was born?"

"Sean," I corrected, wondering if maybe my lawyer had suffered a lobotomy since I'd last seen him. The boy whose fate now dangled in midair, whose future was contingent upon this man's ability to ask the right questions, was named *Sean*, not Sam. Did the idiot need bifocals to read his own handwriting? Was he looking at the correct page? This was the Murphy-versus-Murphy proceeding. I hoped like hell he'd brought the correct tablet.

"I'm sorry, yes. Yes, I mean *your son*, Sean Murphy," he said, as if perhaps I, too, had forgotten the boy's name.

When it came time to ask about specifics, Swindle gave out a fake cough and asked, "How would you describe your childcare arrangements? Where does Sam, I mean, *Sean*, stay when you're at work?"

I considered how to best answer that question since, before I'd separated, I'd often let Sean stay with Kenny or Neta Sue. "Well, I used to have Kenny or his mother babysit," I said, attempting to do as Swindle had instructed, keeping my answers thorough and clear. "But for the past eight months, Sean's been attending kindergarten."

Swindle again searched his notes. Assuming he'd thought things through far enough to anticipate my reply, which took a broad imagination, I sensed he was unsatisfied with my response.

I scanned up and to my right, looking at the judge whom I'd expected to find contemplatively listening to testimony. With his left hand, he tapped a pencil eraser on the dais, creating a sound that annoyed every bit as much as a leaky faucet. Using his other hand, he sifted through and sorted a stack of celery-colored legal folders, the day's pending cases, I presumed.

Neta Sue took the witness stand. Thornton, who'd obviously expended more review effort than Swindle, led his client's mother carefully through examination. "And how would you describe Renee Murphy's relationship with your grandson?" he asked, measuring his steps as he backed away from his witness.

Neta Sue pursed her lips and frowned as if trying to recall some distant memory, like maybe the last time she'd seen her husband or the first time she'd ever said a curse word. "Well now, I'm not sure I can rightly say. I haven't seen all that much of Renee and Sean *together.*" She corrected her posture and thrust out her chin. "She's always got more important things to do than be a *mother.*"

"Ob-jec-tion," Swindle drawled as though talking in his sleep.

"*Sus*-tained," the judge said without looking up.

Thornton began again. "What kinds of things do you believe Renee Murphy prioritizes over being a mother to Sean?"

Swindle momentarily came to life. "*Objection,* Your Honor."

"I'm merely trying to get the witness to clarify her earlier comment," Thornton countered, still facing the bench.

"Overruled," the judge said, his face buried in a folder.

Swindle unlocked himself from his half-risen, half-seated position. The courtroom didn't resemble any I'd seen on television, nothing like the kind where everyone remained attentive and concerned to get at the truth. In fact, I wasn't sure why any of us even needed to be there. Whatever this so-called man of justice used to formulate his decisions must have been contained in those green folders because he didn't seem to be listening to anyone's testimony.

"Let me rephrase the question, Mrs. Murphy. What kinds of things are you stating Renee Murphy held in higher interest than being with Sean?"

I could almost hear a drum roll.

Neta Sue steadied herself to speak. "Things like working and taking typing classes and going to night school...and," she added with a full cymbal crash, "sleepin' 'round with other men." Her song lost its intended crescendo because Kenny had already accused me of as much.

From underneath a pair of glasses, ones he must have purchased for show, Kenny cried like a newly weaned pup. "I didn't want to b'lieve it," he said, eyes darting from his attorney to the judge. "Turned out to be true, though. She was having an affair with some Mes-can man she worked with. They'd been getting it on, the whole time we was married."

I felt relieved that Momma and Daddy weren't in attendance to hear this. No other relatives existed for me to disappoint. Grandma Goodchild's heart had given out after she'd learned of Daddy's deviant ways. There was no one left to kill with mine.

This was the kind of shame one shouldn't have to share with her loved ones. What more did Kenny and his lawyer want from me? It seemed their next move might be to strip me buck-naked and parade me down Main Street wearing a banner that said, "Town Whore."

The judge didn't care that Anthony and I were no longer seeing each other. I'd been indecent with this man in public. Kenny's attorney successfully pried that much out of me, which was enough to cast me in an unfavorable light—one with a bright red tinge to it. I admitted under oath to being unfaithful. The circumstances surrounding my offense, however important to me, remained irrelevant in that courtroom. By afternoon, I'd be divorced from Kenny, but ridicule and guilt would remain my companions for life.

Those were the stories Sean would forever hear about his mother, tales of selfishness, neglect, and sexual misconduct. I followed the path of destruction, imagining the ruin that day would leave behind.

Immediately I understood what Pearly had been trying to tell me about that tornado.

~

During break, Swindle and I sat outside the courtroom on what looked like an antique church bench fit for the occasion. It wasn't even ten o'clock yet, and already I'd called upon God several times. "I don't think this is going to last much longer," Swindle offered matter-of-factly. "We'll next hear from the social worker Ms. Pratt—"

"That's *Platt*," I stressed.

"Thank you. Yes, Platt. And then I think there'll be another witness or two." Swindle glanced down at a handful of typed pages. "You ever heard of anyone named Billy Wayne Edwards?"

I searched my mind for the names of Kenny's thieving cousins, but I couldn't recall any of them. "No, I haven't."

"Hmph. Probably a character witness." Swindle checked his watch. "We should return to the courtroom."

The court back in session, Helen Platt acted as if she'd been called to testify on her only day off work. Possibly she had been. Fidgeting in her seat and picking at her unpolished nails, she kept her responses brief.

"And have you had an occasion to meet with Sean and Renee Murphy in their home and witness them interacting with one another?" Douglas Thornton, the third, asked.

"I have."

"And when you met with Sean at his mother's home, what were your observations of the child, Ms. Platt?" Thornton's voice sounded steady, confident.

"That he seemed healthy and well-groomed, polite and eager to speak with me…" She paused. "And that he missed his father."

It was Thornton's turn to fall momentarily mute. He let Platt's final remark hang in midair before he followed up with, "Do you, in your professional opinion, have reason to believe that Renee Murphy has ever struck the child, Sean Murphy?"

Platt adjusted her gray A-line skirt. "Yes, I think she did on at least one occasion."

I'd never given Sean anything more than a light, open-handed swat on his legs or behind. And I could count those rare occasions on a single hand.

Thornton had coerced her to say what he needed her to say. There was no need for Platt to elaborate. "Thank you for your testimony," he said. "That'll be all."

I only hoped Swindle's cross-examination would force Platt to cite specific incidents. I'd scribbled my comments about spanking on a tablet Swindle had provided for such purpose.

Swindle, however, never bothered to address the matter.

~

By the time the court adjourned for lunch, my stomach ached and head pounded. I hadn't eaten anything that morning, so I bought breakfast at a nearby diner. Swindle excused himself from joining me, stating he needed to make some calls.

Thornton had begun questioning me before the break. He could have written my biography from the information I'd been forced to divulge. What did my sex life have to do with parenting, anyway? Didn't married parents have sex? No one had inquired about Kenny's intimate life. He certainly wasn't going to take an oath of celibacy if he gained custody of Sean. And he darn sure wasn't about to give up his part-time porn business.

When we returned, Thornton resumed his questioning. "To recap, Ms. Murphy, let me see if I understood you correctly. You told this court that you work forty hours a week, commute for five, and take evening classes about eighteen hours a month. I believe you said you confined your social life to Saturdays, when Mr. Murphy keeps his son Sean overnight. Is that correct?"

I nodded. The Dr Pepper I'd drunk during lunch had stressed my bladder. I pressed my knees together, hard.

"So you really aren't around your little boy very much, are you, Ms. Murphy?"

Swindle bellowed, "Ob-*jection*, Your Honor."

"Withdrawn."

~

Billy Wayne Edwards took his oath while my gaze remained affixed to the polished floor beneath me. Too humiliated to look up, I was lost beyond all reason of salvation. I hardly listened to Thornton's inquests, directing my attention instead to the possible return of two scrambled eggs and hash browns with toast. I clicked in long enough to hear him ask, "Mr. Edwards, will you please tell this court how you know Renee Murphy?"

Oh, this ought to be good, I thought. I'd never before heard of a Billy Wayne Edwards, not

257

once in my whole life. I brought my toes together, braced one knee against the other, and practiced bladder control.

"Live right next to her," the mystery man said.

Snapping to attention, I nearly suffered whiplash. I zeroed in on the witness stand. There sat the guy whose raging voice had been echoing through my apartment for months, the Neanderthal who now had a name, Billy Wayne Edwards.

"As Ms. Murphy's next door neighbor, do you share a common vestibule with her?" Like an old riding stable horse, Thornton was racing for the barn. In no time at all, he'd have this clod saying most anything. Soon enough, Thornton would be feeding on his ill-gotten success.

"Yep. Sure do," confirmed Billy Wayne.

"So I take it you can see, from time to time, people coming and going from Ms. Murphy's residence? Is that correct?"

"Uh-huh." Billy Wayne nodded.

"And have you ever witnessed any men, other than this one—" Thornton pointed to Kenny. "Entering or exiting Ms. Murphy's apartment?"

"Sure. Many times," Billy Wayne said. "All types of 'em."

"All *types?*" Thornton feigned surprise. "What do you mean by that?"

"Coloreds...whites...Mexicans." He shrugged. "All kinds."

Before Billy Wayne stopped yapping, he'd accused me of sleeping with just about every man with whom I'd ever made contact, from Jewel Gardens' maintenance staff to Pearly's husband Jarnell.

~

Leaving the courthouse on that spring afternoon, I didn't notice the fuchsia and white azaleas lining the sidewalk or the boxwoods' newly green shoots. I couldn't hear the cardinals' high-pitched chirps or the grackle's shrill caw. I'd been deafened by defeat. The judge's final words echoed in my brain. "Effective the last scheduled day of the school year, this court hereby orders Renee Ann Goodchild to relinquish primary conservatorship of Sean Lee Murphy to his legal father, Kenneth Raymond Murphy, subject to standard visitation...first and third weekends...holidays...Mother's Day..."

I could no longer hear anything else but those words and the sounds of my own heart reassuring me that, though I didn't want to, I still lived.

Swindle uttered, "I'm sorry."

"How...you tell me how does this happen?" I demanded. "That man is a wife-beater. How could anyone think he's a better parent than me?"

Swindle stowed a few file folders in his briefcase. "We had no proof of that because you'd never filed any charges. There were no photos, just your word against his." He snapped shut his attaché. "He had character witnesses. And you didn't."

Oh, no, I wasn't about to let him off that easily. "What about the restraining order I filed against him? Didn't that prove something?"

Swindle gave me a consoling look. "It was a mutual order, if you'll recall. They could have easily said *you* were violent." He took a few steps toward the exit door then turned back. "Look, the good news is, the judge denied him any child support." With a flip of his wrist, Swindle checked his watch. "I have an appointment. I'm sorry." With that, he strode away.

To Swindle, it had been only a minor setback, nothing that would jeopardize his career or, for that matter, affect his sleep. Later, I suspected he'd have a drink with Kenny's lawyer. Together, they'd probably share a few laughs about their boring cases. It was all part of a game for which they were dearly paid and yet never held accountable.

Dazed, I stumbled toward where I thought I'd parked my car. The courthouse anchored the town square with metered parking around the full perimeter. From any angle, the building looked pretty much the same unless you set your bearings by other landmarks. I hadn't.

All I needed was a minimum sense of direction, I decided, only enough to find my vehicle and drive for thirty minutes without veering into someone or something head on. As much as it hurt to admit, at that moment, a fatal car crash held strong appeal.

The first sounds I remember hearing came from several yards behind me, the click-clack of a woman's high-heels. My head tingled, vision blurred. At any second I thought I might faint into the arms of the lady overtaking me on my right. Maybe she'll break my fall, I considered. I turned to see how sturdy she might be.

Plenty stout, indeed.

"Well! Maybe now you see it doesn't pay to be a hussy!" Neta Sue admonished. She gripped the handles of her dull tapestry bag, glaring at me as if I was a convicted felon. Her fat jowls shook as she spoke. "Nobody screws around on *my* son and gets away with it."

I wanted to tell her what a fool she was making of herself, but the words wouldn't form. My pulse quickened, reviving me. Instead of fainting, I felt more like punching a fist through her dentures.

"Come on, Momma." Kenny caught up to Neta Sue and stood next to her. "We got what we wanted. Leave her be." Refusing eye contact with me, he hooked one arm through Neta Sue's and tugged. "Let's go now."

Such a sensible gesture had been more than I would have expected from the likes of Kenny Ray. Briefly, I wondered if maybe he'd truly gotten what he wanted. In little more than half a day, my entire life and that of my child's had slipped away. Our

261

futures had been sealed right there in that courtroom. I was destined to become a social leper—and Sean a carbon copy of Kenny. That was as certain to me as nightfall.

TWENTY-SEVEN

April rains stretched into May, uncharacteristic weather for a Memorial Day weekend in Texas. I carefully folded Sean's size-five shorts and T-shirts while he helped me gather his toys. He pointed to a haphazardly filled produce box and said, "I did 'em *all.*"

"Oh, Seany, you need to leave some of your things here. What'll you play with on weekends when you're with me, sweetie?"

He looked as if the idea of returning to my apartment had never dawned on him. He blinked then rocked back onto his heels. "You can buy me *new* ones!"

How could he be so happy, so seemingly unaffected by his pending departure? A piece of my heart had been in every item he'd packed. Those toys held memories; they weren't items to be shuffled like leaves—any more than children were. I charged for the bathroom before Sean could see the effects of the anguishing thoughts about to consume me.

After tomorrow morning, Sean would only be a visitor when he was at my apartment. He wouldn't live there anymore. He would take with him all of his belongings, every token from his childhood, the parts of a past we'd shared: the Stretch Armstrong doll that oozed its red gooey gel onto my living room carpet, his shirt from the Dallas Zoo, his Nerf baseball, the one that had broken my blown-glass swan, his Superman pajamas, and his wind-up radio that played *Raindrops Keep Falling On My Head.* I'd let him listen to that song over and over on nights when he'd been afraid. Now I was the one who felt fearful and scared of losing him forever.

I'd given birth to this boy, an unexpected gift, but all the same a delight. Wasn't it written somewhere in the annals of history that a child and mother belonged together at all times? Not just on first and third weekends, alternating holidays, and Mother's Day. Who decided differently? It couldn't have been a woman. Whoever was responsible for that violation of natural order, I wanted him brought before me and forced to spell out his reasoning. No one in that courtroom had honored me with any explanations. Yet, even as I thought this, I knew no amount of rational explanation would change the way I felt.

Rubbing my eyes, I sat on the toilet lid and cried harder. Between sobs, I heard Sean's frail knuckles rap against the bathroom door. "I need to go to the bathroom, Mommy."

I blotted my eyes with some toilet tissue and let him in. "I'm sorry." I forced a grin. "Mommy sprung a leak."

Sean held himself and examined my face. "Is that the same thing as crying?"

"Yeah, I guess it is."

Mentally, I scolded myself. I had to keep it together for his sake. No need to make the move difficult for him. If Sean felt comfortable loading up all his belongings, then I ought to find peace in that. There was no reason for me to transfer my pain to him. He had enough of his own to carry.

I returned with Sean to his room to finish packing. He peered into a box he'd already filled with playthings, located his Fisher-Price radio, and pulled the heirloom free. Winding the dial a few times, he lovingly handed me the toy. I clutched the object to my chest, listening to its familiar melody.

"You can keep that one," Sean said.

~

The night stretched expectantly before me, an endless darkness. Unable to sleep, I twice sneaked down the hall and stood in Sean's bedroom doorway. I wanted to sear that mental image in my mind forever. *This is Sean, age five, asleep and unaware on the eve before a major turning point in his life. This is what he looked like. Remember. Remember forever.*

Soon he'd begin first grade, another important passage. Yet I wouldn't be the one to accompany him to class on his first day of school. Unlike me, Neta Sue wouldn't give a hoot about becoming Sean's homeroom mother. She'd probably never bake chocolate-chip cookies for his school parties or shop for valentines and teachers' gifts the way I'd planned to do. I'd expected to stay involved in Sean's school life. Knowing Kenny and Neta Sue, though, they'd make sure to keep me out of the loop. Sean would have to depend on the two of them participating in his activities. Collectively, Kenny and Neta Sue possessed neither the talents nor the inclination to fulfill my parental role. Standing there in the dark, I grieved that recognition, grieved for me, for Sean, and for everything we'd been wrongfully deprived of.

~

Morning. Sunshine. Captain Crunch. It was such an ordinary Saturday in so many other ways, people driving to the mall, hair appointments, and grocery stores. Amid the usual daytime bustle, I faced the extraordinary task of turning over my son to Kenny Ray for permanent keeping. I wanted to be most anybody other than who I was right then: a frightened, hurt, broken human being. I'd spend the rest of Sean's childhood looking into the eyes of random acquaintances, making excuses for why my child didn't live with me, knowing that no matter what I said, strangers and even my own momma would negatively judge me. Most people I knew believed the myth that only mothers who were hookers, dope heads, or both, lost custody of their children.

To become a parent, I'd given up my own childhood. I'd even foregone my last two years of high school. Never would I experience a senior prom or graduation ceremony. My name wouldn't surface on the ten-year high school reunion guest list. No one would wonder and ask what had become of me because I'd dropped off the traditional radar screen. And now, the very child for whom I'd made those sacrifices had been stripped away from me.

In Neta Sue's driveway, I parked my car and motioned through tears for Sean to hug me goodbye. Already he'd noticed his daddy and grandmother standing on their front porch next to a cauldron filled with red begonias. Sean's gaze shifted from me to Kenny, as if before he could show me any affection he first needed to get his daddy's permission. I tried to fend off the taste of bile in my mouth. No use. Any second, I knew I would hurl.

Neta Sue approached my car. She yanked wide the front passenger-side door and grabbed for Sean's waist. "Come on out, now," she said, throwing daggers at me over the top of Sean's head. "You'll see her again in a few days."

Kenny popped open a rear door and hoisted Sean's toy box to his shoulders. Lugging the container to the veranda, he set it down and then returned for the remaining boxes I'd filled with Sean's other belongings. I sat motionless and said nothing. The battle had already been fought. And our side had lost.

Sean sprang from the car and gave his daddy a high-five.

Slapping his hand twice on the Mustang's roof, Kenny indicated the cargo had been cleared so I could leave. I watched in anguish as the three of them strutted toward their newly shared quarters, Neta Sue on one side of Sean, Kenny on the other. Shoving open my driver's side door, I leaned my head over the asphalt and heaved the remains of my breakfast.

For a second I was convinced I needed a paramedic, someone to help remove me from that driveway. But after what felt like a lifetime, I found reverse gear and drove off.

My soul seemed to orbit my body. Vaguely I observed the traffic signals, highline wires, tract homes, and strip centers all passing in a silent haze. Like a satellite, my vision hovered somewhere far out in space. My eyes looked out from a place so remote that no one could have possibly seen into them.

~

On Sunday, Momma came to visit and found me sitting on my sofa, catatonic. I hadn't bothered to change out of my ratty robe or comb my hair. I didn't want to see her or anyone else, didn't want to talk, didn't even really want to breathe.

Momma found her way to my kitchen where she warmed a cup of chicken soup. She set the liquid nutrition on my coffee table and searched for a chair. Finding only the orange, fake-fur beanbag Sean liked to sit on, she dragged it over next to the sofa and plopped down. "Now listen. I know you don't want to talk, so just listen."

I stared past her at the TV set that hadn't been turned on for two days.

"Sometimes life gives us more than we think we can handle," Momma said. "Then time passes, and we see that we were wrong."

I did not need a salvation speech. I knew she was trying to pull me back to the surface before I drowned. However, all I wanted was to close my eyes, inhale water, and sink into the deep.

She leaned closer. "Renee Ann, I don't know what you're feeling right now. But whatever it is, I know it won't be permanent."

I gazed off into the nothingness. "What am I, if I'm not Sean's mother?"

Momma wrestled herself free from the beanbag chair. "You're still his mother, and you're my daughter."

I looked up, studying her face for answers. "What kind of mother loses custody of her child?"

"The Lord is the one who giveth and taketh away. It's not our place to question," Momma offered with rote precision.

"Yeah? Did He take Daddy away from you and give him to another woman?"

Momma folded her arms. "Yes, He did. And I found out life kept right on going, even when I didn't expect it to." She sighed. "Even when I sometimes didn't want it to." She sat down on the couch next to me.

I twisted to face her. "I don't have anything left to take away. My spirit is broken."

"No. Your heart is broken. Your spirit is just fine."

~

When I next saw Pearly, she was selling Mary Kay cosmetics and giving everyone she'd ever met a makeover. "Yes, ma'am," she said, wiping goo from my forehead. "You be prettier than evah when I finish." She searched through the variety of samples she'd placed on my coffee table. "Them mens won't be able to take they eyes off you."

"I don't want another man."

Pearly's eyes grew wide. She dabbed at my face with toner. "I hope you ain't saying what I think you saying."

I groaned. "I just want my son back."

Pearly applied cake foundation with a damp sponge. "Of course you do. Meantime, you gots to be there ever chance you get." She brightened like she'd suddenly figured out the formula for perfect bliss. Giving out one of her trademark hoots, she declared, "There's no glory in raising kids. It's work, hard work. Let 'em have it. You do the fun stuff!"

"Like what?" I asked, trying not to move my lips.

Pearly traced a line of pink around my mouth. "Vacations! Movies! Take him to the *circus*!" She held up a hand mirror for me to see the finished results.

"He *lives* in a circus." We both fell into fits of laughter.

What Pearly did for my appearance and outlook seemed nothing short of miraculous. I purchased twenty-five dollars' worth of cosmetics that afternoon. But the mental makeover advice I received was worth thousands more.

TWENTY-EIGHT

I don't know how mothers survive the death of a child, but I suspect they do it by trudging fearlessly forward despite a deeper urge to fold into a fetal position and succumb to intentional starvation. Though Sean hadn't died, all my dreams for his future had been destroyed. I experienced that loss in a profound way that I could only compare to suffering the death of a loved one. While I knew I would continue to see him, the Sean with whom I'd interact going forward would be a different child than the one I'd previously known.

Though children, by the very nature of maturation, will change over time, I watched helplessly as Sean's personality altered in ways I'd always hoped to discourage. On the weekends when I had Sean with me, which weren't that many, I spent all of my time with him. We swam, toured The House of Wax, where Sean got scared in the dungeon, and watched the lion tamers and trapeze artists perform at the Ringling Bros. Circus. If I couldn't be the primary parent, I decided, at least I'd be the exciting one. I wanted to create the kind of childhood memories that would last Sean a lifetime, ones strong enough to withstand a daily sabotaging from Kenny and Neta Sue.

In addition to my new secretarial job, I'd been freelancing for the local newspaper for extra income. Now I could afford what had once been out of question. I'd even managed to move from government-subsidized housing into a brand new apartment that accepted only adults. I had access to a swimming pool and a clubhouse where guests were welcomed, and it was okay to have children visit on weekends. Neatly bordered by sculpted shrubbery, the apartment complex parking lots remained abundantly lit at night. And each apartment unit had a dishwasher and ceiling fans that actually worked.

Residents of Heatherwood Springs, my new address, appeared more courteous than those I'd encountered at Jewel Gardens. I never heard anyone arguing. I guessed all those amenities helped folks sustain their agreeable natures.

My new surroundings even improved my attitude toward Kenny. Though he remained as overbearing and possessive as ever, when it came to Sean, I no longer felt the need to meet Kenny's pigheadedness with resistance, which worked about the same as dousing a fire with lard anyway. That was why, when Kenny insisted that Sean remain home with him on Friday nights, though our divorce decree instructed him to surrender Sean by six o'clock, I decided not to argue. "You can pick him up at ten o'clock Saturday morning," Kenny commanded, as though along with primary custody he'd been granted the right to make the rules. Unable to fight him from his position, I'd simply acquiesced.

Every time I saw Sean, he seemed different. When he'd first visited after he'd gone to live with Kenny, he'd arrived wearing a stained shirt and a pair of orange shorts that looked like they'd gone one too many rounds with a washing machine agitator. I laundered the outfit one more time, which didn't help matters much, and sent Sean home in a brand-new set of red and navy Buster Brown coordinates. Two weeks later, when he returned for his next visit, he again looked like a poster child for poverty relief.

Besides Sean's outer appearance, his personality underwent changes, too. He repeatedly referred to Neta Sue as "Momma," which I'd explicitly asked him never to do. He constantly wanted to roughhouse with me, as though we might be contenders for a World Championship Wrestling. "Come uh-uh-n-n, Momma," he'd complain when I refused to pin him to the ground. Once, he caught me off-guard and put a chokehold on me. For Christmas, the holiday he pretty much thought about year-round, Sean asked for a set of boxing gloves.

Adding to Sean's peculiar behavior, he incessantly spoke of bingo dabbers, jackpot rounds, and lucky cards as though these were standard vocabulary words for a six-year-old. I had to wonder if Neta Sue might not have been better suited for the medical profession because, with surgical precision, she'd seemingly extracted parts of me from Sean and substituted those closer to her likeness.

"Hi-eee," I chirped when Sean climbed into the car seat next to me one Saturday morning. "I've got a surprise for you today!"

Sean looked around inside the vehicle, as if to say, 'Where is it?'

"We're going to *the fair!*"

He clapped his hands and chanted, "The fair, the fair! Oh, boy!"

"We're going home first, for lunch." I hadn't yet become rich enough to afford overpriced entertainment foods. "Then we'll head to the fairgrounds, right after that."

At the apartment, I served hot dogs and chips, Sean's favorite weekend meal. But as I took a seat at my new dinette, I noticed Sean staring at the weenies as if they were infested with cockroaches. "What's the matter?" I asked. "You too excited to eat?"

Sean shook his head. Gazing into his lap, he said, "I don't want to get sick."

"Have you been sick, sweetheart? I'm sorry. I didn't know. We can go to the fair another time if you're not feeling well."

Sitting taller and looking more energetic than before, Sean explained, "No, I'm not sick. Momma said...I mean, Grandma said you fed me rotten weenies and made me sick when I was a *baby.*"

I wondered if Sean could see steam spewing from my ears. Neta Sue had pushed things too far. If she thought she'd gotten away with that ploy, she was badly mistaken. "I don't know why your grandmother would say such a thing. I never fed you hot dogs when you were a baby. And I wouldn't feed you anything that might make you sick. Okay?"

Sean smiled, picked up his frank, and chowed down.

~

On Sunday, at the end of our visit, I returned Sean to Neta Sue's house. I'd little more than pulled into the driveway when Sean announced, "Daddy's not home. He said Momma would be here."

"You mean your grandma, Neta Sue," I corrected.

Sean shook his head. "She says for me to call her momma because *she's* my momma now."

"She does, huh?" I climbed from the driver's seat to let Sean out of the vehicle. "I'm going to walk you to the door." I rubbed Sean's back as he wandered unaware into the minefield.

At the stoop, I rang Neta Sue's doorbell. She tore herself from behind the window shades she'd been peeping through to answer the door.

"I brought Sean back," I said, "and I'm glad you're here. You see, Sean has been confused, and you seem a bit confused yourself. So before I leave, I want to clear up something."

I bent down low, to Sean's height, so I could look him in the eyes. "Sean, this is your grandmother," I pointed to Neta Sue. "And I'm your mother." I tapped my collarbone. "That's why you call me Momma, because that's who I am. And you call her Grandma or Nana or Granny, because that's who she is."

Neta Sue's eyes sparked. "I'm not the one who's confused. I'm raising this child."

I coaxed Sean inside, past Neta Sue's imposing stature, and stood up to square off with the witch. "You ought to finish raising your own son before you go trying to raise *mine*. Seems you failed miserably the first time around."

Her hands balled into fists, Neta Sue pushed her girth past the doorjamb and stormed out onto the porch. "Get your ass out of here. I'm done talking to you."

I took a step closer to her bulbous figure. "I'll get out of here, all right. But I'm not getting out of my son's life."

She sneered as I turned to leave.

From inside my car, I looked back at Neta Sue. She stood on the stoop, glaring at me. I gave her a go-to-hell look as I pulled my Mustang into reverse gear. Backing from the drive, my anger overtook me.

I shot Neta Sue the middle finger.

Though Neta Sue and Kenny might wish to relegate me to the furthest fringes of Sean's life, they would not push me out, I vowed. I would not let that happen. At his core, Sean remained a part of me as much as he was a portion of Kenny. I couldn't be fully severed from him because even when we were physically separated, we remained connected through sheer genetics. And no one, not even Kenny Ray, his vengeful mother, or a courtroom genius could change that fact.

~

Nine forty-five. I drove past the city limits and sped the last few miles toward Neta Sue's house, anticipating how Kenny would act when I arrived to pick up Sean for summer vacation. More likely than not, he'd repeat his normal routine—act like he'd won some meaningful contest of wills or garnered proof that he could order me around since he lacked any other hint of personal power. Every time I showed up to retrieve Sean, Kenny would carry him to my car as though Sean was a baby. You'd have thought the boy hadn't yet learned to walk.

The show began as soon as I parked my vehicle. First, Kenny would hesitate while standing underneath the weatherworn awning that covered Neta Sue's front porch, talking low enough to Sean that I couldn't hear. From his consoling facial expressions and Sean's befuddled look, I guessed he pretended to soothe Sean. For a final jab, Kenny would enact a major display of affection right before he'd place Sean in the front seat of my car. "Love you," Kenny would say in a singsong voice. And then he'd wave as if Sean might be going off to boarding school.

"Love you," Sean would parrot back.

"Love you *more*," Kenny would say before he'd close the passenger door. After that, the jerk would tilt his head forward and stare at me through the window glass. I could feel him searching me for signs of what? Happiness? Devastation? I was never sure.

Each time I retrieved Sean, Kenny's theatrics made me feel like an intruder. The first few moments when Sean and I were reunited were always overshadowed by Kenny's behaviors. To my extensive list of reasons to loathe him, I added this one. But on this morning, I made an internal promise not to act bitter. I would not give Kenny permission to reach inside my head and rearrange my emotions. I would not.

I navigated past the familiar landmarks: a veteran's cemetery now filled with red, white, and blue flags, a milkweed-infested pasture erupting into purple blooms, and a barn so dilapidated that it practically begged for a tornado. The bridge that had once spanned Hawk Creek now arched over a dry gulch. Along the roadway on either side, sunflowers sprouted in the bar ditches. I swerved to miss a large pothole, my tires narrowly escaping the road hazard.

Nearing Neta Sue's drive entrance, I slowed to make the left-hand turn. Under the great oak that shaded most of her front yard, I could see a small squat figure: Sean. Glints of sunlight danced across his hair through the spaces between the tree leaves. He was outside, playing alone. Perfect, I thought. Maybe today Sean would stride to the car on his own two legs.

I parked the Mustang with its rear bumper barely clearing the road behind me, its nose pointed toward the detached garage that could have been plumbed by a drunken sailor.

Sean stood, straightened his small frame, and stared right at me.

Glancing back toward the house, I observed a shadow in the doorway. I smiled at Sean and yelled, "Hi-i-ee!" With a wave, I motioned him my direction. He put down his toy caterpillar and stared as though he no longer recognized me.

My heart surged. What was he doing? I lowered the passenger side window. "Sweetie, are you ready for vacation?"

His eyes narrowed, face contorted. "No-o-o!" he screamed. "Don't make me go-o-o! I don't want to go!" At full throttle, he traced a direct line to the front door, yelping, "Dad-dy, Dad-dy!"

Kenny opened the storm door as if it were a drawbridge and he the fortress gatekeeper. He knelt to receive Sean, patting him and stroking his head. You'd have thought the child had suffered a skull fracture. But I suspected it had been something closer to a brainwashing.

I looked on in horror, a lump rising into my throat.

Disregarding me as easily as he had my parental rights, Kenny pulled Sean inside and closed the door. The innermost one.

That scene replayed itself many times over the next six years. Though I never knew when Sean would go with me or when his mind would be too poisoned to leave his dad, I kept showing up.

Only death could have stopped me.

TWENTY-NINE

I'd like to say I had a premonition about it, but I didn't. It happened the year I graduated from college, on an otherwise ordinary February day: forty-five degrees, overcast, windy, with a slight chance of rain, the kind of day I almost didn't mind being stuck indoors reading press releases from individuals who had nothing of significance to report. I opened the day's business mail and answered mildly annoying telephone inquiries.

Between calls, I addressed hundreds of envelopes to people who would likely never open them.

The telephone on my desk rang. Another assignment, I figured. Through broken words that began high and ended low, sounds filtered through the vocal chords of an adolescent boy-turned-bullfrog. Sean croaked, "Mom, I'm stranded. Can you come get me?"

"Stranded? Where are you?"

"At school. Dad was supposed to pick me up an hour ago, but he never showed up." He coughed. "I called his work. But they said he got sick on the job and somebody took him to the hospital." In the background, I could hear a photocopier running and what sounded like a couple of junior high school girls giggling. Sean was safe indoors, at least. "I called Grandma," he continued, as if he needed to tell me I hadn't been his first choice, "but she's not home."

"I'll be right there. But call your dad's work back and see if you can find out what hospital they took him to."

By the time I tore out of the parking garage and onto Main Street, I'd shifted both my new car and my imagination into high gear. Had a pallet of sandbags fallen and crushed Kenny? Had he stood behind a dump truck and been accidentally, or in his case maybe intentionally, run over? Was he injured or just ill? And if he'd been injured, could he have been left permanently disabled? It would take something drastic like that to get that blockhead to agree to let Sean live with me.

At thirteen, Sean needed some distance from Kenny's temper tantrums. And he needed true parenting, something neither Kenny nor Neta Sue knew much about. Today, they'd proven this. No one had bothered to check and see if Sean had made it home from school.

To prevent alarming Sean, I spoke little when he climbed into the vinyl bucket seat next to me. The drab hues of a misty winter sky painted a bleak enough picture without my help. An ambulance passed, its lights flashing, siren blaring. I reached across the console and patted Sean on the knee. "I'm sure everything's all right. We'll take a swing by the hospital. He's probably checked out already. Baylor General, right?"

"Yeah." Sean twisted at his lips with a thumb and forefinger.

The automatic doors swung wide to greet us at Baylor General. We passed through the entrance, the cold dampness of early nightfall biting at our heels. I clutched Sean's left hand with my right and gave it a slight squeeze. "We'll just ask that woman over there," I said, gesturing toward a lady wearing a reflective nametag and a shrimp-colored pinafore. The woman behind the information desk looked like a geriatric version of Dorothy from the *Wizard of Oz*, with the minor exception that it had been Dorothy's *dress* and not her *hair* that was electric blue. Drawing closer to the desk, I about gagged on the unmistakable odors of tomato soup and rose-scented perfume. Campbell's and Avon weren't meant to be mixed like that.

My stomach roiled from thoughts of aging and my own mortality. If I hadn't been sick when I entered this place, I expected I could become that way soon. "She'll have the records on her computer," I said to Sean. "Maybe she can tell us if he's still here."

For once, Sean didn't seem to mind having a room full of strangers witness his mother holding his hand. He didn't try to pull free, a maneuver he'd well perfected by age two.

"Can you tell us the status of Kenneth Murphy?" I asked the information assistant.

She tapped a couple computer keys. "He's in ICU. Are you immediate family?"

~

Neta Sue had been first to the hospital, the same way she'd kept one step ahead of me on most anything involving Kenny or Sean. But I'd been the one to retrieve Sean from school. For some reason, I found that hugely gratifying. In Neta Sue's haste to rescue her own son, she'd temporarily forgotten about mine.

I sat in one of the waiting area's dozen or more pea-green chairs and watched that sow's backside as she waddled with Sean into the Intensive Care Unit. If nothing else, I prayed, let me be spared a conversation with her. Sean would give me the facts when he returned. I didn't want to hear anything from Neta Sue. It wasn't that I lacked curiosity or concern. I simply didn't need any more lip from her. She acted like the universe would spin out of control if she wasn't around to give directions. If I had to bet, she was probably in there, right now, barking orders at the ICU nurses.

From somewhere nearby, a man's voice called out, "Ms. Murphy?"

"Right here," I said, wiggling back into the pumps I'd prematurely slipped off. I'd forgotten this was Kenny's mother's name, too, most likely because it was too much for me to consider that I'd ever be mistaken for her.

"Ms. Murphy? Oh, you're the *other* Ms. Murphy. Was that your son?" the doctor asked. He motioned with his head toward a pair of swinging metal doors.

I nodded.

The physician's voice faded in and out. "I'm...and I'll be...husband's doctor...." I caught only every fourth or fifth word he said because my attention was trained on those shiny metal doors—and on Sean.

"Would you care to join me in my office?" Doctor Somebody asked. He pointed down a sterile hallway. "We could speak more privately in there about your husband's condition."

"*Ex*-husband," I corrected. I felt I had to say it to remember sometimes. "We've been divorced for years."

"I'm sorry. I should have seen that on his chart."

This guy must have thought I'd fallen off of the last onion truck passing through town. Even *I* knew that doctors didn't read admission records. I probably should have sensed something strange about the man right then, but I saw only his white coat of authority. I paid little attention to the personality behind that jacket, and even less to his physical appearance. If he'd been one of the hospital's bakery staff, I doubt I would have noticed.

"That's okay. It doesn't matter. Tell me what happened and if he's going to be okay," I said.

The physician directed me to a wingback chair in front of his desk. He took a seat in his executive chair, pushing aside a stack of papers and manila file folders. "Your husband...I mean ex-husband...has sustained heart damage from an aneurysm. He's currently suffering arrhythmia and kidney failure. The next twenty-four hours will be critical for him. You should pray for the best and prepare for the worst. That's about all I can tell you right now."

I had to adjust my hearing. Heart damage? I'd never known Kenny to have any heart issues. At least, not medical ones. "Is he conscious?" I asked.

"No. And I doubt he will be tonight. So if I were you, I'd take that boy home when he's through visiting and try and get some rest." The physician hesitated, then added, "Mr. Murphy's mother said she will be staying here overnight."

My throat felt as if I'd swallowed a cotton ball that enlarged with every breath. Any second it might seal off my windpipe. My whole body grew clammy. I detected perspiration forming around my lips and along my hairline. Had the room temperature suddenly risen twenty degrees? I strained to listen more closely, but the sounds around me faded farther into the distance. Elevator bells, rolling gurneys, and paging calls gave way to a high-pitched ringing noise.

My face must have revealed my trauma. The doctor stepped from behind his desk and scrambled to reach me. By one arm, he led me over to a tufted leather sofa that I could barely see. "I think you better lie down here until you're feeling better." He pulled a chair close, seated himself, and lifted my wrist to check my pulse. "I know this is a shock to you." He caressed my hand with the warmth of his own. "How long did you say you've been divorced?"

Probably he was trying to divert my attention to keep me from fainting, sidetrack me into thinking about something other than Kenny's ruptured brain. Physicians are skilled at distracting their patients that way. But if he was going to ask me personal questions, I felt I should at least know his name. I opened my eyes and tried to read his silvery badge for the first time. The letters were too blurred for me to decipher. "About seven years," I said, closing my lids to shut out my embarrassment.

"Mmm. I see. And you kept the name Murphy, I presume, because of your son?" The doctor's chair creaked. When I next looked, I found his face closely suspended over mine. His penetrating gaze, reminiscent of a man in search of his own reflection, startled me.

"Yeah, that's right," I said. "I've always gone by Renee Murphy. Nobody knows me as a Goodchild anymore. That was my maiden name."

The practitioner gave a forlorn smile. "Oh, you could be wrong. *I* still know you better as a Goodchild. But I didn't think I'd ever see you again. Certainly not under these circumstances."

I sat upright and strained to focus. His hair appeared a darker shade now that he'd cut it so short, and he'd gained at least thirty pounds since I'd last seen him. But those deep indentations, the ones I used to find so endearing, still framed his thin lips when he smiled. Like always, his eye color remained elusive, alternating between shades of hazel, teal, and at times gray. I glanced at his desk. Sure enough, his nameplate had been in front of me, big as a boxcar, the entire time: DAVID W. LASSITER, M.D.

Scanning the surroundings, I noted my former admirer's various college and medical diplomas detailing what he'd accomplished while I'd been growing up too fast, a funny statue, and photographs of family and outdoor scenery. Centered on one wall, flanked by more outdoor photography, was an eight by ten enlargement of a Mayan pyramid.

"We'll talk more later, when you're up for it. I've got to make my rounds now." Doctor Lassiter—David—adjusted his collar and heaved a reflective sigh. He took a few steps toward his office door, then stopped and turned back toward me. Under the florescent lights, his vacant eyes now appeared a dusty blue. For a moment, I recalled how I'd felt when, as a young teen, I'd stared into those eyes. Special. Valued. Genuinely accepted.

"Do you remember what I used to tell you? Do you remember what I used to say about Kenny?" David asked, studying his cushioned loafers.

How could I forget anything that had been repeated to me that often? 'If anything ever happens to Kenny, I want to be the first to know,' I silently recited. He'd said that like a broken record.

"Yes, I remember."

"Hmm." His gaze met mine, his mouth twisting into a wry grin. "This wasn't exactly what I had in mind."

Those earlier nights when I'd lain in bed thinking about David, wondering if we'd one day meet again, imagining our future children together, had long since faded from memory. Over the years, I'd mostly forgotten about him and our juvenile romance. I had to struggle to remember what he looked like when I'd seen him last, with his eyes brimming over with rejection.

From all appearances, we'd both moved on, each establishing new lives and loves. How ironic that Kenny had been the one to reunite us, though it was much too late.

For several minutes, I sat in David's office realizing I hadn't ever wanted this either. Though I'd wished Kenny dead more times than not and imagined my glee over his demise, my guilt from having such thoughts overwhelmed me. Maybe my words had held more power than I'd realized. And possibly David's had, too. He'd said he wanted to know if anything ever *happened* to Kenny. No doubt, he meant he wanted to know if Kenny and I ever broke up. But he'd probably hoped that would occur before he'd married and had that little girl whose photo adorned his desktop.

I'd always wanted Kenny to simply disappear.

Perhaps we both should have been more specific.

THIRTY

The telephone on my nightstand rang once. I strained to read the alarm clock's fiery digits. Six-eighty, it looked like. No, that couldn't be right. More like five-thirty. Only five and a half hours since I'd reassured Sean and tumbled into bed, three hours since I'd actually fallen asleep and dreamed about Kenny.

A partial second ring. I grabbed the receiver. "Hello," I whispered, my voice croupy, heart thumping. On the other end, someone's shallow breathing. Though she'd not yet spoken, I knew the caller was Neta Sue. I could feel it in the pit of my stomach, sense it through the heaviness of the receiver. Between her gasps, I recognized her. In the few seconds we sat suspended in time, propelled toward tragic discourse, words lost their importance. The connection had been made, and already I understood.

She whimpered, making the kinds of sounds produced only by grievous loss, the high-pitched mournful tones caused by a mother torn from her a child, the desperate cry I knew all too well. "He's gone. My boy's gone forever. Please," she said, suddenly sounding stronger, "tell Sean his daddy loved him very much. Will you?"

Despite his many shortcomings, Kenny had always loved Sean. I couldn't deny that and never would. It was me he hadn't cared for like he should have. I pressed my teeth into my bottom lip. "Yes, of course I will," I said, confident I should be registering something more than shock. But I had no idea what I should feel.

Neta Sue had despised me for more than a decade. Did I owe her anything now? Forget my obligations, if ever I'd had any to her. At bare minimum, shouldn't I be the least bit melancholy? My ex-husband, my son's father, had died—vanished for good. Yet I felt strangely narcotic. Possibly, I considered, I'd become desensitized to pain.

Neta Sue sniffed. "I'll call you later, once I've made the funeral arrangements." She paused. "Do you want me to tell Sean?"

Neta Sue couldn't quit vying for my role in Sean's life. When it came to acting like Sean's parent, I figured she'd been standing in for me long enough. "No, I'll do it. But I'm going to wait until he wakes up on his own." That was the least I could give him, a morning of uninterrupted sleep. Soon enough he'd receive the news that would catapult him into premature adulthood.

"Do whatever you think's best," Neta Sue said. "He's *your* son." She spoke with such detachment that, for a second, I almost forgot who she was.

Though I tried, I couldn't go back to sleep. I lay there, searching for the right words to say to Sean when he woke up. Failing to find acceptable language, I mentally replayed my conversation with Neta Sue. If I analyzed her remarks long enough, maybe I could decode her message. "He's your son," I whispered. She'd placed the emphasis on "your." It took a while for me to realize she hadn't meant that to be sarcastic. She'd actually been raising a battle-worn flag of surrender, though she'd been so badly shell-shocked that she hadn't identified her true opponent. It hadn't been me waiting for her submission.

Neta Sue had been right about one thing; Sean was *my* child, mine and Kenny's. Only now it looked like he would be fatherless. Where was the victory in such heartbreak? From this day forward, Sean would have no one to send a card to on Father's Day, no dad to experience his birthday smiles or holiday joys, no one to share his love for licorice, racecars, and cop shows. How could a mother fill such voids? Who would have the tough talks with Sean, the ones about sexuality—not that Kenny was any expert in that department? Who would endure the emergency room visits, stitch removals, and bone relocations resulting from Sean's favorite sport, football? And who would be there later, to compare body scars and wound stories? I'd always expected to be Sean's mother, but I hadn't counted on being his daddy, too. The prospect of that, the sheer impossibility of such, demanded my recognition.

~

Sean folded in on himself like an imploding skyscraper. First, he appeared stoic and upright, then virtually invisible. He clutched at an opaque plastic bag with both fists and fixed his eyes on his high-top sneakers. Kenny had purchased those shoes, I presumed. I knew I hadn't. Neta Sue couldn't have been responsible, because she detested anything that didn't fasten with Velcro.

I sat on the mattress next to Sean, one arm looped firmly around his shoulders. If only I, like one of those storybook godmothers, could dispel his misery he might again let me inside his private world. Was there a password somewhere? And if so, had I earned the right to access?

Sean stared at the sack that contained his father's belongings, the items Dr. Lassiter had so graciously given to him when Neta Sue wasn't around. "These rightfully belong to you, son," he'd said. And then he'd pressed the package's drawstrings deep into Sean's open palm.

I placed my right hand on Sean's left. "Do you want to open the bag? Would you like to hold your daddy's things?" I moved to stand, but he leaned his weary head on my nearest shoulder and exhaled.

"If you'll stay here with me," Sean moaned.

I gave him a hug.

Sean widened the opening gathers. Inserting first a forefinger and then an entire hand into the bag, he eased Kenny's work shirt from its wrinkled confinement. The garment's sleeves displayed Kenny's trademark perspiration stains. Like most of Kenny's clothing, the uniform smelled musty, a cross between mildew and potting soil. I glimpsed the chest insignia and remembered the last time I'd read the word "Ken" and wondered who he was. Though, when it came right down to it, without our labels, neither of us could have identified our true selves.

Sean traced the emblem with his fingers. He swallowed hard, allowing his tears to turn Kenny's shirt polka dot. What could I do to make him feel better? As his mother, wasn't I supposed to know?

Why couldn't it have been me? Why hadn't God taken Sean's mother, the person he saw the least, instead of his father, the one he loved most? Clearly, between the two of us, I'd been the expendable one. Almost everyone agreed. 'As useless as a sixth toe,' as Neta Sue liked to say. Besides, I had evil thoughts and a freakish lack of conscience. I was the one in need of punishment. Hadn't I once plotted to blow Kenny's brains out? And now, potentially because I'd dwelled on such thoughts, his Maker had followed through on something similar.

I shuffled to Sean's dresser and grabbed a few tissues. Before I could hand them to him, he buried his face in Kenny's shirt and wept. From the hollow of his being rose a deep throaty cry that sounded more man-like than anything I'd have expected from a thirteen-year-old. His wails sliced through me.

"Oh, honey, I know. I know," I said. "I know it hurts. I know it does." I felt my own sorrow spiraling up from parts of me I didn't know existed, causing me to choke. "Let it out. It's okay. Let it all out."

Mourning our separate losses together, we clung to each other.

Sean dropped the shirt into his lap and latched onto me. "Why, Mom? Why? Why did this have to happen?"

I'd been asking myself the same question. Of the few reasons that had come to mind, Sean wasn't yet old enough to comprehend any of them.

I was struck by the absurdity of our lives, Kenny's and mine, by the degree of wasted energies, money, and time we'd both spent fighting over...what? Our own basic needs? Our child? And to what end? This one. Ridiculous. Stupid, stupid losses.

Sean stiffened. Pulling away, he looked peculiarly angry. "They better not have taken his wallet!"

"Who?" I asked, stupefied.

He looked at me as though I should know. "Those *hospital* people."

I lifted the package that had fallen to the floor. "Oh, hon...they wouldn't take his billfold. It's probably in here, right inside this bag, with his other things." Rummaging through the contents, my hands emerged with the leather wallet. "Here it is. See?"

Sean rubbed his freckled face on his sweatshirt and squinted. He snatched the billfold from me and opened it. "I wonder how much money's in it. I'll bet they took his money," he said, splitting the seam. He stared inside. "I knew it! They *did*."

I peered into the gaping wallet and counted four George Washingtons—exactly what I would have expected. Nothing about that man had changed. "I doubt that seriously. The whole time I was married to your daddy, he never carried more than a few dollars on him at any time."

"Hmm." Sean ignored my comment and continued inspecting the billfold compartments, as though somewhere inside one of them he might find the clues to a critical mystery. But I knew the answers he sought wouldn't be located that easily. The explanations he needed were too large for a wallet to hold.

Sean moved to the photo section, unsnapped the outer cover, and hollered, "Look!"

If I have to witness that photo of Neta Sue one more time, I'm going to toss my lunch. Just glance, smile, and try to say something nice.

I braced my better instincts against a concrete wall of contempt and directed my attention to Sean's discovery.

"It's the only one in here," Sean said. "Probably the only one he had."

I gulped. "Omigod." Through filmy plastic layers I'd seen many years before, my own eyes

297

laughed back at me. Somewhere between then and now, I realized, Kenny had replaced his mother's photo with mine.

Was it possible that he'd actually loved me in his own warped way? Had I been the high point in Kenny's seemingly otherwise meaningless life? All that time, I'd thought he'd hated me. Confronted with new evidence, I could no longer be sure. Why would a man carry around the likeness of an ex‐wife he despised? Given Kenny's distorted views, could he have been simply doing the best he knew how? And had his final thoughts included me even as I'd stood outside his hospital doorway paralyzed by fear?

My heart ached from all the false judgments, disappointing failures, and lingering hurts we'd caused each other. Our innocence had been stolen from us long before we'd realized its value. If we'd only lived our lives differently, maybe Kenny would still be here.

I pressed my thumbs against the translucent overlay and stared closely at the photo of Sean and me. The image had been snapped on the porch steps in front of our old duplex. I'd been seated on the stoop, hugging Sean by his hips. Sean's tiny fingers were interlocked, his hands high in front of his forehead to shield out the sun. My face was turned toward Sean's, my mouth wide with laughter. It had been then, as it was now, a painfully bright day.

~

You can't predict much about February weather, or for that matter, a funeral. Someone's going to get buried. Maybe it'll rain. That's about it. Anything else can happen.

The funeral director met us inside the foyer. "Good afternoon," he said, first shaking hands with Sean and then me. "I'm so sorry for your loss," he uttered, as if he hadn't repeated that line too many times for it to hold any meaning. His voice was measured and breathy, in a way that might put some people at ease.

I wasn't one of them.

The funeral attendant wore the hairstyle of a televangelist and smelled of cheap aftershave and disinfectant. I didn't want to touch him. And Sean didn't either. We were both in a pretty bad mood, seeing as how, for good reasons, neither of us wanted to be there.

Earlier that morning, Sean and I had fought. He'd been generally mad about everything: the unexpected sunshine, the missing grave monument—something he didn't understand takes time to produce—and the navy suit his dad had been dressed in, an outfit Kenny had never worn in his life, not even on his wedding day.

"Whose idea was it to put that *stupid* red-striped tie around his neck?" Sean asked. "My dad *hated* those things. He said only men who wanna be pulled around by the necks wear shi...crap like that."

The boy's emotions were in a tangled mess, and mine weren't a great deal better. Besides watching my son go through the most difficult day of his life, I was heading into a hostile environment—one that included a dead body—alone. I say "alone" because Sean didn't really count. He was an insider, so to speak, a member of the Murphy family, a clan from which I'd been divorced for more than seven years.

My kinfolk would be conspicuously absent at the services. Momma couldn't get off work, she'd said. But I knew it was more like she couldn't afford to miss a day's pay, and that was all right. She probably couldn't have handled seeing her grandson cry or her former son-in-law lying there inside that copper-handled casket. Besides, if Momma had come, Ricky would have shown up, too, possibly with greasy fingernails and stringy hair. And that would have given Neta Sue another chance to make sour remarks about my family. All things considered, Momma's absence was for the best.

Daddy had offered to fly in from California, but I'd asked him to stay put. That had been before I'd known Momma wasn't going to attend the funeral. I'd figured I would have enough on my hands without dealing with Momma and Daddy seeing each other for the first time since their divorce. There was a limit to how much stress a person can manage in a single day. That definitely would have exceeded mine. Despite the forecast, you might say I was flying a single-seated aircraft straight into a thunderhead. Turbulence was to be expected.

Neta Sue pinpointed us right off. "*Here* he is-s-s." She made her way over to us.

I gripped Sean's hand tightly, and then let go. "I'm going to let you visit with everyone...but I'll see you before the services start. Okay?"

My goals for the day were directly at odds. I wanted to be there for Sean and, at the same time, I hoped to avoid conflict. It seemed clear that Sean would sit up front with Neta Sue and all her sisters and brothers-in-law, in the family section. I figured I'd find a place somewhere in the back of the room with Kenny's friends and acquaintances, since most likely there wouldn't be a designated area for remorseful ex-wives.

Sean spun and grabbed me by one arm. "Where're you going, Mom? I want you to stay with *me*. Pulleeze?"

I studied his fragile face, his flushed cheeks, and pleading eyes. Never before had I wanted to grant one of his requests so badly. But that was Neta Sue's son in there in that coffin. And Sean was her only grandchild, the final proof of Kenny's existence, Neta Sue's sole link to him now. If a choice had to be made, for today, for the first time I could remember, Sean rightfully belonged with her. He didn't need to sit with me, the woman who'd once contemplated murdering his daddy. "I'm just going to walk down the hall," I said. "I'd like a few moments alone, that's all."

Neta Sue tugged at Sean. "Come over here. I got somebody I want you to meet." Apparently sidetracked by introductions, she didn't acknowledge me.

Sean followed his grandmother, but over his shoulder he gave me a bewildered look. I nodded back at him, indicating his momentary departure was okay. Then I quickly slipped down a hallway leading to a small empty chapel.

Inside the undersized sanctuary, I slid into an oak pew and sobbed. In there, I was finally alone, away from the penetrating glares and hurtful accusations. Just me and God. As I considered the word "God," I experienced my greatest sense of abandonment. And right there, I held a silent dialog with my Creator.

Don't you see? I've never fit in anywhere, especially not here and not now. Why didn't you take me? It would've been better. If you were going to take Kenny, why'd you wait until now? Why didn't you spare me all those years of pain? Why didn't you do it when he was beating me, before Sean was old enough to even remember him? Why make Sean suffer? Why? I don't understand.

I cried until I shook from my separateness. My chest heaved. I felt I might drown at any minute, sitting there in my self-pity. Then I noticed an altar at the front of the chapel. Inscribed on the centerpiece were the words, *This do ye in remembrance of Me.* I don't know what it was about that sentence that jostled me from my despair. But all at once, I realized how much God loved me, how painful it must have been for Him to watch me suffer. And I understood that I was not, and never had been, alone.

Draping my elbows over the pew in front of me, I began to pray.

I lifted my head and observed the sunlight flickering like liquid gold through the chapel's intricate stained-glass windows. Patting my eyes dry with a tissue, I paused to check my watch. It was time. And I would be brave. I would be all right—because I was not alone.

Someone touched me lightly on the shoulder. I turned, expecting to see Sean.

Neta Sue looked at me through eyelids puffed like marshmallows. In her gaze I recognized something different, something I'd never before witnessed. She extended her hand. Before I could speak, she said, "Renee, I want you to sit up front with me and Sean...with the rest of the family...if you don't mind."

I clasped Neta Sue's hand. With my opposite palm, I linked to Sean. The three of us made our way down the aisle and past the burnished-brass placard that read "Services for Kenneth Raymond Murphy."

EPILOGUE

I'm not sure why I felt the need to record this story, other than to make some sense of chaos. Shit happens, that's a fact. Some of us are plumbed for it, some flourish well in fertilizer, and some just flat get buried beneath everyone else's crap. Often, though, all we need to do is look up to realize we're standing underneath a sewage discharge pipe and ought to move.

Though I still can't say how much of this saga stemmed from choice, what I know for sure is, like Granny Henderson told me years ago, it was my decision to drive or be driven. If I'd never commanded a steering wheel, my outcome would have been something entirely different. That Mustang was more than a car; without it, I might never have left Hawk Creek Road.

I'm fortunate to have met folks like Granny and Pearly, each of whom entered my life at the right time to shape my thoughts in different ways. Both were wise beyond their formal education and taught me something I badly needed to learn.

Pearly rose through the ranks to become a Mary Kay director. When I last saw her, she was driving a pink Cadillac and wearing a genuine diamond watch. I doubt she'll ever need to pawn that timepiece.

Momma married another deacon, one she seldom lets out of her sight. She now resides on a small farm in Alabama where Ricky lives in an adjacent trailer and helps with the chores. Or at least Momma says he does.

Daddy reconnected with and wed his high school sweetheart, who, ironically, has a face that resembles a horse.

Sean received a full football scholarship to SMU, where he put all those tackling moves he learned from his dad to good use. He and his wife own a successful bingo supply warehouse in New Mexico.

Neta Sue retired from cleaning office buildings and hit a $100,000 jackpot in Shreveport, Louisiana. I heard she cussed out some guy who'd taken over her slot machine and then hit the loot on the very next pull. She passed away before she could spend most of her winnings.

As for me...well, I found real love, married again, and wrote this book.

The End

About the Author

Diana Estill lives in North Texas with her husband. She has written four books and two collections of humor essays, including *Deedee Divine's Totally Skewed Guide to Life*, a *ForeWord* Book of the Year finalist. *When Horses Had Wings* is her first novel.

Made in United States
North Haven, CT
01 February 2022

15505141R00188